TALES FROM CENTRAL RUSSIA

RUSSIAN TALES · VOLUME ONE

Retold by James Riordan

ILLUSTRATED BY KRYSTYNA TURSKA

KESTREL BOOKS

KESTREL BOOKS
Published by Penguin Books Ltd,
Harmondsworth, Middlesex, England

Text Copyright © 1976 by James Riordan
Illustrations Copyright © 1976 by Krystyna Turska

First published 1976

ISBN 0 7226 5130 9

Printed in Great Britain by
Western Printing Services Ltd, Bristol

TO MY SON, SEAN

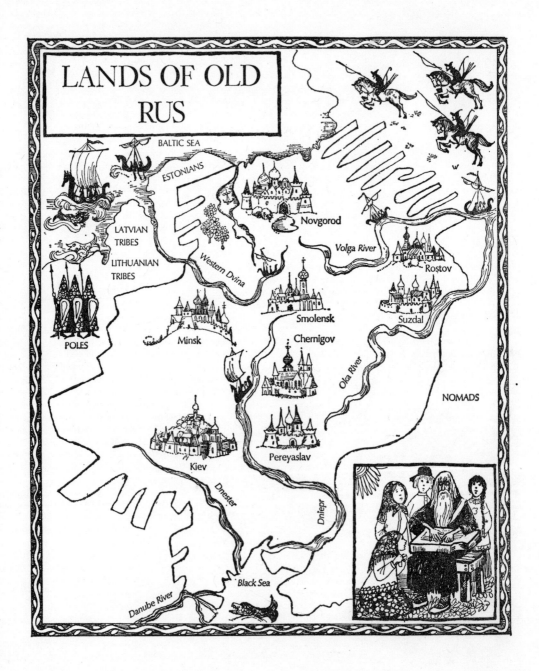

LANDS OF OLD RUS

BALTIC SEA

ESTONIANS

LATVIAN TRIBES

LITHUANIAN TRIBES

POLES

Western Dvina

Novgorod

Volga River

Rostov

Smolensk

Suzdal

Minsk

Chernigov

Oka River

Kiev

Pereyaslav

NOMADS

Dnester

Dniepr

Danube River

Black Sea

Contents

Contents

At River's Bend

ALEXANDER PUSHKIN

An oak tree green at river's bend
Its band of gold doth there suspend
Chained to a cat as wise as can be
Who day and night walks round that tree.
To the right he treads – a song to sing,
To the left he springs – a tale to spin.

Wonders abound: a woodsprite flits,
A water nymph in the branches sits;
And there amid the trampled ferns
Lie trails of beasts of yore;
A little hut on hen's feet turns;
No windows, nor a door.
There, forest and glade in marvels abound;
At dawn waves swish in gentle sound
Dancing lightly in rippled ring,
And thirty handsome heroes leap
In turn from glistening waters deep
Chasing a demon river king.
Lo! A bold young prince comes swiftly riding
Hard on the heels of an evil tsar;
There in the clouds a wizard is hiding
Waiting to seize a noble boyár
And bear him over the steppe afar.

At River's Bend

In a dungeon deep a princess pines,
A big grey wolf his captive minds;
There, Baba Yagá in her mortar looms
Sweeping her traces away with her brooms;
There, Old Bones the Ogre hoards his gold,
There's Russian blood, there's Rus so old!

And I was there, I drank mead ales,
Under the oak tree green I sat
And listened while that wise old cat
Told me these ancient fairy tales.

Fair Vassilisa and Baba Yagá

In a far-off land there once lived an old man and his wife and their daughter Vassilisa. Though life was hard, the family was content with what they had.

But even the bluest of skies may turn to grey, and misfortune one day stepped across their threshold: the old woman fell ill and called Vassilisa to her bedside. Giving her a little doll, she said,

'Do as I tell you, child. Take good care of this doll and show her to no one. If ever you are in trouble, give the doll some food and ask her advice. She will tell you what to do.'

Giving Vassilisa her blessing, the old woman died.

The old man sorrowed for a time, then married again. Vassilisa's new stepmother had two daughters of her own, two of the most spiteful and hard-to-please girls that ever lived. The stepmother loved them dearly, but she never gave Vassilisa a moment's peace.

The girl felt very unhappy, for her stepmother and stepsisters would chide and scold her and keep her toiling from dawn to dusk. They hoped that her face would furrow and darken in the wind and the sun.

Vassilisa did as she was told, waited on everyone and always had her chores done on time. She grew lovelier not by the day but by the hour. All the while the little doll helped her.

Early in the morning Vassilisa would milk the cow and then, shutting herself in the pantry, she would give the doll some milk and say:

'Come, little doll, drink up your milk, my dear,
I'll pour all my troubles into your ear.'

And the doll would drink the milk and comfort Vassilisa and do all her work for her. Vassilisa would sit in the shade twining flowers into her plait and, before she knew it, the vegetable beds were weeded, the pail of water brought in, the fire lit and the cabbages watered. The doll gave her a herb to protect her skin against sun and wind and Vassilisa became fairer than ever.

One day, late in autumn, the old man left home for market and was not expected back for several days. The stepmother and three sisters were left alone in the hut.

In the evening, it became dark outside, the rain lashed the windows and the wind howled under the eaves. The hut stood at the edge of a dense forest in which lived Baba Yagá, an old hag cunning and sly, who gobbled folk up in the wink of an eye.

To each of the three sisters the stepmother gave a task: the first she set to weaving lace, the second to knitting stockings, and Vassilisa to spinning yarn. Then, leaving but a single birch splinter that burnt in the corner where the three sisters were working, she went to bed.

The splinter spluttered for a time, and then went out.

'What are we to do?' cried the stepmother's two daughters. 'It is dark in the hut, and we have to finish our work. One of us will have to go to Baba Yagá's house for a light.'

'I'm not going,' said the first. 'I am making lace and my needle is bright enough for *me* to see by.'

'I'm not going, either,' said the second. 'I am knitting stockings and my two needles are bright enough for *me* to see by.'

'Then, Vassilisa must go for the light! Go to Baba Yagá's house this minute, Vassilisa!' So saying, they pushed their sister out of the hut.

The night drew its black veil tighter around her as she plunged into the dense forest and braved the wild wind and rain. Fair Vassilisa was so frightened she took the little doll from her pocket.

'Dear little doll,' she said, 'they are sending me to Baba Yagá's house for a light, and Baba Yagá eats young children and drinks their blood.'

'Do not worry,' the doll replied, 'all will be well as long as I am with you.'

'Thank you for comforting me, little doll,' said Vassilisa as she continued on her way.

About her the forest rose like a towering giant. No moon, no star shone in the sky above. Suddenly, from out of nowhere, a rider galloped swiftly past. He was dressed in white, his horse was white and the horse's silver harness gleamed white in the darkness.

As soon as the rider had passed, the white light of dawn filtered through the trees, and Vassilisa walked on, stumbling against tree roots and stumps. Droplets of dew glistened on her long fair plaits and her hands were numb with cold.

Presently, another strange horseman came galloping by, this time clad in red, his horse was red and the horse's harness glowed red too. As he swept by, the red sun rose, kissing Vassilisa with its warm rays and drying the dew on her hair.

She walked on through the forest all day without a rest until, towards evening, she arrived at a small glade. There in the centre of the glade stood a wooden hut on hen's feet surrounded by a fence of human bones crowned with human skulls. The gateposts were human legs, the bolts were human arms and the lock was of human teeth.

Just at that moment another horseman came by. His clothes were black, his horse was black and the horse's harness loomed black too. Galloping past the gate, the rider vanished into the gloom.

Sombre night descended. And in the gloom the eyes of the skulls on the fence of bone began to glow and the glade lit up as bright as day.

Fair Vassilisa shivered with fear, her feet rooted to the ground. Yet worse was to come: soon she felt the air tremble and the ground rock beneath her, as out of the dense forest flew Baba Yagá riding in a mortar, driving herself along with a pestle and sweeping away her tracks with a broom. At the gate of the hut she paused and sniffed the air, her long hooked nose pointing towards the girl.

'Foo! Foo! I smell Russian flesh!' she cackled. 'Who is there?'

Vassilisa stepped up to the witch, made a low curtsey and said politely, 'It is I, Grannie, Vassilisa. My sisters sent me for a light.'

'Oh, so it's you, is it?' Baba Yagá replied. 'I know your stepmother well enough. All right, then, stay with me for a while and work, and we'll see about a light.'

With that she screeched:

'Unlock yourselves, my bolts so strong! Open up, my gates so wide!'

As the gates swung open, she entered in her mortar with Vassilisa close behind her.

Inside the fence grew a birch tree which tried to lash Vassilisa with its branches.

'Do not touch the maid, it is I who bring her,' ordered Baba Yagá.

At the door of the hut lay a dog, who made as if to bite Vassilisa.

'Do not touch the maid, it is I who bring her,' ordered Baba Yagá.

Inside the hut, the old cat made as if to scratch Vassilisa.

'Do not touch the maid, it is I who bring her,' ordered Baba Yagá.

'You see, Vassilisa,' she added, 'you cannot escape from me. My cat will scratch you, my dog will bite you, my birch tree will put out your eyes and my gate will not let you pass.'

Baba Yagá then stretched herself upon a bench. 'Come, servant,' she cried, 'serve me something to eat!'

At that, a black-eyed servant set the table for Baba Yagá. She brought her:

> *A bucket of borsh and half a cow,*
> *Ten jugs of milk and a roasted sow,*
> *Twenty chickens and forty geese,*
> *Two whole pies and cottage cheese,*
> *Cider and mead and home-brewed ale,*
> *Beer by the barrel and kvass by the pail.*

The witch ate and drank greedily and all that remained for Vassilisa were bones to pick and a crust to nibble.

'Now then, girl,' she said, 'take this sack of grain and pick it through seed by seed. Mind you take out all the husks, for if you don't I shall gobble you up.' With that, Baba Yagá closed her eyes and began to snore loudly.

Fair Vassilisa took the crust of bread, put it before her doll and said,

'Come, little doll, eat up your bread, my dear, I'll pour all my troubles into your ear. The witch will eat me if I do not do her work.'

'Do not grieve,' said the doll. 'Just close your eyes and go to sleep.'

The moment Vassilisa was asleep, the doll called out in a clear voice:

'Pigeon, sparrow, chaffinch, kite,
There is work for you this night.
On your help, my feathered friends,
Fair Vassilisa's life depends.
Come in answer to my call,
You are needed, one and all.'

The birds came flying in their flocks, more than the eye could see or the tongue can tell. They picked through the seed very quickly: into the sack went the good seeds, into the bin went the husks, and, before the night was spent, the sack was filled to the top.

As they finished, the white horseman galloped past the gate mounted on his white horse. Day was dawning.

Baba Yagá awoke and asked:

'Have you finished, Vassilisa?'

'Yes, it's all done, Grannie.'

Baba Yagá was very cross, but the work was done. So she snapped, 'I'm going out now. While I am gone, take that sack of black peas and poppy seeds, sort out the peas from the seeds and, if you don't do it, I shall eat you.'

She then stepped through the door, whistled shrilly and the mortar and pestle swept up to her. The red rider galloped past, and the sun rose in the sky.

Baba Yagá sat in the mortar and rode out of the yard, driving herself along with the pestle and whisking away her tracks with a broom.

Fair Vassilisa took a crust of bread, fed her doll and begged her help. The doll's clear voice rang out:

'Come to me, you mice of house and field and shed,
Sort the seeds, or the girl will soon be dead!'

The mice came running in swarms, more than the eye could see or the tongue can tell, and, before the hour was up, the work was done.

Towards evening the black-eyed servant laid the table for Baba Yagá's return. As twilight fell the black horseman rode past the gate and night

[16]

descended. The eyes of the skulls began to glow, the trees swished, the leaves quivered and Baba Yagá swept in.

'Have you done what I told you, girl?' she asked.

'Yes, it's all done, Grannie.'

The witch was very cross, but there was nothing to be said.

'Well then, go to bed. I shall have my supper.'

While Vassilisa lay behind the stove, she heard Baba Yagá say to the black-eyed servant, 'Light the stove and make it hot, when I awake I shall roast Vassilisa in the oven.'

Whereupon, Baba Yagá stretched out on the bench, placed her chin on a shelf, her nose on the stove, covered herself with her foot and began to snore so loudly that the whole forest shook.

Fair Vassilisa began to sob and, taking out her doll, put a crust of bread before her.

'Come, little doll, have some bread, my dear, I'll pour all my troubles into your ear. Baba Yagá intends to roast and eat me in the morning.'

The doll told her exactly what to do.

So Vassilisa thrust the doll back into her pocket, went into the kitchen to the black-eyed servant and curtseyed low before her.

'Please, black-eyed maid, help me!' she cried. 'When you light the stove, sprinkle water over the wood so that it doesn't burn properly. Take my silk scarf as a gift.'

The black-eyed maid replied:

'Very well, Vassilisa, I shall help you. I shall tickle Baba Yagá's feet so that she sleeps more soundly. Meanwhile, run away as fast as you can!'

'But won't the three horsemen catch me and bring me back?'

'No,' replied the maid, 'the white horseman is the Bright Day, the red horseman is the Scarlet Sun and the black horseman is the Dark Night. They will not touch you.'

Vassilisa ran out of the hut, and the cat flew at her and would have scratched her had she not thrown her a pie.

As Vassilisa ran down the steps, the dog darted out and would have bitten her had she not thrown him a piece of bread. The dog let her pass.

Then, as she ran along the path, the birch tree tried to lash her face. But she tied its branches with a ribbon and the tree let her pass.

The gate would have swung shut, had she not loosened its hinges with some dew.

She ran into the dense forest just as the black rider galloped by, bringing darkest night. It was then she recalled she had to fetch a light for her stepsisters. So, taking a skull from the fence, she put it on a stick and set off home through the forest. Its eyes glowed and cast a piercing light through the trees.

When Baba Yagá awoke, stretched herself and saw that the girl had escaped, she rushed to the door.

'Cat, did you scratch the girl as she ran past?' she demanded.

And the cat replied:

'No, I let her pass, for she gave me a pie. I have served you ten long years, but you have never given me even a dry crust of bread.'

Baba Yagá ran into the yard.

'Did you bite the girl, my faithful dog?' she demanded.

But the dog replied:

'No, I let her pass, for she gave me some bread. I have served you many years, but you have never given me even a dry bone.'

'Birch tree, birch tree!' the witch screamed. 'Did you put out her eyes?'

The birch tree answered:

'No, I let her pass, for she bound my branches with a ribbon. I have been growing here for ten years, and you have never even tied them with string.'

She hurried down the pathway to the gate.

'Gate, gate!' she cried. 'Did you shut tight so that the girl might not pass?'

'No, I let her through, for she put dew on my hinges. I have served you long, but you have never even put water on them.'

Baba Yagá flew into a rage. She began to beat the dog and thrash the cat, to break up the gate and chop down the tree. She was so tired then that she quite forgot about the girl.

In the meantime, Vassilisa ran home and saw there was still no light in the house. Her sisters at once shouted at her.

'What took you so long?' they demanded. They snatched the skull from her and carried it into the house. But a strange thing happened. The skull's glowing eyes fixed themselves on the stepmother and her two daughters and scorched them. No matter where they tried to hide, the eyes followed them everywhere, never letting them out of sight.

By morning all that was left were three piles of cinders. Only Fair Vassilisa remained unharmed. She took the skull and buried it in the garden, and at once a bush of beautiful red roses grew on the spot.

That same day, Vassilisa's father returned home from the market and his daughter told him the story. Her father was glad to be rid of his wicked wife and her two spoilt daughters. And from that day to this, they have lived in peace and prosperity.

Little Sister Fox and Brother Wolf

ONE winter morning a starving fox was walking along a snow-packed track in search of food. Suddenly, spying an old peasant approaching with a sledgeful of fish, she scampered on ahead and lay flat on her back in the snow, her tail rigid, her paws pointing upwards.

When the peasant drew level, he reined in his horse, looked down at the fox and smiled to himself,

'Ah, fortune is kind today. A dead fox! She will make my wife a fine fur collar.'

Seizing the fox by the tail, he tossed her into the sledge on top of the fish, flung a canvas over her and continued on his way.

The crafty old fox did not lie still for long; she made a hole in the bottom of the sledge and began to drop fish through it onto the track, one by one until the cart was empty. Then she too squeezed through the hole while the sledge trundled on.

Presently the old peasant drove into his yard and called to his wife, 'Hey, old woman, come and see what a splendid fur collar I've brought you – and a cartload of fish!'

The old woman lifted the canvas – but there was no collar and no fish

to be seen . . . Thereupon she set to cursing and beating her husband for his stupidity. Poor old grandad realized then that he had been tricked by the crafty fox, but it was too late to catch her.

Meanwhile, the fox carried all the fish back to her earth and sat down outside to eat them. While she was dining, her neighbour, the wolf, chanced to pass by. He was very hungry.

'Hello, Little Sister! What are you eating?'

'Good-day to you, Brother! Some fine fish.'

'Will you spare me one, Sister?'

'Catch some yourself and dine to your heart's content,' said the fox.

'If only I knew how,' replied the wolf.

'Bless me,' sighed the fox, 'there's nothing to it. Listen, Brother, go to the river, drop your tail through the ice and shout: "Come to my call, fish big and small!" And the fish will come and hang on your tail. But do be patient or you won't catch anything.'

So the wolf scuttered down to the frozen river, let his tail through the ice and shouted: 'Come to my call, fish big and small!'

He squatted like that all night, his discomfort increased by his hunger. By morning his tail was frozen solid. When he tried to rise, he found he was stuck.

'My, my, fancy that,' chuckled the wolf. 'I've caught so many fish I cannot pull them all out!'

As he sat there stuck in the ice wondering what to do, his content turned to alarm when he spotted a group of village women coming for water. As soon as they caught sight of the wolf, they began to scream:

'Wolf, wolf! Kill him! Kill him!'

They rushed down the river bank and set about the wolf with whatever they could lay their hands on: pails, pots, yokes and sticks.

The wolf squirmed and tugged with all his might and, at last, tore himself free . . . leaving his long bushy tail stuck in the ice.

'Just wait till I see that fox,' he muttered breathlessly as he limped across the snow and ice. 'I'll give her the thrashing of her life!'

Little Sister Fox, however, having finished the fish, was up to her tricks again. But this time she was out of luck. Having stolen into a hut where women were frying pancakes, she had tripped and fallen headlong into the pancake mixture, and barely escaped with her life.

On the way home she bumped into the wolf.

'So there you are, Sister Fox,' snarled the wolf. 'I'm going to teach you a lesson! I lost my bushy tail and was beaten because of you.'

'Oh, Brother Wolf,' moaned Little Sister, 'that's nothing to what happened to me. As you see, I've had the stuffing knocked out of me! I am in a far worse state than you: I can barely drag myself along.'

The wolf stared at the white, bedraggled figure of the fox and his rage mellowed to pity. At last, he said kindly:

'Sit on my back, Little Sister, I'll carry you home.'

The crafty fox mounted the wolf's back and smiled to herself:

'The fool is carrying the clever one,' she murmured.

'What's that you say, Little Sister?' asked the wolf.

'Oh, I was only saying: our hard work is never done.'

'Just so, my dear, just so,' said the wolf sadly.

Ivan the Rich and Ivan the Poor

THERE once lived two brothers, Ivan the Rich and Ivan the Poor.

Ivan the Rich had bread in the larder and meat on the table,
A well-furnished house and a well-stocked stable,
Bins full of flour and barns full of wheat,
Fine things to wear as well as to eat.
His sheep were fat and his cows were sleek,
And they grazed in the meadow by a long winding creek.

In a word, he had all he needed, and no one to provide for but his wife and himself, for Ivan the Rich had no children, big or small.

But Ivan the Poor had seven children and nothing to his name save a cat by the fire and a frog in the mire. All seven children would sit in a group, begging for porridge and cabbage soup. Alas, there was nothing to eat, not a crust of bread nor a scrap of meat.

So, Ivan the Poor went to his rich brother to ask for some food.

'Good-morrow, Ivan the Rich!' he said.

'Good-morrow, Ivan the Poor! What brings you here?' replied his rich brother.

'I've come to borrow a bowl of flour, Brother. You shall have it back, I promise.'

'Very well,' said Ivan the Rich. 'Here is a bowl of flour, but you must give me a sackful in return.'

'A whole sack for one bowl! What are you saying? Would you rob your own brother?'

'Take it or beg at someone else's door!'

Ivan the Poor took the bowl of flour and went home. But just as he reached the door of his hut, a gust of wind blew all the flour from the bowl, then swept off again.

[23]

That made Ivan the Poor very cross indeed.

'Oh, you wicked Wind!' he cried. 'You have left my poor children hungry. I shall find you and make you pay for your mischief!'

And Ivan the Poor hurried off to catch the Wind as it swept along the road and into the forest. After a while the Wind stopped at a wide oak and crept into a hollow in the tree to rest and get its breath back. As Ivan squeezed in after it, the Wind looked up in surprise.

'Tell me, peasant, why do you follow me about?'

'I was taking my starving children a bowl of flour when you, mischief-maker, flew at me and scattered all my flour. I cannot return home empty-handed!'

'Oh, is that all!' said the Wind. 'Well, there's no need to worry. Here, take this magic cloth. When you put it on the table it will bring whatever you ask.'

Ivan the Poor thanked the Wind, bowed low and hastened home.

As soon as he entered his hut, he spread the cloth on the table and said:

'Cloth, cloth, magic cloth, bring something to eat and drink!'

No sooner were the words out of his mouth than there appeared on the table cheese and onion and mushroom pie, and an enormous ham to cheer the eye.

Ivan the Poor, his wife and their seven children ate till they could eat no more and then went to bed. In the morning the same thing happened at breakfast, this time with curds and cakes and steaming tea. As they were having breakfast, Ivan the Rich arrived.

Seeing the table groaning under the weight of the meal, Ivan the Rich turned green with envy.

'What is this, brother!' he exclaimed. 'Have you become rich over-night?'

'Not rich, but at least I shall never want for food again. And I shall have enough to provide for you too, if you like. Which reminds me, I owe you a sackful of flour. You shall have it right away. Cloth, cloth, magic cloth, bring me a sack of flour!'

A sackful of flour appeared on the table.

Ivan the Rich took the flour without a word and left the hut.

Towards evening he was back again to see his brother.

'I must ask a favour, Brother,' he said. 'I've some guests arriving unexpectedly and the stove is not heated, nor the bread baked. I have nothing to give them. Lend me your magic cloth for an hour or so.'

Ivan the Poor was glad to help his brother and at once handed him the magic cloth.

That evening, Ivan the Rich regaled his guests and, when they had left, he hid the cloth in a chest and took another just like it to Ivan the Poor.

'Thank you kindly, Brother,' he said. 'We have dined excellently thanks to you and your magic cloth.'

Some time later Ivan the Poor and his family sat down to eat, and spread the cloth on the table.

'Cloth, cloth, magic cloth, bring some supper!' said Ivan the Poor.

Yet the cloth just sat there, white and clean and shining, and, though they waited patiently, no food appeared on the table.

Ivan the Poor ran to his brother's house.

'What have you done with my magic cloth, Brother?' he asked.

'Whatever are you talking about? Why, I gave it back to you.' With that, his rich brother drove him angrily out of his house.

Ivan the Poor made his weary way home.

One day passed, and another, then another, and his children began to cry and beg for food. He had nothing to give them, not a crust of bread, nor a scrap of meat. There was nothing for it but to visit his rich brother again.

'Good-morrow, Brother!' he said.

'Good-morrow to you, Ivan the Poor! What brings you here?'

'My children are crying, they are so hungry. Please lend me a bowl of flour or a piece of bread.'

'I have no flour to give you, nor bread. But there's a plate of milk jelly in the larder. You may take that if you wish.'

Ivan the Poor took the plate of milk jelly and went home. The day was warm, the sun shone brightly and its rays streamed down on the milk jelly, which soon melted and dribbled away. By the time Ivan the Poor reached his door, nothing remained but a tiny pool on the plate.

Ivan the Poor was very cross.

'Oh, you foolish Sun!' he cried. 'My poor children are starving. Just wait, I shall make you pay for your mischief!'

So Ivan the Poor set out to catch the Sun. He walked and walked all day, but the Sun was always ahead of him, and it was only towards dusk that it finally sank down behind a big green hill. It was there that Ivan caught up with it.

When the Sun saw Ivan the Poor beside it, it said:

'Tell me, peasant, why do you chase me?'

'I was taking some milk jelly home to feed my starving children when you, foolish Sun, melted the jelly and turned it to water. How can I now go home to my family empty-handed?'

'Oh, is that all!' said the Sun. 'Since it was I that made you suffer, I shall gladly assist you. Take this goat from my flock. Feed it on acorns and it will give you gold instead of milk.'

Ivan the Poor thanked the Sun, bowed low and drove the goat home. He fed it with acorns and then began to milk it. Gold poured into Ivan's bucket.

From that day on, Ivan the Poor's life changed and his children always had plenty to eat.

It was not long, however, before Ivan the Rich heard about the goat and came to visit his brother.

'Good-morrow, Brother!' he cried.

'Good-morrow to you, Ivan the Rich.'

'Do me a favour, Brother,' he said, 'and lend me your goat for an hour. I must repay a debt I owe, and I haven't a kopeck.'

'Very well, you may take the goat, but do not try to cheat me this time.'

Ivan the Rich took the goat and milked it, and, when he had enough gold to spare, he hid the goat in a shed and took an ordinary goat back to his brother's hut.

'Thank you for helping me, Brother,' he said.

Ivan the Poor fed the goat with acorns and then set to milking it, and the milk ran from its udder down to its hoofs, but not a speck of gold was to be seen.

Ivan the Poor hurried off to his rich brother, but he would not so much as listen to him.

'I don't know anything about it,' he said. 'I gave you back the same goat you lent me.'

Ivan the Poor trudged sadly homewards. The days passed, and the weeks flew by, and his family again started to cry with hunger. Winter snow now lay on the ground; it was very cold, and there was nothing in the hut to give the children, not a crust of bread, nor a scrap of meat. Finally, Ivan the Poor had to go to his rich brother to beg for food.

'My children are crying, they are so hungry, Brother,' he said. 'Please lend me a bowl of flour!'

'I have no flour or bread to give you, but you can have some of yesterday's cabbage soup.'

Ivan the Poor took the pot of soup and went home. As he walked along, the Frost crackled and crinkled, the Wind blasted and blustered, and it grew colder by the minute. Soon the Frost began to make sport with the cabbage soup; first it spread a film of ice over the soup, then it swept some fine dry snow over the ice and finally froze the cabbage soup into a solid block of ice.

Ivan was extremely angry.

'Oh, you cruel Frost! You nipped my cheeks, numbed my feet and left nothing in the pot save a small piece of ice. You would kill my children. Just wait, I shall catch you and make you pay for your mischief!'

Ivan the Poor set out to catch the Frost. But Grandfather Frost swept over the fields, with poor Ivan wading through the snow in his wake; it descended on the forest, hanging icicles on the bare boughs, and finally came to rest under a large snowdrift. To the Frost's surprise, Ivan appeared at his side.

'Why do you follow me, peasant? What do you want of me?'

'I was taking a pot of yesterday's cabbage soup home to my children, and you froze it solid. How can I return home and face my starving children empty-handed? My brother stole my magic cloth and the goat that gave the golden milk, and now you have spoiled the cabbage soup!'

'Oh, is that all!' said the Frost. 'Well, I shall give you an enchanted sack. You have only to say: Jump out of the sack! – and two strong men will spring out. If you say: Jump back in the sack! – the two strong men will jump back again.'

Ivan the Poor thanked the Frost, bowed low and went home. When he arrived, he opened the sack and said,

'Jump out of the sack!'

Immediately two strong men sprang out of the sack and rained blows with thick wooden clubs on Ivan the Poor, all the while repeating:

> *'Ivan the Rich thinks of nothing but gain,*
> *Learn to be wise or he'll trick you again!'*

So hard did they thrash him that it was all Ivan could do to mutter: 'Jump back in the sack!'

At that the two strong men jumped back again and sat at the bottom of the sack as quiet as mice.

Towards evening, Ivan the Rich came to his brother's hut.

'Where have you been, Ivan the Poor?' he asked. 'And what have you brought back with you this time?'

'I paid the Frost a visit, Brother, and he gave me an enchanted sack. I have only to say: Jump out of the sack! – and two strong men will spring out and do all that needs to be done.'

'Do me a favour, Brother, and lend me your enchanted sack for a day. My roof is broken and I have no one to repair it.'

'Very well, Ivan the Rich, you may take my sack, but be careful with it!'

Ivan the Rich took the sack home with him and locked the door. He placed the sack carefully in the middle of the floor and called:

'Jump out of the sack!'

At once the two strong men with thick wooden clubs sprang out of the sack and began to lay about him, saying:

> *'What belongs to your brother is not for you,*
> *Return him his goat and his magic cloth too!'*

Ivan the Rich staggered to his brother's hut, with the two strong men beating and thrashing him soundly all the way.

Ivan the Rich and Ivan the Poor

'Oh save me, save me, Ivan the Poor!' begged Ivan the Rich. 'Please take back your magic cloth and your goat that gives the golden milk.'

'Jump back in the sack!' ordered Ivan the Poor.

At once the two strong men returned to the sack and sat there as quiet as mice. Ivan the Rich dragged himself back home more dead than alive and never tried to cheat his brother again.

From that day on, Ivan the Poor and his family lived in good health and cheer,
Growing richer from year to year.
Their spoons are gaily coloured, their bowls are made of wood,
There's butter in the porridge and the soup is very good.

The Bun

OLD grandad once asked his wife to bake him a nice round bun for his tea.

'But what shall I bake it with?' she replied. 'We have no flour.'

'Get on with it, woman!' old grandad snorted. 'Scratch around in the loft and find a few ears of corn.'

The old woman swept up a few handfuls of corn, ground them into flour, kneaded the pastry with sour cream, rolled a round bun, baked it in butter and placed it on the window-ledge to cool.

By and by, the bun was tired of just lying there, so he rolled from the ledge onto the porch, from the porch onto the grass, from the grass out of the gate – and off down the dusty road. On the way he met a cross-eyed hare.

'Round bun, round bun,' piped the cross-eyed hare, 'I am going to eat you.'

'Oh, please, before you eat me, let me sing you a song,' begged the bun.

The hare lifted his floppy ears and the bun began,

'I am a round bun, round bun.
In the loft I was found,
Into flour I was ground,
With cream and butter I was bound,
To bake me nice and round.
When they made me into bread,
From my grannie I soon fled,
From my grandad I soon fled,
And I'll roll away from you.'

The Bun

And off he rolled down the dusty road, so fast the hare could not catch him.

The bun rolled along the road into the forest until he met a big grey wolf.

'Round bun, round bun,' snarled the wolf, 'I am going to eat you.'

'Oh, no, don't eat me, grey wolf,' pleaded the bun. 'Let me sing you a little song.'

And he sang out loud and clear,

> *'I am a round bun, round bun.*
> *In the loft I was found,*
> *Into flour I was ground,*
> *With cream and butter I was bound,*
> *To bake me nice and round.*
> *When they made me into bread,*
> *From my grannie I soon fled,*
> *From my grandad I soon fled,*
> *From the cross-eyed hare I fled,*
> *And I'll roll away from you.'*

And off he rolled down the dusty road, so fast the wolf could not catch him.

As he rolled on through the forest, he met a bear snapping brushwood and stamping down the bracken.

'Round bun, round bun,' growled the bear, 'I'm going to eat you.'

'Oh, big twig-snapper, don't eat me,' cried the bun. 'Listen to my song.'

He struck up his song, while the bear stood listening,

> *'I am a round bun, round bun.*
> *In the loft I was found,*
> *Into flour I was ground,*
> *With cream and butter I was bound,*
> *To bake me nice and round.*
> *When they made me into bread,*
> *From my grannie I soon fled,*
> *From my grandad I soon fled,*

The Bun

From the cross-eyed hare I fled,
From the big grey wolf I fled,
And I'll roll away from you.'

And off he rolled, leaving the bear standing and wiggling his ears.
On rolled the bun, farther and farther into the forest until he met a fox.
'Well, good-morning, Master Bun!' said the fox. 'How scrumptious
you look today!'

The bun was pleased to be praised, and burst into his little song, while
the fox listened and crept closer and closer.

'I am a round bun, round bun.
In the loft I was found,
Into flour I was ground,
With cream and butter I was bound,
To bake me nice and round.
When they made me into bread,
From my grannie I soon fled,
From my grandad I soon fled,
From the cross-eyed hare I fled,
From the big grey wolf I fled,
From twig-snapper bear I fled,
And I'll roll away from you.'

'What a delightful song!' said the fox. 'The only trouble is, my tasty
little morsel, I've become old and rather deaf. Come, sit on my nose and
sing once again.'

The bun was so happy the fox liked his song, he jumped up onto the
fox's nose and began to sing:

'I am a round bun, round bun . . .'.

And the fox – snip-snap! – swallowed him.

The Firebird

ONCE upon a time there lived a king named Berenday who had three sons, Prince Peter, Prince Dmitri and Prince Ivan. The king also had a magnificent orchard with an apple-tree that bore golden apples. One morning he discovered that someone had visited his orchard in the night and stolen some of his golden apples. So upset was he that he sent soldiers to stand guard night and day. But they did not stop the thief, nor even see him.

The king became so miserable he refused all food and drink. His sons tried to cheer him up by promising to guard the orchard themselves.

The eldest son said, 'Tonight I shall keep watch.'

That night he went into the orchard, paced up and down but saw no one. At last, tired and bored, he lay down on the soft grass and fell asleep. And more apples were taken.

In the morning the king asked:

'Do you bring me good news? Do you know the thief?'

'No, Father. I will swear no one came. My eyes were open the whole night through and they saw nobody.'

On the following night, the second son stood guard, and he too settled beneath the tree and fell asleep, and in the morning swore he had seen no one. Yet more apples were gone.

It was now the youngest son's turn. Prince Ivan resolved not to sit down for a moment. Whenever he felt drowsy, he washed his face in the silvery dew and immediately felt refreshed.

Half the dark night passed and then, suddenly, the whole garden became as bright as day. As the light shone brighter and brighter, Prince Ivan had to shield his eyes from the fiery glare. He looked up, and there, in the branches of the apple-tree, he saw the Firebird, pecking at the golden apples.

Climbing stealthily up the tree he seized the bird by its tail. But the Firebird tore free and flew swiftly away, leaving but a golden feather from its tail.

In the morning Prince Ivan went to his father.

'Well, my Son, have you caught the thief?' asked the king.

'No, Sire,' said the young prince, 'I have not caught him, but I know who he is. See, he leaves you this feather to remember him by. The Firebird is the thief.'

The king took the feather, and from that day forth he became cheerful again and began to eat and drink. Not long after, however, he summoned his sons and said:

'My dear Sons, I want you to saddle your trusty steeds and ride across the wide plain in search of the Firebird.'

The three princes bowed low before their father, mounted their horses and rode off in different directions. The eldest son took one road, the second son another and Prince Ivan a third.

Whether Prince Ivan was long on his way I cannot say, but eventually he came upon a stone at a crossroads. On the stone was an inscription: 'Straight ahead to find a wife, turn left to be killed and turn right to lose your horse.' He read the sign and thought, 'I don't want to die. And it is too early to find a wife. First, I must find the Firebird.' So he took the path to the right. After riding some way through the forest, he felt so tired that he dismounted and, tying the horse's feet so that it would not stray, he lay down to rest.

Whether he slept for long or less I could not guess, but when he awoke he found his horse gone. He followed its tracks until at last he came upon its white bones picked clean. The prince was now in despair. How could he continue his journey without a horse?

There was nothing for it but to go on foot. Soon, however, he was tired and exhausted and he sank to the gentle grass. As he did so, a huge grey wolf suddenly appeared.

'Why do you sit and grieve, Prince Ivan?' asked the wolf.

'How can I help being sad, Grey Wolf. I have lost my trusty steed.'

'It was I who killed your horse. But I will take pity on you. Come, tell me, why are you so far from home?'

'My father sent me across the wide plain in search of the Firebird.'

'Well, you could not have found the Firebird on that horse in three-score years. I alone know where he is. If it is truly your wish to find the Firebird, so be it. Since I have eaten your horse, I shall be your true and faithful servant. Jump on my back.'

Prince Ivan climbed upon the grey wolf's back and they sped off as swiftly as the wild wind. Blue lakes skimmed past very fast, green fields swept by in the wink of an eye and, in the space of one night, they arrived at a palace surrounded by a high wall.

'Now listen carefully,' said the wolf, 'and mind what I say. Climb over that wall. You have nothing to fear – all the guards are sleeping. In a chamber within the tower you will see a window, in that window hangs a golden cage and in that cage is the Firebird. Take the bird and hide it beneath your coat. But whatever you do, do not take the cage!'

The young prince climbed over the wall and recognized the tower with the golden cage in the window and the Firebird in the cage. He took the bird and thrust it inside his coat, but he could not bear to leave behind the golden cage.

'Oh, what a beautiful cage it is! What a shame to leave it here!' he thought.

And he quite forgot the wolf's warning. The moment he set hands on the cage, however, a hue and cry arose within the palace, for invisible golden strings led from the cage to a cluster of bells. Trumpets began to blow, drums to beat, bells to ring; the guards woke up, seized Prince Ivan and marched him off to the king.

'Who are you and where are you from?' King Afron demanded angrily.

'I am Prince Ivan, the youngest son of King Berenday.'

'Shame on you! That a prince should try to steal from my palace!'

The young prince hung his head in shame and explained that his father had sent him to find the Firebird who had stolen golden apples from the king's orchard.

On hearing this, King Afron replied, 'If you had come to me, I would willingly have given you the Firebird in respect for your father, King Berenday. But now, the news of your disgrace must spread throughout the land.'

The king paused . . . an idea had come to him.

'However,' he continued, 'if you were to do me a certain favour, I should pardon you and give you the Firebird as just reward for your services. Now listen. In a certain land there dwells King Kusman who owns the White Horse with the Golden Mane. Bring me that horse – and the Firebird is yours.'

Prince Ivan was crestfallen. He returned to his friend, the wolf, waiting beyond the wall.

'I warned you not to touch the cage,' said the wolf. 'Why did you not heed my warning?'

'I am truly sorry, Grey Wolf, please forgive me.'

'Never mind,' said the wolf. 'Climb upon my back again. I gave you my word and I must keep it.'

Off sped the grey wolf with Prince Ivan clinging to his back. Whether they were long on their way I cannot say, but at last they came to the palace where the White Horse with the Golden Mane was stabled.

'Climb over the wall, Prince, while the guards are sleeping,' said the

wolf. 'Enter the stable and take the horse, but mind you leave the golden
bridle hanging from the wall.'

Prince Ivan climbed over the palace wall and, all the guards being
asleep, went into the stable and led out the wonderful White Horse with
the Golden Mane. As he did so, his eye caught the golden bridle hanging
on the wall.

'How can I ride the horse without a bridle?' he said to himself, and
reached out to take it down from the wall. No sooner had he touched the
golden bridle than a hue and cry went up within the palace, for the bridle
was joined by invisible strings to a cluster of tinkling bells. Trumpets
began to blow, drums to beat, bells to ring; and the guards woke up,
seized the prince and marched him off to King Kusman.

'Who are you and where are you from?' the king demanded in a rage.

'I am Prince Ivan, youngest son of King Berenday.'

'What! A prince stealing horses! If you had come to me openly I would
have granted you the horse and the bridle as well, but now I must inform
the world of your dishonour. If, however, you will perform a small
service for me, I shall not tell anyone and I shall reward you with the
White Horse with the Golden Mane. Now listen. You must ride beyond the Land of One Score and Nine and bring me back Fair Helen,
daughter of King Dalmat.'

Prince Ivan was more miserable than before as he returned to the wolf.

'I am sorry, Grey Wolf, please forgive me.'

'Never mind,' said the grey wolf, 'climb upon my back again.'

Off raced the wolf with Prince Ivan clinging to his back. Presently they
reached the land of King Dalmat; in the grounds of his palace the Fair
Helen was strolling with her ladies-in-waiting.

'This time I shall do everything myself,' said the grey wolf. 'You
return to the forest and wait beneath the oak-tree. I shall soon be with
you.'

So the young prince went back into the forest, while the grey wolf
sprang over the wall into the palace grounds. There he crouched behind
a leafy bush and waited patiently for the Fair Helen to pass with all her
ladies-in-waiting. By and by, the fair princess came past the bush and the

wolf seized her at once, tossed her across his back, jumped over the wall and made off with her into the forest.

When he arrived back at the oak-tree, the wolf told Prince Ivan to jump on his back behind the fair princess.

He then raced off along the forest path with Prince Ivan and the Fair Helen upon his back. Blue lakes skimmed past very fast, green fields swept by in the wink of an eye and soon they came to the realm of King Kusman.

'Why so silent and sad, Prince Ivan?' asked the wolf.

'How can I help being sad, Grey Wolf. I have fallen in love with the Fair Helen and she with me. It breaks my heart to part with her. And to think I must trade her for a horse!'

'You need not part with her, we can hide her in the forest, while I change myself into a princess, the living likeness of the Fair Helen, and you shall take me to the king instead.'

So they left the Fair Helen in the forest; the grey wolf struck the damp earth, turned head-over-heels and was at once changed into a princess, the very image of the Fair Helen. Prince Ivan took the wolf-princess by the hand and led her to King Kusman who was delighted.

'Thank you for bringing me such a lovely bride, Prince Ivan,' he said. 'Now the wonderful White Horse with the Golden Mane is yours, and the the golden bridle too.'

Prince Ivan mounted the horse and, riding back to the forest, lifted the Fair Helen into the saddle and galloped swiftly away.

Meanwhile, at the palace, King Kusman held a magnificent wedding feast to celebrate his betrothal to the Fair Helen. After banqueting all day long, he retired late with his new bride to their chamber. But, once in bed, a strange thing happened. Instead of kissing the lips of his young wife, the king kissed the cold wet muzzle of the wolf. So startled was he that he fled screaming from the chamber. The grey wolf at once sprang up and ran away.

It was not long before the fleet-footed wolf caught up with Prince Ivan; he saw that the prince still looked sad.

'What grieves you, Prince Ivan?'

'How can I help being sad! I cannot bear to lose the White Horse with the Golden Mane in exchange for the Firebird.'

'Never fear. I shall help you once more,' said the wolf.

Soon they were in the land of King Afron.

'We shall hide the horse and the Fair Helen,' said the wolf. 'I shall turn myself into a horse, the living likeness of the wonderful White Horse with the Golden Mane and you shall take me to King Afron.'

So they hid the Fair Helen and the White Horse with the Golden Mane deep in the forest and the grey wolf struck the damp earth, turned a somersault and changed into a horse, the very image of the White Horse with the Golden Mane. Prince Ivan led him by the golden bridle to the court of King Afron, who was so delighted, he rewarded the prince with the Firebird in the golden cage.

No sooner had Prince Ivan left the palace than he hurried into the forest, lifted the Fair Helen onto the wonderful White Horse with the Golden Mane and, together, they set off homewards, carrying the Firebird in the golden cage.

Meanwhile, King Afron had the wonderful White Horse brought to him, and he leapt upon its back to go for a ride. Imagine his horror when he found himself clinging not to the smooth white coat of the horse, but to the bristling grey fur of the wolf. So frightened was he that he at once slithered to the ground, staring after the grey wolf as he raced off in pursuit of Prince Ivan.

When he had caught them up, they journeyed on together until they reached the bleached bones of Prince Ivan's old horse.

'Now I must say farewell,' said the wolf, 'for here it was I devoured your horse. Now I have repaid my debt and served you well.'

Prince Ivan dismounted, bowed low three times before his faithful friend and humbly thanked him.

'Do not bid farewell, for you may need me yet,' said the wolf before disappearing into the forest.

'Why should I need him again?' pondered Prince Ivan. 'All my wishes have been fulfilled and I now have everything I could possibly hope for.'

With that he leapt astride the wonderful White Horse behind the Fair

Helen and rode on to his father's land. On the way the fair princess became
thirsty and tired, for the sun was hot and the plain dry. Prince Ivan
stopped his horse by a spring, where they sipped the cool water and then
lay down to rest in the shade of a birch-tree.

Just at that time, the prince's two elder brothers chanced to pass,
empty-handed from their quest for the Firebird. Journeying along the
road towards their father's palace they caught sight of the group resting
beneath the tree. When they realized that their young brother had not
only caught the wondrous Firebird, but had the lovely princess and
the White Horse with the Golden Mane as well, they were angry and
envious.

'Let us kill our brother Ivan,' muttered the eldest brother, 'then all his
spoils will be ours.'

So, without more ado, they drew their swords and killed him, then
drew lots for their prizes, one taking the White Horse with the Golden
Mane, the other the Fair Helen. They forced the princess to tell their
father it was they who had rescued her and the White Horse and the
Firebird. Then, on they rode to the palace to tell their false tales of
heroic deeds.

For full ninety days Prince Ivan's body lay on the plain. But on the
ninety-first day the grey wolf chanced to pass and see his friend, the
prince. An old crow and her young were picking at the body. The grey
wolf quickly darted forward and, seizing a young crow in his teeth, made
as if to tear her apart.

'Listen here, old crow,' snarled the grey wolf. 'Fly to the Land of One
Score and Nine and bring me back the waters of life and death! If you do
that, I'll free your child.'

The old crow flew swiftly away and, at the end of three days, she
returned with two small flasks in her beak. The wolf took the two flasks
and at once ripped the young crow apart. First he sprinkled the water of
death over its corpse – and the two halves joined together. Then he
sprinkled the water of life over its mended body – and straightaway the
young crow opened her eyes and flew off cawing.

Next the grey wolf sprinkled the water of death on the prince's body –

and the wounds healed. Then he sprinkled the body with the water of life – and Prince Ivan sat up rubbing his eyes.

'How soundly I have slept!' he exclaimed.

'But for me you would have slept forever,' replied the grey wolf. 'Your brothers slew you and robbed you of the fair princess, the White Horse with the Golden Mane and the Firebird. Jump upon my back and let us hurry to your father's palace, for today your eldest brother is to marry the Fair Helen.'

Prince Ivan at once leapt upon the wolf's broad back and they raced off to the palace. When they arrived, the young prince took leave of his loyal friend and rushed into the palace.

At the head of the table sat his eldest brother next to the fair princess, whose lovely face was wet with tears. But the moment she saw her true love, she gave a cry of joy and rushed to him. And she then told the king the story of the elder brother's wickedness.

The king was greatly shocked to hear of the cruel misdeeds of his two sons and immediately ordered them to be flung into the deepest dungeons.

That same day Prince Ivan married his Fair Helen. They lived together in health and cheer for many a long and prosperous year.

Good and Evil

THERE once lived two brothers who never saw eye to eye. One was wealthy and sly, the other poor and simple. They chanced to meet on the village street one day and at once set to arguing.

'Life is hard,' said the poor brother, 'and the world can be a cruel place; all the same, it is better to do good than evil.'

'Bunkum!' retorted his brother. 'Doing good will get you nowhere. You've got to be hard and artful to get by.'

They quarrelled thus for several hours and, at last, agreed to put their question to the first folk they encountered. The one who was proved right three times in a row would take all that belonged to the other.

Off they went along the road, through the village and out into the open country until they came upon a man returning from a season's labour in the squire's fields.

'Greetings, friend,' they said. 'We have a question to put to you.'

'Go ahead,' said the man, stopping to fill his pipe.

'Which is better: to do good or evil?'

'That's easy,' said the man. 'There's no sense in doing good; people just take advantage of you. Look at me: I laboured long and hard and all I got for my sweat were a few miserable rubles – and the master tried to cheat me of those. No, no, honesty doesn't pay; it's better to do evil than good.'

'What did I tell you, Brother?' said the rich brother with a triumphant smile.

The poor man was unhappy, but he still had two chances left. Presently they met a merchant riding along the road.

'Greetings, honest merchant,' the brothers called. 'We would like to ask you a question.'

'Go ahead,' said the merchant, pulling up his horse.

'Which is better: to do good or evil?'

'What a stupid question!' replied the merchant with a sneer. 'You cannot make a living doing good. If you want to sell to people, you must lie and cheat until they don't know right from wrong.'

With that he rode on.

'There, you see,' shouted the rich brother. 'I'm right a second time.'

The poor man was silent, but he still had one chance left. On they walked until they encountered a prince in his carriage.

'Greetings, Your Highness!' they called together, bowing low. 'There is a question we would put to you, if Your Lordship pleases.'

The prince stopped his carriage and beckoned the two men forward.

'Which is better: to do good or evil?'

'You peasants are not men of the world or you would not ask such a ridiculous question,' answered the prince. 'Why, if I were to follow the path of goodness, my servants would all revolt against me.'

So saying, he prodded the coachmen hard with his stick and was gone.

'That settles it, Brother,' said the rich brother. 'We shall return home and you will give me all you have.'

The poor man walked sadly home, afraid for his wife and children. What would become of them now? His brother soon came and took all his humble belongings, leaving the hut cold and bare.

'Stay here for the time being,' the rich brother said, 'but I shall be back shortly to take your home. So find another place to live.'

The poor man sat in the bare hut with his family; not a crust of bread or scrap of meat remained. His children soon began to howl and his wife to weep; so he took a sack and went to his rich brother to beg for flour.

'Please give me a handful of flour, anything you can spare,' he pleaded. 'My children are dying of hunger.'

The rich brother was angry at being pestered by his poor relation and decided to teach him a lesson.

'You may have a measure of flour in exchange for an eye,' he said spitefully.

The poor man was horrified, but to save his children he had to consent. What else could he do?

'So be it,' he agreed. 'Put out my eye, and may God forgive you. Only give me some flour.'

So the rich peasant put out his brother's eye and handed him a measure of mouldy flour. When the poor man arrived home, his wife gasped.

'What has happened to you, husband? Where is your eye?'

'My brother put it out in exchange for flour,' he said, explaining to his wife the cruel bargain.

His family grieved and sorrowed for a time, but hunger took their minds off the brother's harsh deed. They had to make the flour into bread and eat it – it was all the food they had.

A week passed, maybe two – and once more the children were crying for food: all the flour was gone. So the poor man took a sack and went to his brother again.

'Please spare me some flour, Brother,' he begged. 'The flour you gave me is all gone.'

The rich brother's patience was at an end. He had no time for poor people who came pestering the rich for help. This time he would make sure his brother would not be back.

'All right, you can have a measure of flour in exchange for your other eye,' he said.

'But how can I live without my eyes, Brother?' cried the poor man. 'You have taken one eye already. Surely, you would not blind me for a measure of flour?'

But the rich brother was firm.

'No eye, no flour,' he said.

The poor man really had no choice. Either he gave up his eye or his children would starve.

'So be it,' he sighed. 'Put out my other eye, and may God forgive you for your cruelty!'

So the rich peasant put out his brother's second eye and filled his sack with flour. The blind man took it and turned for home.

He stumbled along in a world of darkness, groping his way from tree to tree, from fence to fence, until finally he felt the rough-hewn posts of his own gate. His wife met him at the door of the hut, her eyes wide with horror.

'How will we live now that you are blind? Who will feed the children?'

She wept and wept until there were no more tears left in her. Her husband tried to console her.

'Do not weep, dear wife,' he said gently. 'I am not the only blind man in the world. There are many like me and they manage somehow without sight. We shall make out, you'll see.'

The sack of flour was soon gone.

'I won't go to my brother again,' the blind man said to his wife. 'Tomorrow morning, at dawn, lead me to the tall poplar on the road beyond the village and leave me there. In the evening you may come and take me home. With luck, I shall be able to beg a crust of bread or some coins from passers-by.'

Thus it was, at dawn the next day, his wife led the blind man out of the village and stood him beneath the tall poplar. And there she left him.

The blind man sat on the ground, a begging bowl before him, hoping to gain a few coins with which to buy his children bread. After sitting all day without so much as a kopeck in his bowl, he felt the evening coolness descend, yet still his wife did not come. Tired and dejected, he decided to make his own way home. When he heard the trees rustling and the birds twittering all around him, he realized he was lost and would have to spend the night in the forest. Fearing he would fall prey to wolves or bears, he climbed a tree and settled in the topmost branches.

As midnight came, he suddenly heard sounds that made his blood run cold: the shrill cries and wails of evil spirits as they came flying to the hollow beneath the tree in which he squatted. The poor man scarcely dared breathe as he heard their chief ask them all what tricks they had been playing.

'I made a man blind his brother for a handful of flour,' chortled one.

'Quite good, but you could do better,' said the leader. 'For the blind man only has to rub his eyes with the dew beneath this tree and he will see again. All the same, since no human knows the secret, he will remain blind.'

[48]

Then the leader turned to another and asked what tricks he had played.

'I dried up all the water in a village well, leaving not a drop for forty versts.* Many will die of thirst before they reach water.'

'You did well, but you could do better,' said the chief. 'There is a large rock on a hill above the village; if that is moved, enough water will flow to satisfy everyone. All the same, since no man knows of that, the secret will be safe.'

'And what of you?' asked the chief turning to another evil spirit.

'I put out the eyes of the king's only daughter, and the doctors can do nothing for her.'

'Very good, but you could do better,' retorted the chief. 'If her eyes are rubbed with the dew beneath this tree, she will see again. Still, since nobody knows of that, the secret will remain safe.'

Unnoticed at the top of the tree, the blind man heard all that was said. As soon as the evil spirits had departed, he climbed down, quickly rubbed his eyes with the magic dew and, to his great joy, his eyes were healed and he could see again.

'Now I must go to help other unfortunates,' he said to himself.

Gathering as much dew as he could in a small flask, he made his way through the trees until he emerged from the forest. Not far off, he spotted a woman carrying two pails of water.

'Give me a drink of water, Grannie,' he said.

'Alas, my friend,' the old woman replied, 'I have brought this water some forty versts and have spilled more than half on the way. Mine is a large family, they will barely survive even with these drops of water.'

'When I come to your village,' he told her, 'you shall have enough water for everyone, for I know of a secret source.'

The old woman was overjoyed to hear such news, at once gave him a drink then hurried off to tell the villagers. A great crowd gathered to meet him, hoping he could save them.

'Take me to the rock that stands on the hill above your village,' he ordered.

* A 'verst' is an old Russian measure roughly equivalent to two-thirds of a mile.

They conducted him through the village, up to the hill on the other side until they reached an old weather-beaten rock, too large for one man to move. There was no doubt that it was the rock the evil spirits had talked of. Then the people set to, put their shoulders against the rock and pushed; after several moments the rock began to shudder and creak and suddenly – as the rock shifted – water gushed out drenching them all, bowling over several men as it rushed down the hillside, filling every nook and cranny in its broad stream as it ran through the valley. The villagers would never want for water again.

Everyone was overjoyed; they gulped down and splashed about in the water, and did not forget the gratitude they owed the visitor. They made gifts of every kind and provided him with a horse on which he could ride to the king's palace beyond the hills.

Whether he was long on his way I cannot say, but he eventually arrived at the gates of the palace.

'I hear the princess is very sick,' he said to the guards in front of the palace gates. 'Perhaps I can cure her?'

The guards laughed: 'How can a poor peasant like you help the princess when the cleverest doctors in the land can do nothing?'

Yet the peasant was so insistent that the guards finally let him pass and he was brought before the king.

'If you can truly cure my daughter and make her see again, I shall give you half my treasure,' said the king as he took the peasant to his daughter's chamber.

Once at the princess's bedside, the peasant poured the magic dew from his flask and rubbed her eyes with it. As if a heavy curtain had been drawn aside, the princess gazed joyfully at all around her, her bright eyes shining with their former youthful light.

The king's happiness was boundless. And he was as good as his word: he granted the peasant so much treasure that it took a whole caravan of mules to transport the gold, silver and jewels. After much feasting and rejoicing, the peasant set out for home.

Meanwhile, in the peasant's village, his wife and children mourned and sorrowed, believing him dead, probably torn apart by the forest beasts or tormented by the woodland spirits. One evening, however, there came a sharp knocking at their door and a familiar voice rang out:

'Open up, old woman. I am home again.'

Imagine the wife's astonishment to see her husband standing in the doorway, his sight restored, laden with all manner of riches. They were now so wealthy they would never go hungry again.

It was not long before the news reached the ears of his brother, who came hurrying to stare at the fortune.

'Tell me, dear Brother,' he said enviously, 'how did you regain your sight and become so wealthy?'

His brother, being a simple man, told the story – just as it had happened.

Thinking he could profit even more from the secrets of the forest spirits, the rich brother was determined to find them himself. That same evening he stole out of the village, made his way through the forest, climbed the selfsame tree and waited eagerly for the evil spirits to arrive.

On the stroke of midnight the spirits came, buzzing in an angry frenzy.

'How did it happen?' they screamed. 'The blind brother and the princess have their eyes healed and water flows from under the rock. Someone must have overheard us! We must find that person and kill him!'

As he listened, the rich brother trembled so greatly that the branches shook and leaves showered down upon the evil spirits, making them look up. With howls of rage, they flew up the tree, pulled him to the ground and tore him to pieces.

The Snow Maiden

In a Russian village lived an old man and woman. They lived peaceably enough, but their lives were empty – for they had no children of their own to cheer their passing days.

When Winter came, it laid its deep carpet of snow across the fields and meadows and invited the village children to play in its soft folds. The old man and woman gazed wistfully at them from their window, feeling more lonely than ever. But then the old man had an idea.

'Cheer up, old woman,' he said. 'Let's make a daughter out of snow!'

The old woman agreed, so they put on their coats, went into the yard and began to build a daughter out of snow.

First they rolled a ball, then added arms and legs and, finally, placed a snow-head upon snow-shoulders. The old man stuck on a nose and drew a mouth and eyes.

And then a wonderful thing happened. . . The Snow Maiden's lips grew red, her eyes opened and she gazed at the old folk . . . and smiled a warm grateful smile. Then, shaking off the snowflakes, she stepped out of the snow – a real, live girl!

The old pair were overjoyed; they took her into their cottage, unable to believe their good fortune. In the passage of time, the Snow Maiden grew up, not by the day but by the hour – and every day she grew more lovely than ever. Her skin was whiter than the winter snow, her hair russet like the autumn leaves, her eyes blacker than a raven's wing.

And yet it seemed she had no colour at all. There was no end to the old folks' love of their daughter, they doted on her every minute of the day. And the Snow Maiden grew up clever, modest and kind. She did all the work about the cottage and, when she lifted her voice to sing, the whole village stopped to listen.

Winter passed.

Spring sunshine began to warm the land. Patches of green grass appeared amid the snowy wastes and larks took up their woodland song.

Yet the Snow Maiden grew sad.

'What is it, Daughter?' asked the old folk. 'What ails you?'

'All is well, Father. All is well, Mother,' she replied in a hoarse whisper.

By and by, the last snows melted, the first flowers blossomed, sprinkling the meadows with golds and pinks and blues, and the birds of summer returned from their winter migration.

The Snow Maiden grew quieter and sadder every day. She would hide from the sun, seek out a chill shadow and stretch out her pale arms to the rain.

Once a black storm-cloud burst, sending down big hailstones. That excited the Snow Maiden; she ran out to catch the hailstones as though they were precious gems. Yet, no sooner had the sun melted the hailstones than she burst into tears – so bitter you would think a sister was mourning her own dear brother.

Summer followed Spring and her friends made ready to gather berries in the woods.

'Come with us, dear Snow Maiden,' they called to her. 'We are going to play and sing and dance in the forest glades.'

The Snow Maiden shrank back into the shadows, but the old woman urged:

'Go on, Daughter, enjoy yourself with your friends!'

The girls took the Snow Maiden with them into the woods, picked flowers, plaited them into garlands for their hair, sang songs and skipped along the woodland paths – as merry and carefree as scarlet poppies in a summer breeze.

Only the Snow Maiden did not join in – she walked alone, head drooping, no smile upon her frozen lips.

As the damp of evening descended upon the forest, the girls gathered brushwood for a fire; and, when it was alight, they took turns jumping over it. The Snow Maiden alone hung back, fearful of the orange flames that flicked their tongues towards her.

But when her turn came, the girls pushed her forward, not letting her go.

With tears glistening upon her pallid cheeks, she leaped over the fire. . .

And, in a sighing hiss, was gone . . . melted away into a wisp of white mist.

When her friends looked about them, the Snow Maiden was nowhere to be seen. They cupped their hands and shouted:

'Aa-oo-oo, Snow Maiden, Aa-oo-oo! Where are you?'

But nothing was heard save the echo of their voices and the distant hooting of an owl deep in the forest.

Axe Porridge

AN old soldier was on his way home on leave and passing through a village. Tired and hungry, he rapped at the first cottage he came to.

'Give an old soldier a bite to eat, dear lady,' he said to the woman who opened the door.

Pretending she had not heard, the woman went to close the door, but it was too late: the soldier had squeezed his way in.

'Come now, you surely have some food for a soldier of the king,' he said.

In actual fact, the old woman had plenty of food in her larder, but she was as mean as the winter wind.

'Oh, brave soldier, I have nothing even to feed myself on – no bread, no onion, no cabbage.'

'Then, make me some porridge,' said the soldier.

'But I've nothing to make it with,' wailed the woman.

Noticing an axe by the door, the soldier thought of how to outwit the mean woman.

'Well, if you've nothing, that's too bad,' he said. 'I tell you what, pass me that axe and I'll make us some porridge out of that.'

'Axe porridge!' exclaimed the woman. 'Whoever heard of that?'

Her curiosity got the better of her, though, and she picked up the axe and handed it to the soldier. The soldier washed the axe carefully, dropped it into a pot of water and placed it on the stove to boil.

The woman stared as the pot bubbled and boiled. Now and again the soldier stirred the water and tasted it with a spoon. At last, with a look of satisfaction, he turned to her and said:

'It smells delicious; it won't be long now. A pity there's no salt.'

'Oh, I have some salt,' said the woman. 'Here, take some.'

The soldier sprinkled salt into the pot and then tasted a spoonful of the water again.

'Not bad, not bad. Mind you, if we had just a handful of oats, it would be perfect.'

The old woman at once brought a bowl of oats from the larder.

'Here, take as much as you need,' she said, eager to see how the axe porridge would turn out.

The soldier went on with his cooking, stirring the pot from time to time, testing it and smacking his lips.

'This really is coming along fine; all it needs now is a knob or two of butter to make the most delicious axe porridge you've ever tasted.'

The old woman brought him butter, too, and he buttered the porridge.

'That will do,' he suddenly exclaimed, his face beaming. 'Now, bring two bowls and two spoons, my good woman, and let us dine!'

Axe Porridge

They both sat down to a steaming bowl of porridge and the old woman vowed she had never tasted such wonderful porridge in her life.

'But when will we eat the axe?' she asked.

'Oh, the axe is not ready yet,' explained the soldier. 'In a day or two I'll boil it up again and eat it for supper.'

With that, he slipped the axe up his sleeve, took his leave and set off for another village. He went chuckling on his way, proud of how he had tricked the mean old woman into parting with her porridge – and how he had earned himself an axe into the bargain.

Ivan Bear's Ear

An old peasant and his young wife went mushrooming one day in the forest. As they wandered apart through the trees, they soon lost sight of of one another. The old man hooted, the woman tooted, they both hooted and tooted – but they did not find one another. To pass the time the woman struck up a song in her shrill voice:

'Sunshine, moonshine, all will soon be fine. I am a poor maid all alone in the forest.'

There was someone in the forest who did hear her, for a deep bass voice echoed back:

'Sunshine, moonshine, all will soon be fine. I am a young man all alone in the forest.'

The two voices, one shrill, one deep, sang in harmony until presently the singers met. Imagine the woman's surprise to find herself face to face with a bear.

The bear at once carried her off to his house in the depths of the forest. And there they lived for time out of mind. By and by, a son was born and they gave him the name Ivan Bear's Ear. He grew and grew – not by the day but by the hour.

When he was full grown, he said to his mother:

'Let us return home; the bear's life is not for us. Climb upon my back and I shall carry you through the forest.'

Eventually they arrived at the old man's hut; through the window they could see him weaving bast shoes. Ivan Bear's Ear rapped loudly at the door and called:

'Let two weary travellers in for the night.'

The old man was overjoyed to see his wife again. Nor did he mind her bringing in the young stranger.

After supper, Ivan Bear's Ear asked the old man to make him a one-pood*club. When the club was made, Ivan took it and struck the ground with all his might, breaking the club in two. He then asked the old man to make a two-pood club. That done, he struck the ground again: once, twice, thrice. And the third time it broke.

Again he asked for a club, this time weighing three poods. Once, twice, thrice he hit the ground with it, but it did not break.

Then he took the club and a fiddle, said good-bye to his mother and returned to the forest.

He walked along a forest path, playing a tune on his fiddle – and the music rang out merry and clear. As he passed a tree, out ran a hare, did a hop and a jig and asked to be taken along.

They continued together, Ivan Bear's Ear and the hare, and soon they encountered a fox. As soon as she heard the fiddle she too started to dance and twirl her bushy tail.

'Ivan Bear's Ear, please take me with you,' she pleaded.

So the three of them – Ivan Bear's Ear, the hare and the fox – went along the path together. Towards them danced a wolf, slapping his paws in time with the music.

'Ivan Bear's Ear, may I join you?' he asked.

Next they met a bear, scattering twigs and leaves as he waltzed along the road. He too joined the band. They journeyed on – Ivan Bear's Ear, the hare, the fox, the wolf and the bear – until they came to a lake. And there they built themselves a pretty wooden hut.

Once the hut was built, Ivan Bear's Ear gave each of them instructions: the hare was to go to the village and fetch bread and ham, the fox was to bring some chickens, the wolf some calves, the bear a honeycomb. This they did: the hare bread and ham, the fox several chickens, the wolf two calves, the bear a honeycomb.

After they had eaten, all that remained were a few licks of honey. These they gave to the spirits of the lake, so that they too would not go hungry. That done and the spirits appeased, the band of friends were thirsty.

* A 'pood' is an old Russian weight measurement roughly equivalent to sixteen kilograms.

Ivan Bear's Ear

Ivan Bear's Ear sent the hare for water. As the hare went to dip his pot into the lake, however, a water nymph suddenly appeared from the water – a lovely girl, with skin the colour of moonlight, hair like silk, eyes like emeralds – but with a scaly tail like a fish.

She thanked the hare for his gift of honey but warned him the lake was charmed by Baba Yagá, the evil, hooked-nose witch. She would let no one take water from her lake.

The hare was afraid; all the same, he hid beneath a bush waiting for the witch. As night fell, she appeared, flying through the air in her iron mortar and driving herself along with a pestle.

'Here I come to drink the honeyed water,' she cackled.

Then, catching sight of the hare quivering behind his bush, she screeched:

'Ah, so it is you, squint-eyed hare!'

Taking up her iron pestle, she beat the hare in and out of the bush, then flew across to the other side of the lake.

The hare hopped painfully back to Ivan Bear's Ear, complaining of his sore head. The next night it was the fox's turn to go for water. Again Baba Yagá came flying in her mortar to taste the honeyed water. Seeing the fox, she cried:

'Ah, so it is you, brush-tailed fox!'

And she set about the fox with her iron pestle, then flew across to the other side of the lake.

The fox dragged herself back to the hut, complaining of a splitting head.

On the third night the wolf went for water. He too sat under a bush waiting for Baba Yagá; he did not have long to wait for soon she came flying down screaming:

'Ah, it is you, stumpy-tailed wolf!'

And she beat him with her iron pestle until the poor wolf was more dead than alive. When she had flown back across the lake, the wolf slunk home without a drop of water.

Next it was the bear's turn. But he fared no better. Baba Yagá called:

'Ah, so now it is you, clumsy-pawed bear!'

And she beat him so hard the poor bear scarcely managed to drag himself back to the hut.

Ivan Bear's Ear himself went for water on the fifth night, but he did not hide behind a bush. Instead, he stood at the water's edge, waiting boldly for the witch. When she arrived, she screeched louder than ever:

'Ah, so you have come at last, Ivan Bear's Ear! I am going to kill you.'

As she stepped from her mortar, Ivan Bear's Ear sprang quickly at her before she could raise her iron pestle; he gave her such a thrashing with his three-pood club that she soon begged him to stop.

'I will spare your life,' he said, 'on condition you remove your spell from this lake and let whosoever wishes drink its waters.'

The witch had to agree. Then, climbing painfully into her mortar, she flew off and was never seen again in those parts.

As for Ivan Bear's Ear, he lives on still in the hut with his animal brothers, playing his fiddle and drinking his fill of the lake's honeyed waters whenever he wishes.

Fenist the Bright-Eyed Falcon

MANY years ago in a small Russian village there lived a rich peasant and his three daughters. When his wife, died the old man wanted to hire a servant, but his youngest daughter, Marushka, said:

'Don't worry, Father, I can keep house for you.'

So Marushka began looking after the family, and a fine housekeeper she made. Her father loved her dearly and was proud of such a pretty and hard-working daughter. But her two sisters were vain and ugly; nothing ever satisfied them – not caftans or sarafans, not gowns or shawls.

One day the old man made ready for market and, before setting out, asked:

'Tell me, my Daughters, what gifts shall I bring you?'

'Bring us each a shawl,' said the two elder daughters at once, 'with flowers in red and gold.'

Marushka was silent.

'What would *you* like, my child?' asked her father.

'Bring me a feather of Fenist the Bright-Eyed Falcon,' she said at last.

The peasant went off and presently returned with the shawls. But, though he had sought the Falcon's feather everywhere, he had to disappoint his youngest daughter.

Some weeks later he again made ready for market.

'Well, my Daughters, what shall I bring you this time?' he asked.

The two elder daughters replied eagerly:

'Bring us each a pair of silver shoes.'

But Marushka repeated:

'Bring me a feather of Fenist the Bright-Eyed Falcon, Father.'

All that day the peasant searched the market. He bought the shoes easily enough, but could find no Falcon's feather, and so returned without it. Once more his youngest daughter comforted him:

[63]

'No matter, perhaps you will find it another day.'

Several months passed, and, as he set out for market a third time, his two elder daughters cried:

'Bring us each a new gown.'

But Marushka persisted:

'Bring me a feather of Fenist the Bright-Eyed Falcon.'

Though he asked at every booth and stall at the market, no person had such a feather. On his way home, he chanced to meet an old man by the roadside.

'Good-day, old man!' said the peasant.

'Good-day to you, Brother! Where are you bound for?'

'Back to my village. I go with heavy heart – my youngest daughter asked for a feather of Fenist the Falcon, but I return empty-handed.'

The old man smiled as he took a box from his pocket.

'I have the very feather you seek,' he said. 'It is charmed, but I know your daughter to be honest and I'll gladly make her a present of it.'

So saying, the old man took the feather from the box and handed it to the peasant. It looked just like any other feather, but he received the gift thankfully and rode off.

On arriving home, he distributed the gifts among his daughters. The two elder daughters tried on their new gowns and mocked Marushka:

'Silly you are, and silly you always will be! Stick the feather in your hair and see how fine you'll look!'

Marushka smiled and murmured:

'We shall see.'

Late that night, when the whole household was asleep, Marushka took the feather from its box, flung it to the floor and said softly:

'Come to me, Fenist, my Bright-Eyed Falcon!'

And an amazing thing happened: the feather turned into a handsome young man, more dashing and bold than can ever be told. They talked together until dawn, but, at first light, he struck the floor and changed into a Falcon. When Marushka opened the window, he soared up into the grey sky.

For three nights she made her dear Falcon welcome. During the day he winged about the blue heavens; but as soon as dark night descended he returned to Marushka as a handsome young man.

On the fourth day, however, Marushka's two sisters heard her talking with someone in her room and, at dawn, they watched the Falcon flutter from the window and fly up into the heavens.

That day the two spiteful girls stuck a row of sharp knives along the window ledge in their sister's room. Marushka did not notice them and went to bed as usual. During the night the Falcon came and beat against the window ledge until both his wings were cut by the knives. Marushka slept on and heard nothing.

'Farewell, my love,' he sighed at last. 'If you love me truly you will find me, but it won't be easy. I live at the ends of the earth. To reach me you must wear out three pairs of iron shoes, break three iron staffs and eat through three stone loaves.'

Marushka caught these words through the mist of her slumber, sprang quickly out of bed and ran to the window. But it was too late; the Falcon was gone. All that remained were drops of blood trickling from the sharp knives onto the window ledge. Marushka wept long and bitterly and her tears washed away the drops of blood.

The next morning, she went to her father and said:

'Give me your blessing, Father. I go in search of my true love. If I succeed we shall meet again; if I die, then so be it.'

The peasant was heartbroken to part with his favourite daughter, but seeing her tears he knew he must let her go.

So Marushka ordered three pairs of iron shoes, three iron staffs and three stone loaves. Then she set off on her long journey to seek Fenist the Falcon.

Across the open plain she wandered, through the dark forests and over the high mountains. The little birds cheered her with their song, the brooks washed her dusty feet and the dark forests bade her welcome. And not a soul harmed her, for all the wild beasts had consented to help her. On and on she went until at last one pair of iron shoes wore out, one iron staff broke and one stone loaf was eaten through.

At that moment she emerged into a clearing in the forest – in the clearing stood a little hut on hen's feet spinning round.

'Little hut, little hut,' said Marushka, 'turn your back to the trees and your face to me, please.'

The little hut turned its back to the trees and its face to Marushka, and in she went through the open door. On the stone stove lay Baba Yagá, a bony hag with a long hook nose and a pointed tooth that covered her chin.

When Baba Yagá saw the girl, she screeched:

'Foo, foo, I smell Russian blood! Who are you come to my door, never met by me before?'

'My name is Marushka and I seek Fenist the Falcon, Grannie.'

'You have far to go, pretty one! You must journey through the forest to a distant realm to find him. The queen of that realm is a cunning sorceress, who gave your Fenist a magic potion and, while the spell was upon him, made him marry her. But I shall help you. Go first to my elder sister. Take this silver saucer and golden egg. When you arrive at the queen's palace, take work there as a servant. After your day's work, put the golden egg on the silver saucer. It will roll around the saucer by itself. Should the queen wish to buy it, do not sell – just ask for Fenist.'

Then Baba Yagá took a ball of golden thread, rolled it along the path and said:

'Follow the golden thread into the forest; it will show you the way.'

Marushka thanked the witch and continued on her way. The forest closed about her and seemed to grow darker and denser as she walked on. After some time, her second pair of iron shoes wore out, her second iron staff broke and her second stone loaf was finished. She came to another clearing. In the middle was a little hut that turned on hen's feet.

'Little hut, little hut,' said the girl, 'turn your back to the trees and your face to me, please.'

The hut turned its back to the trees and its face to Marushka, and in she went. There on the stone stove sat another Baba Yagá, more bony and fearsome than her sister.

The moment she caught sight of Marushka she muttered:

'Foo, foo, Russian blood, never met by me before, now I smell it at my door! Who dares to enter my house?'

'It is I, Marushka, and I seek Fenist the Falcon, Grannie. Your sister sent me.'

'Very well, my pretty one, I shall help you. Take this golden needle and silver frame. The needle embroiders gold and silver on red velvet. Should the queen wish to buy it, do not sell – ask to see Fenist the Falcon. But, first, go to my other sister; she will tell you what to do next.'

Marushka thanked the second witch and, casting the ball of golden thread upon the ground, followed it back into the forest. The farther she wandered into the forest, the blacker and bleaker it became; its trees and shrubs caught at her sleeves and scratched her knees. But she pushed on, never glancing back.

Whether she walked for long time or less I could not guess, but finally the third pair of iron shoes wore out, the third staff broke and the third stone loaf was eaten right through. Just then, Marushka came into a glade; again she saw a little hut on hen's feet turning round.

'Little hut, little hut,' she said, 'turn your back to the trees, and your face to me, please.'

The hut turned its back to the trees and its face to Marushka, and in she went through the open door. There sat the third witch, the boniest and ugliest of all.

As soon as she saw the girl, she exclaimed:

'Foo, foo, Russian blood, never met by me before, now I smell it at my door! Who dares to enter Baba Yagá's house?'

'It is I, Marushka, I seek Fenist the Falcon, Grannie.'

'He is not easy to find, my dear, but I shall help you. Take this silver distaff and golden spindle. Hold the spindle and it will spin a thread of pure gold. Should the queen wish to buy it, do not sell. Ask to see Fenist the Falcon.'

Marushka thanked her, dropped the ball of golden thread upon the damp ground and followed it into the dense forest. She had not gone far when she heard a roaring and a rumbling. The owls fluttered and wheeled

about, the mice scampered beneath her feet and the cross-eyed hares ran across her path. As she stopped in alarm, a grey wolf suddenly appeared.

'Have no fear, Marushka,' the wolf said. 'Come, climb on my back and I shall carry you.'

The girl sat astride the wolf's broad back, and off they sped like the wind after the ball of thread. They crossed rolling meadows and wide plains, rivers of honey between banks of milk jelly, and tall mountains that pierced the clouds. On and on raced the wolf, with Marushka clinging tightly to his back, until at last they reached a crystal palace, its golden domes glittering in the sun. And there was the queen herself staring down from a window of her white tower.

Marushka jumped from the grey wolf's back, took her bundle and, thanking the wolf, went to the foot of the white tower. She curtseyed politely and said:

'Excuse me, Your Majesty, do you need a servant girl who can spin, weave and embroider?'

'If you can do all three well, then enter and set to work,' replied the queen.

So Marushka became a servant at the palace. She toiled without rest throughout the first day and, when evening came, she took her golden egg and silver saucer from her bundle and said:

'Roll, roll, golden egg, round the silver saucer, and show me Fenist, my own true love.'

As the golden egg rolled round the silver saucer, the face of Fenist the Falcon appeared. Marushka gazed at him and tears furrowed her silken cheeks.

'Oh Fenist, my Fenist, why have you deserted me?' she sobbed.

At that moment the queen entered and said:

'Sell me your silver saucer and golden egg.'

'They are not for sale,' she replied, 'but you may take them if you let me see Fenist the Falcon.'

The queen consented.

'Very well, let it be so. Tonight, when he is asleep, you may enter his chamber.'

Night came, Marushka went to the chamber and saw Fenist the Falcon fast asleep. He could not be wakened, for the cunning queen had stuck a magic sleeping pin in his shirt. No matter how loud and long Maruskha called him, kissed his dark brow and caressed his pale hands, he slept on without waking. As the rays of morning light came through the window, she still had not roused her beloved and she had to leave.

All that day she toiled without cease and in the evening took out her silver embroidery frame and golden needle; as the needle worked silently, she murmured:

'Please embroider a towel for my Fenist to wipe his brow in the morning.'

The queen again entered and, seeing the silver frame, said:

'Sell me your silver frame and golden needle.'

'That I cannot do,' Marushka replied, 'but you may take them if you permit me to see Fenist the Falcon once more.'

The queen agreed. 'Very well. You may see him tonight.'

As night fell, Marushka entered his chamber and saw Fenist lying on the bed deep in slumber.

'Oh, my Fenist, my bold and handsome Falcon,' she sighed. 'Wake up and speak to me!'

But Fenist slept on soundly, for the cunning queen had left a magic pin in his black hair as she had combed it, and Marushka could not rouse him, however much she tried.

At daybreak Marushka had to give up in despair and leave. That day she again laboured without pause and, when evening arrived, she took out her silver distaff and golden spindle. The queen once more asked to buy them. But Marushka only repeated:

'They are not for sale, but you may take them if only you will allow me to see Fenist the Falcon for the last time.'

'Very well,' agreed the queen, knowing that Marushka would not be able to rouse him – for she had drugged him with a sleeping potion.

Night drew on and Marushka went to the chamber for the last time. But Fenist was deep in slumber as before.

'Oh, my Fenist, my bold and handsome Falcon, wake up, wake up,' she cried in despair.

Fenist slept on throughout the night. And, though she tried again and again to rouse him, it was no good. When it was almost light she stroked his dark hair as she wept her last farewell. A hot tear rolled down her cheek and fell on Fenist's shoulder and burned him. At last he stirred and opened his bright eyes. Seeing Marushka, he at once took her in his arms.

'Can it really be you, my Marushka? So you have worn out three pairs of iron shoes and broken three iron staffs and eaten through three stone loaves? Weep no more, for nothing can part us now.'

But, as they prepared to leave the palace, the queen caught them and had them brought before her court. The nobles held council to decide the fate of Fenist and Marushka. Fenist addressed them:

'Whom do you consider a worthy wife: the one who loves me so dearly she would follow me to the ends of the earth, or the one who would sell and bewitch me?'

Fenist the Bright-Eyed Falcon

And the nobles consulted and gave their verdict:
'The one who truly loves you shall be your wife.'
So Fenist the Bright-Eyed Falcon married his true love, Marushka, and they returned to her land. There they held a feast so grand it is still remembered to this day.

*

It was at the feast I heard this tale,
There it was I drank mead ale.
Though it flowed down my beard, my mouth stayed dry,
For never a drop passed my lips, swear I.

The Goat's Funeral

An old man and his wife lived a lonely life with no one for company save their old goat. That beast had become so fond of its master that it trotted after him wherever he went.

One day the old man set off for the forest to gather birch bark for making bast sandals; while he went about his work, the goat wandered near by, chewing the grass. Suddenly it began to paw the ground as if digging for something. By the time the old man's work was finished, the goat had made a large hole, and there at the bottom lay an old chest.

You can imagine the old man's joy when he brought it up and found it full of gold. He cast aside his birch bark, snatched up the chest and hurried home, the faithful goat trotting at his heels.

'Well, old man,' his wife told him, 'this is God's will. He is rewarding us in our old age for suffering such poverty all our lives. Now we can live in comfort.'

'No, old woman,' replied her husband, 'it is the goat's fortune; we must treat him as one of the family.'

So, from that day on, they gave the goat the choicest food, the warmest bed by the stove and the greenest grass in the meadows. Mind you, the old peasant and his wife did not live badly either: they lived and prospered and knew no sorrow.

Not long after, however, the poor goat fell sick and died. What were they to do with him?

'It would surely be a sin to throw his body to the dogs,' the man told his wife. 'After all, we owe all our fortune to that goat. I'd best go to the priest and ask him to give the goat a proper Christian burial, as grand as the village has ever seen.'

And the old man went to the priest to explain his plan.

'Greetings, Father. I have come to ask a favour of you. My wife and

I have suffered a bereavement – our goat has died. We want you to bury him.'

When the priest heard this request he flew into a rage, seized the unfortunate man by the beard and began to shake him up and down.

'You miserable sinner!' he bellowed. 'How dare you come here asking me to bury your stinking goat!'

'Wait, Father,' squeaked the old man. 'This is no ordinary beast. He was a devout Christian and left you two hundred rubles in his will.'

The priest hastily changed his manner.

'Listen, old man,' he said, 'I wasn't beating you for asking me to bury your dear goat – but for not summoning me earlier to give him the last rites.'

The priest took the two hundred rubles and told the peasant to go to the deacon to make arrangements for the funeral. When the old man found the deacon, he greeted him cordially.

'God be with you, Deacon, come home with me to the funeral repast.'

'Why, who has died?' asked the deacon.

'I do not think you had the pleasure of meeting my goat. Never mind about that now; he's the one that's passed away, you see,' explained the old man.

On hearing that, the deacon began to box the old man's ears.

'Don't beat me, Deacon,' wailed the peasant. 'You see, my goat was no ordinary beast; he was a good Christian and, before he passed away, he bequeathed you a hundred rubles.'

'Oh, my dear Sir!' said the deacon. 'Why did you not inform me earlier about his glorious passing? Go quickly and tell the bell-ringer to ring the church bell for the goat's soul.'

The old man hastened to the bell-ringer and asked him to ring the church bell for his goat. That churchman at once lost his temper and tugged hard at the old man's beard.

'Let go, let go! I beg of you,' cried the peasant. 'The goat was a good Christian and left you fifty rubles for tolling the bell.'

'Why did you not tell me of his passing before?' said the bell-ringer. 'I would have sounded the bell at once.'

The Goat's Funeral

And rightaway he seized the bell-ropes and pulled for all he was worth.

The priest and the deacon arrived at the old man's house to lead the funeral procession to the graveyard. They placed the goat in a fine oak coffin, lowered him into his grave and the priest pronounced as grand an oration as had ever been heard.

Not long after the burial, rumour of the strange affair reached the ears of the bishop, who summoned the priest and the old man before him.

'How dare you grant a Christian burial to a goat, you sinners!' roared the bishop.

'But, you see,' said the old man, 'the goat was not at all like other goats. Before he died, he left Your Holiness a thousand rubles.'

'Oh, my good Sir,' stuttered the bishop, 'I am not criticizing you for giving your goat a Christian burial – but for not anointing him with holy oil before he died!'

With that, the bishop took the thousand rubles, dismissed the priest and the old man and pronounced his blessing:

'May the goat rest in peace!'

The Castle

A MOUSE once came upon an empty horse's skull in a meadow. Thinking it would make a cosy home, she called:

'Castle, castle! Does anybody live in the castle?'

When there was no reply, she crept in and made her home in the skull.

Next a frog hopped by and croaked:

'Castle, castle! Does anybody live in the castle?'

'I do,' came a squeaky voice. 'Who are you?'

'I am old Croaker the Frog.'

'Then come and live with me,' said the mouse.

The frog hopped in and together they made their home in the old skull. Presently, a hare ran by and asked:

'Castle, castle! Does anybody live in the castle?'

He was answered by a squeak and a croak:

'We do. Who are you?'

'I am Ever-Cheerful, the cross-eyed hare.'

'Then come and join us,' called the mouse and the frog.

Now the skull held the three of them. Shortly after, a fox passed by and called:

'Castle, castle! Is anybody home?'

The mouse, the frog and the hare all answered and asked who the visitor was.

'I am Ever-Artful, the brush-tailed fox.'

'Well, come on in,' they said.

Now there were four in the skull.

A wolf was next to pass by.

'Castle, castle, is anybody home?' he cried.

When four voices asked him who he was, he replied:

'I am Ever-Fearful, the big grey wolf.'

So they invited him in.

By and by, a bear lumbered by and growled:

'Castle, castle, who lives in this castle?'

And five voices shouted together:

'Little Squeaker, Old Croaker, Ever-Cheerful, Ever-Artful and Ever-Fearful. And who might you be?'

'I am Crush-You-All, the big brown bear,' he answered.

Then he sat on the skull and squashed them all.

The Flying Ship

THERE once lived an old peasant and his wife with their three sons. The two eldest were clever and hard-working, clean and smart, but the youngest was a Fool who went about in a black smock and was forever dirty.

One day, news came to the village that the king had given instructions for a flying ship to be built. Whoever could build it would receive the hand of his daughter and half his kingdom.

The two eldest brothers made up their minds to try their luck; the father gave them his blessing, the mother filled their bags with white bread, meat and wines and sent them on their way with a tender farewell. Not long after, the Fool also begged to go.

'Don't be stupid,' scolded his mother. 'You'd be eaten by wolves as soon as you set foot outside the village.'

But there is no reasoning with a Fool. He had made up his mind to go and so pestered the old folk that, in the end, they were glad to be rid of him. His mother prepared a bag of burnt rusks and a flask of plain water and sent him on his way.

He had not gone far when he met an old beggar by the wayside who asked whither he was bound. He told the beggar about the king's request and the reward.

'Can you really build such a ship?' asked the beggar.

'No, I cannot,' replied the Fool.

'Then why are you going?' asked the wayfarer.

'God knows,' said the Fool.

'Well, if that's the case, then you're in no hurry. Come, let's rest together and have a bite to eat. What have you in your bag?'

The Fool was ashamed to show his poor fare, but the old beggar reassured him:

'Never mind how poor it is; what God gives, we must be thankful for.'

So the Fool undid his bundle – and could hardly believe his eyes: instead of black rusks he found white buns and all kinds of sweetmeats. These he shared with his companion.

'You see how God takes pity on a Fool,' said the beggar. 'Somebody has love for you even if your own mother has not. Come now, let us have a drink.'

The Fool was even more surprised to find the water in his flask had turned to wine. And he shared that too. After the meal, the beggar told the Fool how he had encountered his brothers and how they had refused to share their food with him.

'For your simple heart I shall reward you,' he said. 'Listen well: enter the forest, approach the first tree you see, cross yourself three times and strike the tree once with your axe. That done, throw yourself to the ground, cover your face and sleep till dawn. At first light you will see before you a splendid ship; sit in it and fly wheresoever it takes you. But mark my words: take on board every wayfarer you pass.'

Thanking the beggar, the Fool continued on his way. When he reached the forest, he approached the first tree and carried out the old man's instructions: crossed himself three times, cut a snick in the tree with his axe, fell to the ground, covered his eyes and went to sleep. He was awakened by the first rays of dawn, and there before him stood a magnificent ship! No sooner had he sat on board than it rose up into the air, soaring high above the treetops, the rivers and the fields. As he flew along, he spied a man below kneeling on the ground, his ear pressed to the earth.

'Ahoy there, fellow,' shouted the Fool. 'What are you doing with your ear pressed to the ground?'

'I am listening to news from far and near,' called back the man. 'My ears serve me so well I can hear all that is happening in the world.'

'Come and join me in my flying ship,' invited the Fool, bringing his vessel down to land alongside the kneeling man.

The man readily agreed, climbed on board and off they flew into the blue sky. They had not flown far when they saw a man hopping on one leg with the other tied to his ear.

'Ahoy there, fellow!' shouted the Fool. 'Why do you hop on one foot with the other tied to your ear?'

'Because if I didn't,' replied the man, 'I would step across the world in no time at all.'

'Then come and join us in my flying ship,' said the Fool, bringing it down to land.

The man on one foot hopped into the ship and off they flew again over forest and plain until they noticed a man shooting his gun at nothing in the sky. The Fool brought his ship down and asked the marksman why he was aiming his gun at the sky when there was not a bird in sight.

'Because I am so long-sighted I can only see birds and beasts a thousand miles away,' sighed the man.

'Then come and join us,' said the Fool.

When he was safely on board, the Fool cast off and the four were soon soaring through the blue sky. On and on they sailed in the flying ship until they saw a man below carrying a sackful of loaves on his back. The Fool steered the ship until it was level with the man.

'Ahoy there, fellow!' he called. 'Where are you going with such a load?'

'I am going to town to get bread for my dinner,' replied the man.

The Fool was puzzled: 'But you have a whole sackful of loaves on your back!'

'That's nothing,' was the retort. 'I could swallow that in one go and still be hungry.'

'Come and join us,' called the Fool, landing his ship beside the hungry man – who accepted the offer and joined the crew on board the flying ship.

They had not gone far when they caught sight of a man walking round and round a lake. When the Fool enquired what he was doing, the man called back:

'I feel thirsty, but I can find no water.'

'But, there's a whole lake right in front of you,' said the Fool in amazement. 'Why don't you drink that?'

'Alas, I'd swallow this lake in one gulp and still go thirsty,' said the man.

So the Fool invited him to join his voyage and the thirsty man agreed. On they flew until they saw a man walking into a forest with a bundle of brushwood on his back.

'Hey there, old man!' shouted the Fool. 'Why are you taking brushwood into the forest?'

'This is no ordinary brushwood,' called the man. 'I only have to scatter it over the plain and a whole army will spring up.'

He, too, joined the ship and next they met a man carrying a bale of hay – but no ordinary hay. No matter how hot the sun, he only had to spread the hay upon the ground and a cool breeze would spring up; snow and frost would follow.

He was the last wayfarer to join the band; it was getting dark and no more travellers could be seen below. Thus they sailed on through the dark, starry night until they reached the royal courtyard as morning dawned.

They arrived as the king was having his breakfast. Seeing the flying ship landing on his lawn, he immediately despatched a servant to discover who the visitors were. On learning that not a single one was of noble blood – they were all common peasants – the king was extremely displeased: how could he marry his daughter to a simple peasant?

'What if I set some impossible tasks?' he thought. 'That will rid me of these peasants without going back on my word.'

So the king sent an order to the Fool to bring him a flask of the Water of Life – before the meal was over!

Now, while the king was informing his servant of this command, the first wayfarer (the one who had heard news from far and near) listened to the conversation and told the Fool.

'What am I to do?' he wondered. 'I would not find such Water in a year or even a lifetime!'

'Do not worry,' said Giantsteps. 'I shall see to it in a trice.'

And as the servant brought the command, Giantsteps was already unhitching his leg from his ear; he sped off and collected the Water of Life in no time at all.

'There is no hurry,' he thought to himself. 'I'll just have forty winks beneath this windmill before I return.' And he dozed off.

Back at the palace, the king was just finishing his breakfast and the flying sailors were becoming uneasy. The first wayfarer put his ear to the ground and heard the snores beneath the windmill; the marksman took his gun, fired it at the windmill and woke up Giantsteps, who brought the Water in the nick of time – just as the king was about to leave the table.

Foiled on the first task, the king set a second – this time even more impossible: to eat a dozen roast oxen and a dozen freshly baked loaves at a single sitting.

'I could not eat a single ox in one meal,' groaned the Fool.

'Do not worry,' said the Hungry Man. 'That is only enough to whet my appetite!'

And so the Hungry Man devoured the twelve roast oxen and twelve freshly baked loaves in one gulp – and then called for more. The king was furious: he called for forty pails of wine to be poured each into forty barrels and for them to be consumed in a single draught.

Again the Fool was crestfallen. But the Thirsty Man cheered him up:

'I can drain them all in one draught – and still have room for more,' he said.

And so it was. This time the king was desperate. He gave orders for an iron bath-house to be heated until it was white hot; the Fool was to spend the night steaming himself in it – that would surely put an end to him, the king thought.

The Fool entered the bath-house, however, in the company of the Straw Man, who scattered his hay across the iron floor – to such effect that the temperature dropped so low the Fool had barely washed himself before the water turned to ice. When the king unlocked the bath-house the next morning, out stepped the Fool, washed and steamed, as fresh as a daisy.

That sent the king into a terrible rage and he locked himself in his royal chamber for several days before emerging with a new and cunning plan: he commanded the Fool to assemble an entire regiment of troops by the morrow – where would a simple peasant raise an army?

'This is the end,' thought the Fool. Turning to his companions, he thanked them for their help and was sorry their mission had been in vain.

'But you have forgotten me,' piped up the Brushwood Man. 'I can raise a whole host of fighting men in the twinkle of an eye. And if the king refuses to give up his daughter after that, our army will conquer his kingdom and take her by force!'

That night, the Fool's comrade went into the royal meadow opposite the palace, spread his brushwood over the grass and there sprang up a vast army of cavalry, infantry and artillery. When the king awoke the

next morning to see this mighty host arrayed before his palace, he took fright, immediately sent forth his emissaries bearing rich velvet robes to the Fool, begging him to take the princess with the royal blessing.

As soon as the Fool put on this splendid attire, he became the hand-somest man in the kingdom. Appearing before the king, he consented to marry the princess, receive a handsome reward and become the heir to the king's lands. No one ever referred to him as the Fool after that; he became a clever and learned man, much loved by all who met him – most of all by the fair princess.

Grandfather Frost

THERE once lived an old man with his second wife, and they each had a daughter. The wife pampered her own daughter, who was lazy and bad-tempered. But she was unkind to her stepdaughter.

The old man's daughter had to rise before daybreak to tend the cattle, fetch the firewood, light the stove and sweep the floor. Yet her step-mother found fault with all she did and grumbled at her the whole day through.

Even the wildest wind grows calm with time, but there was no quieting the old woman once she was roused. She would not be content until she had driven the poor girl from the house.

'Get rid of her, old man,' she said one day to her husband. 'I cannot bear the sight of her any longer. Drive her into the forest and leave her in the snow.'

The old man pleaded but the wife always had her way. So, one bitterly cold morning, he harnessed his horses to the sledge and called his daughter:

'Come, my child, we are going for a ride, climb into the sledge.'

The sledge raced over the crisp snow into the forest until it came to a lofty fir-tree. There the old man stopped and left the luckless girl trembling by a deep snowdrift. He drove home with heavy heart, certain he would never see his daughter again.

It was very cold, and the girl sat beneath the hoary fir-tree shivering. All of a sudden, she caught her breath, for she could hear a cracking and snapping of twigs, and she knew Grandfather Frost was leaping through the trees. In a twinkling he was in the topmost branches of the very tree by which she sat.

'Are you warm, my pretty one?' he called.

'Yes, quite warm, thank you, Grandfather Frost,' she answered.

He came down lower and the cracking and snapping grew louder than ever.

'Are you warm?' he called again. 'Are you snug, my pretty one?'

The girl was scarcely able to catch her breath, but she said:

'Yes, I'm quite warm, thank you, Grandfather Frost.'

He then climbed lower still, cracking and snapping the frosty boughs very loudly indeed.

'Are you warm?' he asked. 'Are you snug, my pretty one? Are you cosy, my sweet snow child?'

The girl was growing numb and could hardly move her tongue, but still she managed to whisper:

'I'm quite warm, thank you, Grandfather Frost.'

Then Grandfather Frost took pity on the girl and wrapped her in his fluffy furs and fleecy eiderdowns.

Meanwhile the wicked stepmother was frying pancakes and preparing for the funeral repast. She said to her husband:

'Go to the forest, old fool, and bring your daughter back to be buried!'

The old man harnessed the horses and obediently went into the forest and there found his daughter on the very spot where he had left her. She was alive and well, wrapped in a warm sable coat over a glittering velvet gown. Beside her stood a large chest stuffed with furs and rare gems.

The old man was overjoyed. He seated his daughter in the sledge, put the chest in beside her and drove home.

Back in the house the old woman was still frying pancakes when, suddenly, her little dog began to bark:

> '*Ruff-ruff! The old man's daughter comes rich and fair,*
> *A wondrous fortune found she there!*'

The old woman threw the dog a pancake and said:
'You are wrong, dog! You should say:

> "*The old man's daughter is cold and dead,*
> *The forest snow lies on her head!*" '

The dog munched the pancake, but still barked:

> '*Ruff-ruff! The old man's daughter comes rich and fair,*
> *A wondrous fortune found she there!*'

The old woman hurled more pancakes at the dog and, when this did not stop it, she beat it until it ran howling into the snow.

Suddenly there came the sound of the sledge racing into the yard; the door burst open and in walked the old man's daughter, dazzling in her white furs and precious stones. Behind her walked her happy father bearing the heavy chest of furs and jewels. The old woman was astonished to see her alive and dressed in such finery.

'Harness the horses, old man!' she said to her husband. 'Take my own daughter to the forest and leave her at the same spot.'

The old man put the woman's daughter into the sledge, drove her into the forest and left her by the deep snowdrift under the lofty fir-tree. She was soon so cold her teeth chattered and her feet grew numb.

Presently Grandfather Frost came leaping through the treetops, cracking and snapping the twigs, and stopped to ask the old woman's daughter:

'Are you warm, my pretty one?'

'Oh no, I'm terribly cold!' she snapped. 'Don't pinch and pierce me so!'

Grandfather Frost came lower, making the branches snap and crackle more loudly.

'Are you warm?' he called. 'Are you snug, my pretty one?'

'Oh no, I'm freezing!' she snapped back. 'Go away, you stupid old man!'

But Grandfather Frost came down still lower and the branches cracked and snapped louder than ever and his breath grew colder and colder.

'Are you warm?' he called again. 'Are you snug, my pretty one? Are you cosy, my sweet one?'

'Oh no!' she cried. 'I'm frozen stiff! Go away, you stupid grey-beard!'

Grandfather Frost was so cross that he sent a piercing cold blast through her and turned the old woman's daughter into a block of ice.

Day had barely dawned when the old woman said to her husband:

'Make haste and harness the horses, old man. Go and fetch my daughter and bring her back clad in furs and jewels.'

When the old man had gone, the little dog began to bark:

> *'Ruff-ruff! The old man's daughter will soon be wed,*
> *But the old woman's daughter is cold and dead!'*

The old woman threw the dog a pie and said:
'You are wrong, dog! You should say:

> *"The old woman's daughter comes rich and fair,*
> *A wondrous fortune found she there."'*

[89]

The dog continued its barking:

'*Ruff-ruff! The old woman's daughter is cold and dead!*'

Before long she heard the sound of horses' hoofs and rushed out to greet her daughter. But, when the old woman turned back the cover on the sledge, she found her daughter frozen stiff. So overcome with grief was she that she died.

The old man and his daughter lived on together happily for many years, well rid of the cruel old woman and her lazy daughter.

Liza the Fox and Catafay the Cat

An old tom-cat who had been a fine mouser in his prime was now growing lazy. No longer did he chase the mice from the house, and if his master or mistress forgot to feed him he would help himself – only not by catching mice as before, but by stealing milk, cream or curd, which was evidently more to his liking.

It was hardly surprising when, one day, the mistress told her husband to get rid of him.

'Why should we put up with a pampered, good-for-nothing cat who has brought us not even one mouse-tail for a year or more? Even the mice are laughing at us. Take him to the forest when you next go for wood – and leave him there.'

So, when he went to the forest, the peasant took the cat along in a sack and left him at the bottom of a gully.

'Now there's a fine state of affairs!' growled the cat when his master had gone. 'If I were a dog, though he is my foe, I would run behind the cart. But that is not my nature. Clearly this is my fate and I must stay here to die.'

Meanwhile a fox had been watching the scene from some bushes. Now she popped out her head and greeted the new guest:

'Welcome, Catafay Ivanovich!'

'Welcome yourself,' growled the cat, arching his back because he was still annoyed with the peasant.

'What brings you to these parts?' inquired the fox.

The cat told his story:

'There was a time I would feast like a king – that's why my coat is so smooth. Yet nobody wants me now I'm old, so my master has sent me into exile.'

The fox looked thoughtful.

'Can I not profit somehow from this stroke of fortune?' she pondered. 'No creature in the forest has ever seen or heard of such a fierce-looking beast as Catafay Ivanovich. He would surely strike fear into their hearts.'

'Look here, my friend,' said the fox, making up her mind, 'I feel sorry for you; come and live with me – I've nothing fancy, you understand. We are only common folk round here. But I will not complain at what the Good Lord grants.'

'Thank you for your kindness. I am most grateful,' replied the cat.

The fox conducted the cat to her home, and digging the entrance wide, she instructed the cat to crawl in and rest. Meanwhile she dashed off to summon a meeting of the Commune.

All the beasts, big and small, gathered to listen to the fox's announcement. Mistress Fox bowed low to the animals, wished them good health and then made her speech.

'I bring you bad news, comrades. We have a new Governor – a really fearful fellow, the like of which you have never seen. Truly hard times are upon us! His title is Catafay Ivanovich. He has a snout bristling with whiskers, a needle-sharp tongue, eyes like candles, claws like a rake, a snake's tail and a spitting, snarling manner. When he sleeps he snores like a human, when he's awake I have heard just one word from

him: "mo-o-ore, mo-o-ore!" – no matter what I bring him. And just listen to this: he has made my home his headquarters! I would take shelter under a tree somewhere, but he won't let me. I have to wait on him and feed him. That really is too much for me to bear alone. Our new Governor has devoured all the food I put by for winter, and now he orders me to summon the Commune and let you all know what each must bring.'

A murmur of wonder ran through the gathering and each animal began to tremble at the thought of meeting the awful envoy of the king.

'Life is hard enough without the new Governor!' growled Michaelo the bear, scratching himself.

Nobody refused his task, however, and the animals dispersed, each remembering what and when he had to provide for the Governor's table.

Next day they came and arranged their gifts in great dread: the wolf brought half a calf, the bear some home-brewed mead, the polecat had plucked and cleaned a duck, his mate brought eggs. Then they stood waiting some distance from the entrance to the fox's house.

The fox peered out and greeted them all in a hushed voice:

'Our Governor is resting and I dare not wake him; he will be so angry. Be patient, kind souls, just wait until he is ready to receive you.'

'Now look here, Mistress Gossip . . .' the bear began.

But the fox cut him short: 'Pardon me, Michaelo Ivanovich, do not address me as Mistress Gossip any more, I am now the Governor's Lady. By God's will, Catafay Ivanovich came here a bachelor. I am, as you know, a lonely spinster. Our dear Governor has taken pity on me and rewarded my loyal service by making me his wife. Henceforth you must address me as Liza Patrikeyevna, the Governor's Lady!'

The beasts glanced at one another helplessly, shrugged and were silent. Michaelo hung his head, shifted uneasily and inspected his claws.

Soon the wily fox again emerged, and this time she instructed the animals on how to greet the Governor properly when he appeared. Then she bade them lay their gifts before her door.

But the beasts were too scared to move. Each urged his neighbour to go first. Finally it fell to the shaggy old boar who was so deaf he had missed most of the speech. He shuffled forward grunting – in the most respectful way – yet the Governor's Lady shooed him away because, she said, of his lack of manners.

Michaelo went next. As he ambled near he caught a glimpse in the dark hole of a pair of fiery eyes that lit up a most horrible whiskery face. His legs wobbled beneath him, he stuttered and stammered, bowed low and hastily turned back.

'Make way, make way!' cried the fox suddenly. 'His Highness the Governor is coming. . .'

At that, the beasts turned tail and fled into the trees and bushes. Catafay Ivanovich moved slowly and sedately into the clearing, raising his tail high and swishing it imperiously through the air. He stalked over to the feast laid for him and began to eat. Now and again, as was his habit, he meowed loudly:

'Mo-o-ore, mo-o-ore, mo-o-ore!'

While the cat was enjoying his meal, Michaelo plucked up his courage and peered through the bushes. All of a sudden the cat, glancing sideways to where the bear was rustling the leaves, forgot himself and sprang quickly towards the bush – thinking it was a mouse. . . The poor bear nearly died of fright, then took to his heels and was never again seen in the forest. So did all the other animals, firmly believing their last hour had come.

That, then, was how the crafty fox took in a mangy, abandoned cat and used him to frighten all the animals from the forest.

Ivan the Peasant's Son and the Three Dragons

LONG, long ago, in a certain kingdom, in a certain realm, there lived an old man and his wife with their three sons. One day the word spread that the dragon, Chudo Yudo, Monster of Monsters, was coming to stalk the land, kill the people and burn the villages. The old man and his wife began to sorrow and grieve, and their two elder sons tried to comfort them.

'Do not grieve, Mother, do not grieve, Father! We shall fight the dragon and slay him! Ivan, your youngest son, shall stay with you while we are away. He is too young to accompany us.'

'No,' said Ivan, 'I shall not stay home and wait for you. I, too, will go to fight Chudo Yudo!'

The old man and the old woman did not try to stop him. The brothers took their thick cudgels, filled their satchels with black bread, salt and onion and mounted their trusty steeds.

Whether they were long on their way I cannot say, but by and by they met an old man.

'Good-day, bold youths!' said the man.

'Good-day, Grandfather!'

'Whither are you bound?'

'We are on our way to fight the dragon Chudo Yudo.'

'You will need more than cudgels to fight Chudo Yudo. You need swords of damask steel.'

'Where are we to find them, Grandfather?'

'That I will tell you. Ride straight ahead until you come to a high mountain. In that mountain is a deep cave, with a large rock blocking its entrance. Push the rock aside, enter the cave and there you will find the swords. Then ride to Cranberry Bridge over Blackcurrant River; there you must seek the dragon.'

The brothers thanked the old man and rode straight ahead until they came to a high mountain with a large grey boulder on one side. The brothers thrust the rock aside and entered the cave, and – lo and behold! – they found more treasure than the eye could see or the tongue could relate! But they contented themselves with a damask sword each.

'The old man has done us a great service,' they said. 'It will be far easier to slay the dragon with these swords!'

On they rode until they came to a deserted village where everything was burnt and in ruins except for one small hut. The brothers entered the hut and found an old woman lying there groaning.

'Good-day, Grandmother!' the brothers said.

'Good-day, bold youths! Whither are you bound?'

'We are going to the Cranberry Bridge over Blackcurrant River to fight Chudo Yudo, Monster of Monsters.'

'Ah, bold youths, yours is a worthy cause! The black-hearted dragon plunders and lays waste wherever he goes. He has been here; I alone am left alive. . .'

The brothers spent the night at the old woman's house, and early in the morning they rose and continued their journey.

Arriving finally at Blackcurrant River, they found the bank strewn with broken bones, swords, bows and arrows. An empty hut stood near, and there they decided to rest.

'Listen, my Brothers,' said Ivan. 'We have come to a strange land, and we must be wary. Let us take turns to guard our hut and to stop the dragon crossing Cranberry Bridge.'

On the first night the eldest brother went to keep watch. He walked along the bank and looked across Blackcurrant River: all was quiet, no one was to be seen. So he lay down under a bush, fell asleep at once and began snoring loudly.

Back at the hut Ivan could not sleep, nor even rest. When midnight came, he took his sword of damask steel and went to the river. There, under a bush, he came upon his elder brother, fast asleep. But he did not wake him; instead he hid under the bridge, guarding the crossing.

Suddenly, the waters of the river began to seethe and boil, the crows began cawing in the oak-trees and Chudo Yudo, the dragon with six heads, appeared. As he rode to the middle of Cranberry Bridge, his horse stumbled under him, the black raven on his shoulder flapped its wings and his black dog bristled.

The six-headed dragon roared:

'Why do you stumble, nag? Why do you flap your wings, black raven? Why do you bristle, black dog? Do you smell the blood of Ivan the Peasant's Son? But he has not yet been born, and, even if he has, he cannot slay me. I will seize him with one hand and crush him with the other!'

At that, Ivan stepped on to the bridge.

'Do not boast, Chudo Yudo!' he cried. 'Match your strength with mine, and let the winner boast to his heart's content.'

They rushed at one another, and their swords clashed with such force that the earth around them trembled; Chudo Yudo staggered back, for Ivan the Peasant's Son had cut off three of his heads at one blow.

'Stop!' cried the dragon. 'Let me rest!'

'No!' replied Ivan. 'You still have three heads, and I only one. We shall rest when you have no heads left!'

So they closed again and measured swords, and Ivan the Peasant's Son smote off Chudo Yudo's remaining three heads. Then he hacked the body into small pieces, threw them into the river, laid the six heads beneath Cranberry Bridge and returned to the hut.

In the morning his eldest brother came in, and Ivan asked:

'Well, did you see anything?'

'No,' replied the other, 'not a fly flew past me.'

To this Ivan said nothing.

On the next night the second brother went to keep watch. He walked up and down, looked all about him and decided all was quiet. So he crawled into a clump of bushes, curled up on the ground and fell asleep.

Ivan relied no more on him than on his eldest brother. When midnight came, he took up his sharp sword, went down to Blackcurrant River and hid beneath the Cranberry Bridge once more.

Suddenly the waters began to seethe and boil, the crows began cawing in the oak-trees, and Chudo Yudo, the dragon with nine heads, appeared. As he rode to the middle of the bridge, his horse stumbled, the black raven on his shoulder flapped its wings and his black dog bristled. Chudo Yudo raised his whip and brought it down across the horse's flanks, the raven's wings and the dog's ears.

'Why do you stumble, nag?' he cried. 'Why do you flap your wings, black raven? Why do you bristle, black dog? Do you smell the blood of Ivan the Peasant's Son? But he has not yet been born, and even if he has, I shall crush him with one finger!'

At that, Ivan leaped on to the bridge.

'Stop, Chudo Yudo!' he cried. 'Do not boast before we have crossed swords. We shall see who is stronger!'

Ivan rushed at the nine-headed dragon, swung once and then again, and smote off six of the dragon's heads. Then Chudo Yudo struck Ivan a blow and drove him knee-deep into the damp soil. But Ivan the Peasant's Son scooped up a handful of sand and flung it into his foe's fiery eyes, and, while the monster was rubbing them, Ivan chopped off his three remaining heads. Then he hacked the body into little pieces, cast them into the river and, putting the nine heads underneath the bridge, returned to the hut. There he lay down and fell asleep as if nothing had happened.

In the morning the second brother returned.

'Well, did you see anything during the night?' Ivan asked.

'No,' the other replied. 'Not a mosquito flew past me.'

'If that be so, then come with me, my Brothers,' said Ivan, 'and I shall show you the mosquito and the fly.'

And Ivan led his brothers to the bridge and showed them the dragons' heads.

'Those', he said, 'are the flies and mosquitoes that fly here at night. And you, my brothers, are only fit to warm your bones on a stove ledge.'

The two brothers hung their heads in shame.

'We were overcome by sleep,' they murmured.

On the third night, Ivan himself prepared to keep watch.

'I have a fearful battle before me,' he said. 'You, my Brothers, must not sleep, but listen for my whistle. As soon as you hear it, send me my horse and hasten to my aid.'

So saying, Ivan the Peasant's Son went to the river, hid beneath the Cranberry Bridge and waited.

No sooner had midnight arrived than the earth trembled and the waters seethed and boiled, the wild winds howled, and the crows in the oak-trees screeched. Chudo Yudo, the twelve-headed dragon, was riding towards the bridge over the Blackcurrant River. All his twelve heads were whist-

ling and spurting smoke and fire. His steed had twelve wings, a mane of copper and a tail of iron. As the dragon reached the centre of Cranberry Bridge, his horse stumbled, the black raven on his shoulder flapped its wings and the black dog bristled. The dragon brought his whip down across the horse's flanks, the raven's wings and the dog's ears.

'Why do you stumble, nag?' he cried. 'Why do you flap your wings, black raven? Why do you bristle, black dog? Do you smell the blood of Ivan the Peasant's Son? But he has not yet been born, and even if he has, he is no match for me. I have only to blow once, and he will turn to dust.'

At that, Ivan stepped on to the bridge.

'Then, we shall put your boast to the test, Chudo Yudo,' he cried. 'I have come to slay you and save good folk from your evil!'

He brandished his sharp sword and cut off three of the dragon's heads. But Chudo Yudo set them back on their necks, sealed them with his fiery finger and at once they grew fast.

After a while Ivan began to tire, for Chudo Yudo deafened him with his whistling, burned him with his fiery breath, showered him with sparks and drove him up to his knees into the damp soil.

'Perhaps you should rest, Ivan, Peasant's Son?' the dragon jeered.

'Speak not of rest,' Ivan replied. 'I shall fight to the death!'

Thereupon, he gave a loud whistle and flung his right glove at the hut where his brothers waited. Although the glove smashed the windows, his brothers slept on and heard nothing.

Then Ivan the Peasant's Son summoned all his strength, swung his sword more fiercely than ever, and chopped off six of the dragon's heads. But Chudo Yudo caught them, set them back on their necks, sealed them with his fiery finger and they grew fast as if they had never been cut off. Then he set upon Ivan the Peasant's Son and once again drove him up to his waist into the damp soil.

Ivan now realized death was near. He snatched off his other glove and flung it at the hut, and it brought down the roof, but his two brothers slept on and heard nothing.

Then Ivan the Peasant's Son swung his sword a third time, and smote off nine of the dragon's heads. But Chudo Yudo caught them up and set them back on their necks, sealing them with his finger, and they grew fast again. After that, he hurled himself upon Ivan the Peasant's Son and drove him up to his shoulders into the damp soil.

With one last effort, Ivan pulled off his hat and threw it at the hut; the hut shook and swayed and almost crashed to the ground. Only then did his brothers awake. They heard Ivan's horse neighing loudly and trying to break loose.

Dashing into the stable, they untied the horse and rushed after it towards their brother.

Ivan's horse galloped to his master and began kicking out at the dragon, who let out a whistle and a hiss and showered the horse with sparks.

Meanwhile Ivan the Peasant's Son heaved himself out of the ground and swiftly cut off Chudo Yudo's fiery finger and his heads until none was left! Then he hacked the body into little pieces and threw them into the river.

Just at that moment, his brothers arrived.

'What a sorry pair you are!' Ivan said. 'I nearly paid with my life for your deep sleep.'

The two brothers led him to the hut, washed and dressed his wounds, then gave him food and drink, and put him to bed.

In the morning Ivan rose early and began to dress.

'Why are you up so early?' his brothers asked. 'You need rest after so fierce a combat.'

'I cannot rest,' said Ivan. 'I lost my belt by Blackcurrant River and must go there in search of it.'

So Ivan went off alone to the river. But he did not stop to look for his belt. He crossed Cranberry Bridge and stole unnoticed to the dragons' black stone palace. Creeping to an open window, he crouched there, listening for any evil plan to catch him and his brothers.

He spied the three wives of the dragons and the old she-dragon, their mother. They were sitting before an open fire talking among themselves.

Said the first wife:

'I shall take revenge on Ivan the Peasant's Son for slaying my husband! When he and his brothers are returning home, I shall make the air hot and dusty and turn myself into a poisoned well. They will thirst for a drink and drop dead at the first sip!'

'Well said,' murmured the old she-dragon.

Said the second wife:

'And I shall run ahead of them and turn into a poisoned apple-tree. When they take an apple, they will drop dead at the first bite!'

'That is well said, too,' murmured the old she-dragon.

Said the third wife:

'As for me, I shall cast a sleeping spell on them; then I shall run ahead and turn into a soft carpet with silk cushions. When the brothers lie down to rest, they will be burned to cinders!'

'That, too, is well said,' murmured the she-dragon. 'But if you all three fail, I shall turn myself into a giant sow and swallow them in one gulp!'

Ivan the Peasant's Son heard their talk and hurried back to his brothers.

'Well, have you found your belt?' they asked.

'I have.'

'And was it worth wasting so much time?'

'It was, my Brothers, it was indeed.'

Thereupon the three brothers set off homewards. They rode across steppe and plain and the air was so hot and dusty that they felt they had to drink some water or die. Soon they came upon a well with a silver dipper floating upon the water. The two elder brothers said to Ivan:

'Let us stop to water our horses and drink some cool water.'

But Ivan stopped his brothers. Leaping from his horse, he swung his sword at the well, hacking it to pieces. At that, a terrible howling and shrieking arose from the well, a sudden mist descended, the heat abated and they were thirsty no longer.

'Now, my Brothers, you see what kind of water was in that well,' said Ivan.

They rode on; soon they came to an apple-tree laden with large, rosy apples.

The two elder brothers sprang from their horses and were about to pluck the apples when Ivan leaped between them and cut down the tree at its roots; and the apple-tree began to shriek and howl.

'Now, my Brothers, do you see what kind of apple-tree that is?' Ivan said. 'Its apples are not for us!'

The three brothers remounted their horses and rode on.

After riding for some time, they began to feel very tired. Imagine their surprise and relief to see a soft carpet with silk cushions in a field before them.

'Let us rest awhile on that soft, inviting carpet,' exclaimed the two elder brothers.

'No, my Brothers, you will not find that carpet soft,' Ivan warned. The two elder brothers became angry.

'Why do you stop us?' they cried. 'We must not do this and not do that!'

Ivan said nothing. Instead, he took off his belt and threw it on to the carpet; the belt at once caught fire and was burnt to a cinder.

'That is what would have happened to you,' said Ivan to his brothers. He went closer and cut up the carpet and cushions with his sword. Then he scattered the shreds to the four winds.

'As you see, my Brothers, the well, the apple-tree and the carpet were not what they seemed; they were the dragons' wives who wanted to gain their revenge by killing us. Instead, they themselves have perished.'

As the brothers rode on, the sky suddenly darkened, the wind howled and the earth trembled. A giant sow was at their heels. She opened her jaws wide and was about to swallow the three brothers when Ivan took a pound of salt from his satchel and threw it straight into the sow's gaping mouth.

The sow stopped, for she thought she had caught Ivan the Peasant's Son and his two brothers; but, when she began to chew the salt, she soon realized she had been tricked. And again she rushed off after them.

As she ran, her bristles stood on end, her snout poured smoke and her teeth showered sparks. Soon she was at their heels and about to snatch them up.

Ivan shouted to his brothers to ride in different directions: one to the right, the other to the left, and himself – straight ahead. As they did so, the giant sow stopped, for she did not know which to catch first.

While she stood hesitating and waving her snout from side to side, Ivan rushed at her, lifted her up and dashed her to the ground with all his might. So great was the blow that the sow crumbled to dust and the dust was scattered across the plain by the wind.

From then on no more dragons were seen in those parts, and the people knew no fear. As for Ivan the Peasant's Son and his two brothers, they returned home to their mother and father; they lived well, ploughed their fields, sowed their wheat and earned the thanks of all the Russian people.

The Frost, the Sun and the Wind

A PEASANT was once journeying along a road when he met the Frost, the Sun and the Wind.

'Greetings to you!' said the peasant as he continued on his way.

'Which of us did he greet?' they asked themselves after a while.

'It must have been me,' said the Sun, 'so that I may not scorch him.' But the Frost said the greetings were for him:

'Mortals go in fear of me more than of you, for I can turn them into ice!'

'Nonsense,' argued the Wind. 'It was me he greeted, not you.'

They quarrelled and cursed and would surely have come to blows had not the Sun suggested they go after the peasant and ask whom he had greeted.

So off they swept, overtook the peasant and asked: 'Whom did you greet, peasant?'

'The Wind,' answered the peasant.

'You see, Brothers, just as I told you,' said the Wind.

'Just you wait, peasant,' said the Sun. 'I shall make you as red as a lobster. You shall not forget me!'

'Have no fear, friend,' said the Wind. 'I shall blow and cool you down.'

'I shall freeze you, peasant,' said the Frost.

'Have no fear, friend,' said the Wind. 'If I do not blow, he cannot freeze. There is no Frost without the Wind.'

Sister Alyonushka and Brother Ivanushka

A N old man and his wife lived happily with their two children, Alyonushka and Ivanushka. A dark cloud descended, however, and carried off the old man and woman, leaving Alyonushka and Ivanushka all alone.

There was nothing for it but to go out into the world and seek their living. Alyonushka took her young brother by the hand and together they set out.

They had many versts to cover and an open plain to cross, and, after they had been walking for a time, Ivanushka said:

'Sister Alyonushka, I am so thirsty.'

'Be patient, little Brother, we shall come to a well soon.'

They walked on and on, and the sun rose higher in the heavens. Their throats were dry, their feet dusty and both were tired and thirsty. Presently they came upon a cow's hoofmark, filled with water, and Ivanushka pleaded:

'May I drink the water from the hole, Sister?'

'No, little Brother. For, if you do, you will surely turn into a calf.'

Ivanushka obeyed and they continued their journey across the plain. The hot sun beat down more fiercely still and their mouths were now quite parched. Shortly they came upon a horse's hoofmark filled with water, and Ivanushka said,

'May I drink the water from the hole, Sister?'

'No, little Brother. If you do, you will surely turn into a foal.'

Ivanushka sighed, but did as his sister said, and they journeyed on.

They walked on and on, but the air was so dry they could barely breathe. At last they came upon a goat's hoofmark filled with water, and Ivanushka begged:

'I am dying of thirst, Sister. May I drink from the hole?'

'No, little Brother. For, if you do, you will surely change into a kid.'

But, this time, Ivanushka did not heed his sister's warning and quickly drank from the goat's hoofmark.

No sooner had he sipped the water than he turned into a little white goat. When Alyonushka called her brother, the goat came skipping towards her, nuzzling his nose into her hand and bleating: 'maa-aa, maa-aa'.

Alyonushka sat sobbing by the roadside while the white kid skipped round her in play.

By and by, a rich merchant happened to ride by and noticed the pretty young maid and white kid.

'Why are you weeping, young lady?' he asked kindly.

Alyonushka told him of her misfortune.

The merchant, who had fallen in love with the maid, said:

'Do not worry. If you consent to be my wife, I shall dress you in satin and lace and the goat shall come and live with us.'

Alyonushka agreed and they lived together contentedly, the little goat staying with them, sleeping by his sister's bed and eating and drinking from his sister's bowl.

One day the merchant took his merchandise to trade at a faraway town. While he was away, an evil witch appeared from the forest and stood beneath Alyonushka's window. She called to her in a gentle voice to come and bathe in the river.

The day was warm, the air dry and Alyonushka followed the witch to the river. Once on the riverbank, the witch seized the maid and, tying a stone round her neck, hurled her into the water.

Then she put on the girl's clothes, turned herself into a young maiden, the living image of Alyonushka, and returned to the house. No one guessed she was not Alyonushka. Even the merchant, on returning home, did not recognise the evil witch.

Only the little white goat knew the truth. He wandered sadly about with drooping head and would not touch his food. Every morning and evening he would go to the riverbank, stand at the water's edge and call down into the deep waters:

> '*Alyonushka, my Sister so dear,*
> *Swim back, swim back to me here.*'

The witch soon learned of this and told the merchant to have the goat killed.

The merchant was sorry for the little goat, for he had grown quite fond of him. But the witch kept coaxing and nagging so that he finally gave in.

'All right,' he sighed, 'kill him if you must.'

The witch had great fires kindled, iron pots heated and long knives sharpened.

When the goat learned he was to be slaughtered, he went to the merchant with a last request.

'Let me go to the river before I die for one last drink.'

The merchant readily agreed and the little goat ran to the river, stood at the water's edge and cried:

'Alyonushka, my Sister so dear,
Swim back, swim back, to me here.
The flames are rising,
The pots are boiling,
No more shall I see you, I fear.'

And the voice of Alyonushka came from the riverbed:

'Ivanushka, dear Brother so sweet,
A heavy stone on my neck is pressed.
Silken weeds entangle my feet,
Silver sands lie damp on my breast.'

Meanwhile the evil witch sent a servant to fetch the goat. When the servant came to the river, he saw the white goat running up and down the bank bleating piteously:

'Alyonushka, my Sister so dear,
Swim back, swim back, to me here.
The flames are rising,
The pots are boiling,
No more shall I see you, I fear.'

And from the river came a voice:

'Ivanushka, dear Brother so sweet,
A heavy stone on my neck is pressed,
Silken weeds entangle my feet,
Silver sands lie damp on my breast.'

The servant at once hurried back to the house and informed his master of what he had heard. The merchant lost no time in summoning his household and hastened down to the river with a wide silken fishing net. Casting it into the waters, they pulled Alyonushka onto the shore, untied the stone from round her neck, washed her in clear spring water and dressed her in a pure white robe. At last, she opened her eyes and was lovelier than ever.

Sister Alyonushka and Brother Ivanushka

The little white goat went wild with joy and turned head over heels three times. On the third turn he changed back into Ivanushka.

As for the evil witch, she was tied to a horse's tail and the horse set loose across the open plain. From that time on, sister Alyonushka and brother Ivanushka lived with the rich merchant in peace and happiness.

The House of Ice and the House of Wood

As winter approached, a fox and a hare each built a house: the fox built a house of ice, the hare a house of wood. And there the two neighbours spent the cold months of winter sheltering from Grandfather Frost.

Spring came, the sun melted the snow, the air grew warmer every day. Of course, the fox's house melted away, while the hare's stood firm and strong. So the fox paid her neighbour a visit to ask for shelter, and the kind-hearted hare let her in. Once inside, though, the fox drove out the poor hare and took his wooden house for herself.

As the hare shuffled sadly down the road, he met two dogs.

'Chaff, chaff, chaff! Why do you weep?' they asked the hare.

'Who wouldn't weep?' said the hare. 'I had a warm house, while the fox had one of ice. When hers melted, she invited herself into my home and drove me out.'

'Don't worry, hare,' barked the dogs. 'We'll chase that vixen out for you.'

And off the pair of them scampered to the hare's house. Outside the door, they began to bark:

'Chaff, chaff, chaff! Come out of there, fox!'

But she called down from her bed on the stove:

'Go away, go away, or I'll come out and tear you to pieces!'

The dogs took fright and fled.

Once more the hare walked wearily along the road. This time he met a bear.

'Why do you cry, hare?' asked the bear.

He told his story – how the fox had cheated him of his house.

'Dry your tears,' said the simple-hearted bear. 'I shall drive her out for you.'

'I fear you will fare no better than the dogs,' replied the hare.

Nonetheless they returned together to the hare's house.

'Mistress Fox, come out at once!' shouted the bear.

But the fox called down from the stove:

'Go away, go away, or I'll jump down and scratch out your eyes!'

At that the bear's courage deserted him and he stumped off into the forest.

Back down the road trudged the hare in despair, and was met by an ox. The ox asked why the hare was in tears, and heard the story.

'Just come with me,' said the ox. 'I'll get rid of her for you.'

'No, ox, you will not succeed,' moaned the hare. 'The dogs tried and failed, the bear tried and failed, and you will fail too.'

All the same, they went to the hare's house.

'Mistress Fox, come out of there!' bellowed the ox.

But she shouted down from the stove:

'Go away, go away, or I'll come out and tear you to pieces!'

The ox lost his nerve altogether and charged off down the road. Poor hare only cried more than ever. As he walked dejectedly along the road, he was met by Petya the cock, strutting gaily along, a scythe over his shoulder.

'Why are you crying, hare?' asked the cock.

'The fox has stolen my house. The dogs, the bear and the ox all said they would help drive her out, yet they ran away as soon as the fox shouted at them.'

The cock at once marched to the house and crowed loudly:

> *'Coo-coo-ree-coo!*
> *I'll cut the fox in two*
> *With my scythe so sharp and true!'*

When the fox heard that, she took fright and called:

'I'm just getting dressed.'

Again Petya crowed:

The House of Ice and the House of Wood

'Coo-coo-ree-coo!
I'll cut the fox in two
With my scythe so sharp and true!'

The fox shouted:

'I'm just putting on my coat.'

A third time the cock crowed and this time the fox rushed out of the door, scurried down the road and disappeared into the distance in a cloud of dust.

The hare entered his house, invited the cock in and the two of them sat long round the samovar, sipping tea and chuckling at the way they had scared off the fox.

Death and the Soldier

AFTER serving full twenty-five years in the king's army, an old soldier was released from service with nothing but three hard biscuits to eat on his journey home.

He went on his way, bitter at the unkind way the army had treated him after serving the king loyally and truly for the best part of his life.

'All I get for my pains are three miserable rusks,' he grumbled. 'Where am I to lay my head now? God knows whether my folks are alive after all these years. . .'

He turned his steps towards the village he had left twenty-five years before, ate two of his biscuits and saved the third for the long journey ahead. After several versts he met an old beggar by the roadside.

'Take pity on an old man, Soldier!' cried the beggar. 'Give me a bite to eat for the love of God.'

The soldier hesitated, then made up his mind:

'I can struggle on as best I can,' he thought, 'but no one will feed an old beggar.'

So he took out his last biscuit and handed it to the beggar. In exchange, the old man gave him a pinch of tobacco – which he said was no ordinary mixture.

The soldier lit his pipe, puffed long and hard, then continued his march. By and by, he came to a lake on which, to his great fortune, swam a flock of wild geese. Creeping stealthily through the rushes, he took his rifle and fired, killing three whilst the others flew off in alarm.

'What luck!' exclaimed the soldier. 'Now I've something for dinner.'

Stuffing the dead geese into his knapsack, he walked on until he came to a small town; he stopped at an inn and handed the geese to the inn-keeper.

'Keep two for yourself,' he told the man, 'roast the third for me and bring in a pitcher of wine.'

Having washed off the dust of his journey, the soldier sat down refreshed to his dinner, ate and drank his fill, then lit his pipe and addressed the innkeeper.

'Whose is that grand house I passed along the road?'

The landlord shifted awkwardly in his chair as if scared by the soldier's question. After some prompting he recounted the story.

'It was built by a very rich merchant. But he has never been able to move in because a host of demons live there. As soon as night falls, they come out, make a terrible commotion, gallivant about, shriek and make merry. I'm telling you, Soldier, folk are afeared to go near the place after dark.'

Listening to this story and emboldened by the wine, the soldier grew curious and asked his host where he might find the rich merchant.

'I might put myself at his service. Perhaps an old warrior like me could do a spell of guard duty for him.'

After his dinner, the soldier took a nap for an hour or so and then, just as it was growing dark, went in search of the merchant. When he found him, he said:

'I'm an old army-man with nowhere to lay me head. I'd like permission to spend the night in your house, Sir. I hear it's quite empty.'

'Heaven's above!' shouted the merchant. 'Are you mad? Why should you wish to go to your death? Take lodgings at someone else's place; there are enough rooms in the town. Ever since I had that house built, it's been taken over by all the demons in hell – and nothing will drive them out!'

'You never know,' said the soldier, 'the devils might jump to an old soldier's command.'

'You are not the first to volunteer. Brave lads have tried and failed. I had a stranger come to me last summer boasting he would last the night and banish the evil spirits. The next morning, all that remained were white bones sucked clean by the demons.'

'You know what we say in the army,' persisted the soldier, 'a Russian soldier will go through fire and water; he's not afraid of anything. In my time in the ranks, I've had more than my share of fighting, but here I am safe and sound. Don't worry, a few demons don't scare me.'

In the end, the merchant reluctantly agreed to let the soldier try his luck. Before he left, however, the soldier requested a dozen candles, three pounds of peanuts and a large boiled beetroot. Taking these from the merchant's store, he made his way to the haunted house.

When he got there, he opened the front door, climbed the stairs to the bedroom and hung his greatcoat and knapsack on a nail behind the door. Then he lit the candles, puffed away at his pipe and waited calmly for midnight, all the while cracking the peanuts with his teeth. The house was as still as death.

At the stroke of midnight all hell was let loose: doors banged, the floorboards screeched, walls shook as shrieks of demonic laughter filled the house and a score of devils' hoofs stamped the floor in a fiendish frenzy. The din was enough to burst your eardrums. But the soldier sat there calmly as if nothing had happened, cracking his nuts and pulling on his pipe.

Suddenly the bedroom door burst open and a little devil's head peered round the corner. Seeing the soldier, it shrieked with delight:

'I've found a human, I've found a human! Oh, what a feast we'll have now!'

The house was soon in even greater uproar as the host of demons came rushing to the bedroom. They all crowded into the doorway, bumping and shoving one another in their eagerness to see their victim.

'Let's get at him! Tear him to pieces!' voices screamed.

'Just come and try it!' warned the soldier. 'I've never clapped eyes on such a skinny bunch of cowards in all my life. Who'll be the first?'

That stopped the devils: they had not expected such boldness. Huddling in a heap in the doorway, they thrust their chief forward.

'All right, Soldier,' he said, 'let us test our strength.'

'Certainly,' agreed the soldier. 'Is there any among you who can squeeze blood from a stone?'

The chief sent someone to fetch stones from the road. When he

returned with a handful of small stones, the chief took one in his hand and squeezed so hard the stone crumbled to dust.

'Let's see you match that, Soldier!' he said with a sneer.

The soldier slowly got to his feet, took his pipe from his mouth and fetched the large boiled beetroot from his knapsack.

'Just watch this,' he said. 'My stone is twice as big as yours.'

And he began to squeeze the beetroot until the juice ran red, like blood, through his fingers.

The devils were amazed. In the deathly silence that followed, all that could be heard was the soldier calmly cracking the nuts. After a while the demons asked him what he was chewing.

'Nuts,' he replied. 'Only none of you can crack such nuts as these.'

So saying, instead of a nut, he passed the chief demon a bullet from his rifle. The devil popped it into his mouth, chewed and chewed as hard as he could, but could not crack the soldier's nut. All the while, the soldier chewed away, putting one nut after the other into his mouth and cracking them easily.

The devils grew quiet and confused, shifting uneasily from one hoof to the other, staring at the soldier.

'I hear tell,' said the soldier, 'that jokers like you are pretty smart at playing tricks, like making yourselves shrink so that you can squeeze through the tiniest crack.'

'So we can, so we can!' shrieked the devils.

'Well, go on then,' said the soldier. 'Let's see all of you squeeze into my old knapsack.'

At once the devils rushed, fighting and scrambling to get into the soldier's knapsack; within seconds the house was as quiet as if no one had been there. All the demons were safe inside the knapsack.

The soldier went over to the door, fastened the straps of his knapsack and pulled them tight.

'Now I can get some peace and quiet,' he muttered as he lay down on the bed, covered himself with his greatcoat and closed his eyes.

At first light the next morning, the merchant sent his servants with an empty coffin to gather up the soldier's bones. Imagine their amazement to find the soldier pacing up and down the room puffing contentedly on his pipe.

'Good-morrow, Soldier!' they said. 'We hardly expected to find you alive. We even brought a coffin for your bones.'

The soldier chuckled:

'It's a bit early to bury me yet, lads. Give me a hand to carry this knapsack to the smithy.'

When the soldier and the merchant's servants arrived at the smithy's with their burden, they placed it on the anvil and the soldier called on three blacksmiths to hammer it as flat as they could. After a few blows, there came a great chorus of muffled wails from inside the knapsack.

'Let us out, Soldier! We'll never go near that house or the town again. And we'll give you anything you ask. Only please spare us!'

After several more hearty blows, the soldier instructed the three blacksmiths to stop.

'That'll teach you to meddle with a Russian soldier!' he called, undoing the straps and letting the devils out, one by one until all had fled save their chief.

'Bring my reward before I let him out,' ordered the soldier.

And before he had time to smoke a pipeful of tobacco, a little demon came running up with an empty sack.

'What jape is this?' demanded the soldier angrily. 'I'll have your chief beaten to pulp for that!'

'Don't beat me,' squeaked a frightened voice from inside the knapsack. 'Listen, that is no ordinary sack; shake it and it will bring you anything you wish. All you have to say is "Jump in!" – and the sack will hold all you want.'

Still suspicious, the soldier gave the sack a good shake and wished for three pitchers of wine, crying 'Jump in!' as he did so.

At once the sack grew heavy and, when he looked, there at the bottom were three pitchers of wine. Handing the wine to the three blacksmiths, he let the last demon out of his knapsack.

'If I ever catch you again, I'll thrash you black and blue,' warned the soldier.

Death and the Soldier

The demon took to his heels and sped off as fast as his hairy black legs would carry him. Meanwhile the soldier took up his sack and returned to the merchant.

'Your house is clear now,' he said. 'You can move in; no demons will disturb you again.'

The merchant thanked the soldier, ordered his servants to prepare a great feast in the soldier's honour and begged him to stay and live with him in the great mansion.

No sooner had the festivities ended, however, than the soldier bade the merchant farewell and continued on his way. He marched over hill and plain, through forest and glade, until at long last, reaching the top of a hill, he gazed down upon his native village – as neat and homely as when he had left it many, many years before.

'There's no place like home,' he sighed. 'I've been to many foreign lands, set eyes on many cities and palaces, yet no sight is grander than my own village.'

He stopped outside a cottage, stepped onto the porch and knocked on the door. An old woman answered his knock and immediately recognized her soldier son. She hugged and kissed him and cried tears of joy.

'My son has come home,' she cried. 'If only your father could have been here to greet you; it's five years now since we buried him.'

The old woman began to fuss about the cottage, laying the table, setting pots on the stove. But the soldier sat her down and told her she would not have to toil or labour again: taking his magic sack, he gave it a shake and wished for as much food and drink as the table would hold. And mother and son sat down to a hearty meal.

On the next day the soldier again took the sack, shook it hard and wished for a mound of silver – and silver coins poured from the sack onto the floor. With this fortune he bought a cow and a horse, and all that he and his mother required for a comfortable life. In good time the soldier took a wife, the best there was, and began to live as happy a life as ever a man could wish. His old mother soon had grandchildren to fuss over – and everyone lived in peace and prosperity.

*

And there our story might have ended. But it did not, for an even stranger adventure befell our soldier before his journey's end.

Some six or seven happy years passed; at the end of that time, however, the soldier fell ill. He lay in a fever for a day or two not wishing to eat or drink, and grew weaker and weaker. On the third day he opened his

eyes and saw Death standing by his bedside, sharpening his scythe and staring down at him.

'Your time is up, Soldier,' said Death. 'I've come to collect you.'

'Give me more time,' said the soldier feebly. 'Give me another thirty years, time to bring up my children, marry off my sons and daughters, see my grandchildren. Then come for me. I'll be ready then.'

'No, Soldier, Death waits for no man,' droned the voice of the skeleton.

'Well, if you won't spare me thirty years, let's settle for three,' begged the soldier. 'I've so much to do still.'

But Death showed no mercy and would not grant the soldier even three more minutes of life. The soldier saw it was useless to argue, yet he did not wish to die. So, summoning up his last ounce of life, he pulled out his magic sack (which he always kept under his pillow). Grasping it in one hand, he gave it a feeble shake and murmured,

'Jump in!'

No sooner had the words passed his lips than he felt the sickness drain out of his body, his fever vanished and, when he glanced round the room, Death was nowhere to be seen. Only when he opened his sack did he see him sitting there at the bottom.

The soldier fastened the sack as tight as he could and placed it in the corner while he ate a hearty breakfast.

'I'll teach you not to meddle with a Russian soldier, you noseless skeleton!' he said, munching a thick slice of black bread and swallowing a full pitcher of kvass.

'What will you do with me?' came a reedy voice from inside the sack.

'I'm sorry to lose my sack,' replied the soldier, 'but there's nothing for it. I shall push you so deep in the mud of the swamp that you will never escape.'

'Let me out, let me out, Soldier!' cried Death. 'I will grant you three more years of life.'

The soldier laughed and did not answer.

Death begged even harder:

'All right, have it your way. You can have another thirty years if you let me out.'

The soldier thought it over and finally agreed.

'Right. Only, if I free you, you must promise not to come for anyone for thirty years.'

'But how will I exist?' asked Death. 'What am I going to live on?'

'You can gnaw moss and the roots of trees,' answered the soldier.

To that Death could find no answer.

'Take it or leave it,' cried the soldier slinging the sack over his shoulder and opening the door.

Death and the Soldier

At once Death cried out:

'So be it; I shall not carry off any humans for thirty years. I'll live on roots and moss as best I can. Only set me free.'

'Mind you keep your word,' warned the soldier, 'or else I'll come after you with my sack and push you into the swamp.'

With that he carried the sack from the house, untied it and let Death out. Snatching up his scythe, Death scuttled off into the forest, where he learned to live on the forest roots and moss.

From that time on, folk lived without sickness or worry. Every human was healthy, nobody fell ill and nobody died.

And so it went for nigh on thirty years. As the years passed, the soldier's children grew up; his sons took wives, his daughters were wed and the family grew not by the day but by the hour, as the saying goes. In their large and merry household there was always someone to help round the house, to give advice, to tell the children stories and to keep the family happy. The soldier had his hands full looking after them all, but he was so content he never gave Death a thought.

One day, however, when he was alone in the house, Death suddenly appeared before him.

'Your thirty years are up today, Soldier!' said Death. 'Get your things, I've come for you.'

The soldier did not resist.

'I've been a service-man and I obey the regulations,' he said. 'If those are my marching orders, so be it. Bring in the coffin.'

Death brought in an oak coffin with iron handles. Taking off the lid, he ordered:

'Get in, Soldier!'

The soldier pretended to be angry.

'That's no way to give an order. Listen, you don't come to an old soldier, bark your orders and expect him to jump to it. That's not the way we did things in the army. When I was drilling new recruits I had to show them myself before giving orders. So let's do things soldier-fashion: you go first and show me, then I'll obey your order!'

Death lay down in the coffin.

'Now, watch me, Soldier, you lie like this, stretch out your legs and cross your hands over your chest, got it?'

That was exactly what the soldier wanted. He quickly banged shut the lid of the coffin and nailed it tight.

'You lie there yourself!' he shouted. 'I'm fine out here!'

With that he carried the coffin to a steep riverbank, heaved it down the slope into the water and the current bore Death far out to sea.

For several years Death was tossed and thrown about on the ocean waves, while, on land, people lived in good cheer, praising the soldier for saving them from Death. Meanwhile the soldier saw his grandchildren get married and set to teaching his great-grandchildren the ways of the world. From dawn till dusk his hands were full as he enjoyed life with his large family.

One day, however, a great storm raged out at sea; the waves raced with the coffin over the sea and dashed it onto the stony shore. Death emerged more dead than alive, tottered up the beach and lay on dry land to recover. Then he headed straight for the village where the soldier lived, intent on getting his revenge. He stole quietly and unnoticed into the soldier's yard and hid behind the barn door, waiting for him to come into the barn.

He did not have long to wait, for the soldier, needing some flour for bread, took a sack and went to the barn to fill it. No sooner had he entered the barn than Death sprang out from a dark corner, cackling in his evil way:

'Got you, Soldier! Now there's no escape.'

Seeing there really was no escape this time, the soldier shrugged his shoulders and resigned himself to his fate. At least, though, he would give that bag-of-bones one last scare before he went.

Taking the empty sack he had brought for flour, he shook it under Death's nose, shouting:

'So you've come to climb back into my sack, have you? This time I'll bury you so deep in the marsh, you won't escape in a million years.'

Seeing the empty sack in the soldier's hands and thinking it really was the magic sack, Death took fright and fled like the wind.

Death and the Soldier

Folk say that the soldier was the last person ever to see him. From that day on, Death has crept up on people, snatching them on the quiet, keeping himself well out of sight. He is frightened of ending up in the soldier's sack and landing in the swamp.

The soldier lived on and on, without Death to cast a shadow over his happiness. Some folk say he died only the other day; others say he lives on still in his native village somewhere in the heart of Russia.

Mother Confessor Fox

ONE frosty autumn night a fox was prowling through the forest in search of a meal. But her luck was out. Just before dawn she ventured into a nearby village to grab a chicken breakfast.

Stopping at the first yard, she squeezed into the chicken house and was about to seize a fat hen when, right at that moment, dawn broke and woke up the cock. With a fearful flapping of wings and stamping of feet, Petya the cock stretched up and screeched:

'Coo-coo-ree-coo!'

At that, the fox fled from the chicken run in such alarm that she lay in a fever for three weeks.

Some months later the cock was taking a walk on the edge of the forest, unaware that the sly fox was watching him. Hoping to gain her revenge, she followed the cock as he strutted through the trees. Just as the fox was about to pounce, however, Petya flew up to a branch of a fir-tree.

The fox soon tired of waiting and decided to coax the cock down. So she strode out and greeted her old enemy:

'Good-morrow to you, Petya. What a splendid day it is.'

'What's that cunning old fox up to now, I wonder?' said the cock to himself.

'Petinka, my son, I really ought to show you the error of your ways,' continued the fox solemnly. 'Now, look here, Petya, you have fifty wives, yet not once have you been to confession. Are you not ashamed of yourself? Just come down to me now, bow your head low and I shall absolve you of your sins.'

The cock, who was an extremely pious bird, climbed lower and lower and landed right in the fox's lap. The fox at once seized him by the neck and said:

'Now you will experience the fires of hell! You'll atone to me for your wickedness, you sinner! Remember how one autumn morning I came for one of your wives, but you flapped your wings, stamped your foot and gave me an awful fright!'

'Ah, Your Holiness!' stammered the cock. 'what a noble sermon you deliver. Mother Confessor, did you know our Archbishop is to hold a harvest festival soon? I shall surely ask him to let you bake the Communion bread; then we shall have crisp bread with sweet honey. And your fame will spread throughout the land.'

Listening to these flattering words and smacking her lips, the fox released the cock's neck; and Petya immediately escaped to the topmost branch of the tree.

The Frog Princess

LONG, long ago, in ancient Russia, there lived a king who had three sons. When they were grown to manhood, the king called them to him and said:

'My dear Sons, it is time you were married so that I might see my grandchildren before I die.'

To which the sons replied:

'If that is your wish, Sire, give us your blessing and tell us whom you would have us marry.'

'Take your bows and go beyond the palace walls into the open plain. There you must each loose an arrow and seek your bride wheresoever it falls.'

The three princes bowed low before their father and, each taking an arrow, they went beyond the palace walls, drew back their bow strings and let fly their arrows.

The Frog Princess

The first son's arrow landed in a nobleman's courtyard and was picked up by the nobleman's daughter. The second son's arrow fell by a rich merchant's house and was picked up by the merchant's daughter. The third son, Prince Ivan, shot his arrow so high and wide that he quite lost sight of it. After walking all day he finally found his arrow in a marsh; and sitting on a waterlily leaf holding the arrow in her mouth was a slimy green frog. When Prince Ivan asked for his arrow, the frog replied:

'I shall return your arrow only if you take me as your bride.'

'But how can a prince marry a frog!' said Prince Ivan in disgust.

Prince Ivan was angry, but there was nothing for it: he picked up the frog and carried her back to the palace.

When he recounted the story to his father and showed him the frog, the king said:

'Well, if the Fates would have you wed a frog, so be it.'

Thus it was that three weddings were celebrated the very next day: the first son married the nobleman's daughter, the second son the merchant's daughter and poor Prince Ivan the frog.

Some little time passed, and the king again summoned his sons and said:

'My dear Sons, I want to see which wife can make me the finest shirt. Let them each sew me a shirt by the morning.'

The princes bowed to their father and went their separate ways. The two eldest sons were not in the least dismayed, for they knew their wives could sew, but the youngest prince came home dejected and downcast. The frog hopped up to him and asked:

'Why do you hang your noble head, Prince Ivan? What ails you?'

'Well I might be sad,' he replied. 'Father would have you make him a shirt by morning.'

'Oh, is that all!' said the frog. 'Do not grieve. Eat your supper and go to bed. Morning is wiser than evening.'

As soon as Prince Ivan was asleep, the frog hopped through the door and onto the porch, cast off her frog skin and became Vassilisa the Wise, a princess fair beyond compare.

She clapped her hands and cried:

'Come my loyal servants, make haste and set to work! Sew me a shirt by morning as fine as that my father used to wear.'

At dawn, when Prince Ivan awoke, there was the frog sitting on the table by a shirt wrapped in an embroidered cloth. Overjoyed, he took the shirt to his father who was busy receiving the two elder sons' gifts. The first son laid out his shirt before the king, who took it and grumbled:

'This shirt is not fit for a humble peasant!'

The second son laid his shirt before the king, and the king moaned:

'This shirt is not fit for a common merchant!'

Then Prince Ivan laid out his shirt, so handsomely embroidered in gold and silver that the king's eyes shone and he exclaimed:

'Now this is a shirt fit for a king to wear on the grandest occasion!'

The two elder brothers went back to their wives, muttering to each other:

'We were wrong to mock at Prince Ivan's wife. She must be a witch, not a frog.'

Presently the king again summoned his sons.

'Your wives must bake me a white wheaten loaf by tomorrow morning,' he said. 'I want to see which is the best cook.'

Again Prince Ivan left the palace miserable and morose. And the frog asked him:

'Why so sad, Prince Ivan?'

'Well I might be sad,' he said. 'You are to bake a white wheaten loaf for my father by morning.'

'Is that all?' replied the frog. 'Do not grieve, Prince Ivan. Have your supper and go to bed. Morning is wiser than evening.'

This time his two brothers had sent an old woman from the palace kitchens to see how the frog baked her bread. But the frog guessed what they were up to. She kneaded some dough and cast it into the fire. The old woman immediately ran to the two brothers to give them the news. And their wives proceeded to do as the frog had done.

Meanwhile the frog hopped through the door onto the porch, changed into Vassilisa the Wise and clapped her hands.

'Come, my loyal servants. Make haste and set to work!' she cried. 'By morning bake me a loaf of crisp white bread, the kind I used to eat at my father's table.'

At dawn, when Prince Ivan awoke, there was the bread all ready, lying on the table and decorated with an entire town made from sugar.

Prince Ivan was overjoyed. He wrapped the bread in a white cloth and carried it to his father, who was just receiving the loaves his eldest sons had brought. Their wives had thrown the dough into the fire as the old woman had told them, and the loaves were black and lumpy.

The king took the bread from his eldest son, looked at it closely and dispatched it forthwith to the servants' quarters. He took the loaf from the second son and did likewise. But when Prince Ivan handed him his bread wrapped in a white cloth, the king was so delighted he exclaimed:

'Now this is bread fit to grace the royal table!'

At once he invited his three sons to bring their wives to a banquet that very evening.

Once more Prince Ivan returned home sad and sorrowful, hanging his head. Again the frog met him at the door and asked:

'Why so sad, Prince Ivan? Was your father not content?'

'Oh, my Frog Wife!' cried the young prince. 'Well I might be sad. The king has ordered me to bring you to the palace tonight. How am I to show you to the royal guests?'

But the frog replied:

'Do not grieve, Prince Ivan. Go to the banquet alone; I shall follow later. When you hear thunder, do not be afraid, and if they ask you what it is, say: "That is my Frog Wife arriving in her carriage".'

So Prince Ivan went to the banquet alone, and his elder brothers came with their wives dressed in all their finery.

'Why are you alone?' his brothers teased Prince Ivan. 'You could surely have brought your wife in a handkerchief. Wherever did you find such a beauty? You must have searched all the swamps for her.'

The king with his sons, their wives and all the noble guests sat down to dine at the white-clothed oaken tables. As they were about to start their meal, they suddenly heard thunder and the whole palace trembled and shook. The guests were alarmed, but Prince Ivan calmed them:

'Do not be afraid, noble people. That is my Frog Wife arriving in her carriage.'

At that moment a golden carriage drawn by six white horses arrived at the palace, and out of it stepped Vassilisa the Wise. Her blue silk gown glittered with stars and on her golden hair she wore the bright crescent moon. Her beauty was greater than tales can tell or words can relate. She took her husband's arm and led him to the white-clothed oaken table.

The king was enchanted with the Frog Princess's grace and beauty; her learned words attracted all the guests. Her sisters-in-law looked on in envy, determined to imitate her every gesture. They noticed that, after picking the bones of the roast swan, she slipped them into her right sleeve, and, after drinking the wine, she poured the last few drops from the goblet into her left sleeve. They did likewise.

When the dinner was over, the guests made ready to dance. Vassilisa the Wise took her husband by the arm and began to dance. She whirled round and round as the guests watched and marvelled: when she shook her left sleeve a shimmering lake appeared; and when she shook her right sleeve a flight of white swans swam upon the lake. The king and his noble guests were filled with wonder.

Then the wives of the two elder sons began to dance. When they waved their arms, their wet sleeves flapped against the king's face and bones flew out hitting the noble guests. The king was very angry and ordered them from the palace.

Prince Ivan, meanwhile, was extremely happy to learn that his wife was a clever and lovely princess. But, fearing she would turn back into a frog, he slipped out of the palace, hurried home and, finding the frog's skin, threw it into the fire.

When Vassilisa the Wise returned and saw her skin was gone, she burst into tears.

'Oh, Prince Ivan, what have you done! Had you waited just three more days, I would have been yours for ever. But now we must part. If you wish to find me, you must go beyond the Land of One Score and Nine to the realm of Old Bones the Immortal.'

With these words, she turned into a grey cuckoo and flew out of the window. Prince Ivan grieved many days and then, with his father's blessing, he set out to seek his wife. Whether he walked high or low I do not know, far or near I did not hear, long time or less I cannot guess, but his boots were soon worn, his caftan torn and his face forlorn. One day, when he had almost given up hope, he met a withered man as old as old can be.

'Good-morrow, young prince,' said the old man. 'What do you seek and whither are you bound?'

When the young prince had told him his tale, the old man shook his head and sighed:

'Oh, Prince Ivan, why did you burn the frog's skin? It was not yours to do as you like with. Vassilisa the Wise was born wiser and cleverer than her father, and this angered him so much he turned her into a frog for three years. It will be hard to find her now, but take this ball of thread and follow it wheresoever it rolls.'

Prince Ivan thanked the old man and continued on his way, following the ball of thread. It rolled on and on through a dense forest, and at last

emerged into a clearing, where the prince saw a bear. He was about to loose an arrow at it, when the bear spoke in a human voice:

'Do not kill me, Prince Ivan, you may have need of me some day.'

The prince took pity on the bear and continued on his way. A little farther on he spotted a drake flying overhead. He was about to shoot it, when it cried out in a human voice:

'Do not kill me, Prince Ivan, you may have need of me some day.'

So the prince spared the drake and journeyed on. Presently, a cross-eyed hare ran across the prince's path. Prince Ivan took aim quickly and was about to shoot, when the hare spoke in a human voice:

'Do not kill me, Prince Ivan, you may have need of me some day!'

So Prince Ivan spared the hare's life and followed the ball of thread until he came to a lake, where he found a pike lying on the bank gasping for breath.

'Take pity on me, Prince Ivan,' gasped the pike. 'Throw me back into the lake.'

So Prince Ivan threw the pike into the water and walked on. By and by,

the ball of thread rolled into a forest and stopped in a glade by a little hut on hen's feet, spinning round.

'Little hut, little hut, stand with your back to the trees and your face to me, please,' said Prince Ivan.

The hut slowly came to a halt and stood with its face to the prince and its back to the trees, and he entered. There, on the stove ledge, lay Baba Yagá, one bony leg curled beneath her, the other dangling, and her crooked nose reaching almost to the ceiling.

'What brings you here, Young Russian?' she screeched. 'Do you come as you willed or have you come to be killed?'

'That's not the way to greet a Russian guest, Grannie,' Prince Ivan replied. 'First heat up the bath-house, let me wash and steam myself, then give me food and drink, prepare a bed for me, and in the morning you may put your questions.'

So the witch heated up the bath-house, gave him food and drink and prepared a bed. In the morning Prince Ivan told her how he was seeking his wife, Vassilisa the Wise.

'I know where she is,' said Baba Yagá. 'Old Bones the Immortal has her in his power. It will be hard to rescue her, for no one can slay him. His death is at the end of a needle, the needle is in an egg, the egg in a duck, the duck in a hare, the hare in a stone chest and the chest at the top of a tall oak-tree which he guards like the apple of his eye.'

After learning the whereabouts of the oak, Prince Ivan set off on his journey and, late that evening, he arrived at the oak-tree. It stood tall and strong, the stone chest firmly lodged in its topmost branches and out of reach.

The prince was in despair when suddenly, from nowhere, a bear appeared, went up to the tree, hugged it in his strong arms and pulled it up by the roots. Down crashed the chest onto the damp earth and split asunder, so loosing a hare which bounded away as fast it could. At that moment, another cross-eyed hare appeared and gave chase. It caught the first hare and tore it to pieces. Out of the dead hare flew a duck, which flapped up into the sky. In a trice the drake was upon it and struck it so hard that it dropped an egg. Down the egg fell into the lake.

At that, Prince Ivan wept in despair: how would he find the egg at the bottom of the lake! Imagine his joy when the pike came swimming to the shore with the egg in its mouth. Prince Ivan cracked the egg, took out the needle and began to bend it. The more it bent, the more Old Bones writhed and twisted in his palace of black stone. And, when Prince Ivan broke off the end of the needle, Old Bones fell down dead.

The young prince then hurried to the palace of black stone for Vassilisa the Wise. Reunited at last, they returned home where they lived long and happily.

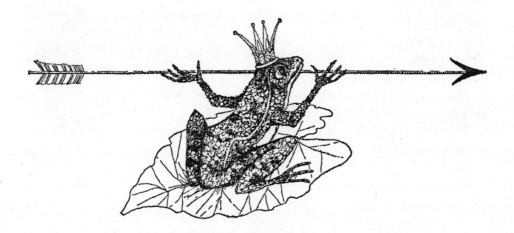

The Rosy Apple and the Golden Bowl

THERE once lived an old man and woman and their three daughters. The two eldest daughters were vain and cruel, but the third, Tania, was quiet and modest in all she did. The eldest daughters were lazy and stupid and sat at home all day, but Tania busied herself in the house and garden from dawn to dusk. She would weed the vegetable bed, chop firewood, milk the cows and feed the chickens. Her sisters would make her do their chores for them, and she would go about her work without a word or a sigh.

One day the old man made ready to take some hay to market, promising to bring back gifts for each of his daughters.

The first daughter said:

'Buy me a length of blue silk, Father.'

The second daughter said:

'Buy me a length of red velvet.'

Tania said nothing.

The old man asked again.

'Come now, what shall I fetch you, my child?'

'Bring me a rosy apple and a golden bowl,' she said at last.

At that her sisters laughed so hard that they nearly split their sides.

'What a fool you are, Tanushka!' they cried. 'Why, we have a whole orchard of apples, you can pick as many as you please. And as for a bowl, why do you need that – to feed the ducks from?'

'No, dear Sisters. I shall roll the apple in the bowl and say magic words. An old beggar once taught me them for giving her an Easter cake.'

Her sisters laughed even louder, and the old man reproached them:

'That's enough. I shall bring all of you the gifts you request.'

The old man sold his hay and bought his three daughters the gifts.

For the first daughter he bought blue silk, for the second red velvet and for Tania a rosy apple and golden bowl.

The two eldest sisters were delighted with their gifts and at once set to making new dresses, all the while poking fun at their sister.

'Sit there and roll your apple, silly!' they called.

Tania sat quietly in a corner of the room rolling her rosy apple in the golden bowl, as she sang softly:

> *'Rosy apple, roll, roll*
> *Round my little golden bowl.*
> *Show me meadows and seas*
> *And forests and leas,*
> *And mountains so high*
> *They reach to the sky.'*

[139]

Suddenly bells began to ring and light flooded the whole cottage. Round and round the golden bowl rolled the rosy apple and, in the bowl as clear as day, there appeared:

> *Downs and dales,*
> *Soldiers in fields with swords and shields,*
> *Grassy leas and ships on seas,*
> *And mountains so high they reached to the sky.*

The two eldest sisters could hardly believe their eyes. Their only thought now was to find a way of taking the apple and bowl from their sister.

Tania, however, would not exchange her gift, never let the apple and bowl out of her sight and would play with them every evening.

One day, tired of waiting, the two sisters decided to lure her into the forest.

'Come, sweet Sister,' they said, 'let us go and gather some berries and flowers in the forest. We may find some wild strawberries for mother and father.'

In the forest there were no berries or flowers to be seen anywhere. Tania took out her golden bowl and rolled her rosy apple in it as she sang softly:

> '*Rosy apple, roll, roll*
> *Round the little golden bowl.*
> *Show me strawberry red and cornflower blue,*
> *Poppies and daisies and violets too.*'

At once bells began to peal. Round and round the golden bowl rolled the rosy apple and, in the bowl, as clear as day, there appeared strawberry red and cornflower blue, poppies and daisies and violets too.

As Tania's two cruel sisters watched, a wicked gleam came into their eyes; while their sister sat quietly on a log staring down at her golden bowl, they killed her, buried her body beneath a silver birch and took the golden bowl and rosy apple for themselves. It was evening by the time they reached home, bringing baskets piled high with berries and flowers. They told their mother and father:

'Tania ran away from us and was lost. We searched the forest, but could not find her. The wolves or bears must have eaten her.'

On hearing that the mother burst into tears and the father said grimly:

'Roll the apple round the bowl and perhaps it will show us where Tania is.'

The sisters turned cold with fear, but they had to do as their father ordered. Yet when they tried to roll the apple in the bowl, it would not roll, and the bowl would not spin, and nothing appeared in it: no meadows or seas, no forests or leas, no mountains so high they reached to the sky.

Just about that time, a young shepherd was in the forest looking for a stray sheep and he came upon a silver birch with a fresh green mound beneath it and blue cornflowers growing around. Long slender reeds were shooting up amidst the flowers and from one of these the shepherd cut himself a pipe to play.

No sooner had he put the pipe to his lips than it began to play of itself. And these were the words it sang,

> 'Play, pipe, play, for the shepherd to hear,
> Play, pipe, play for the shepherd to cheer.
> By my sisters I did die,
> Beneath the silver birch I lie.'

The shepherd was frightened and ran straight to the village to tell his story. All the villagers gathered round to listen and gasped in horror.

When Tania's father heard the tale, he seized the pipe and put it to his own lips. The moment he did so it began to play by itself:

> Play, pipe, play, for my father to hear,
> Play, pipe, play, for my father to cheer.
> By my sisters I did die.
> Beneath the silver birch I lie.'

The father put down the pipe and turned to the shepherd.

'Take me to where you cut the reed for your pipe,' he said.

The shepherd led him to the fresh green mound in the forest where cornflowers were growing beneath the silver birch-tree. They dug a hole and found Tania in her shallow grave, quite cold and dead, but looking more lovely than ever, as if she were in peaceful slumber. And the pipe began to play again.

> *'Play, pipe, play, songs sad and gay,*
> *Listen, Father, to what I say:*
> *If you wish to see me well,*
> *Fetch some water from the royal well.'*

At these words, the two wicked sisters trembled and paled, fell on their knees and confessed their crime. The old man immediately set out for the king's palace to fetch the water.

When he finally reached the palace he was taken before the king.

The old man bowed to the ground and told his story. The king listened closely and said:

'You may take the water from my royal well and, if your daughter comes to life, bring her here together with her wicked sisters.'

The old man thanked the king and bowed low many times before going to the well and filling a flask with the water.

On returning to his dead daughter, he sprinkled her fair brow with the water from the royal well. Tania stirred, opened her eyes and embraced her parents.

The old man once more set off for the palace, this time with his three daughters; he arrived there and was again taken to the king. The king's gaze settled on Tania, as lovely as a spring flower, her eyes as radiant as the rays of the sun, her face as fair as the sky at dawn, and tears rolling down her cheeks like the purest of pearls.

'Where is your golden bowl and rosy apple?' the king said kindly.

As Tania took them out and spun the rosy apple round the golden bowl, there came a great ringing and pealing of bells and, one after the other, all the great Russian cities appeared in the bowl. Into the cities marched regiments of soldiers with their banners flying and their generals galloping ahead. Such was the firing and shooting, so thick the smoke that the battlefield was hidden from sight as if day had turned to night.

The rosy apple rolled on round the golden bowl and there appeared the sky in all its splendour: the bright sun chased away the pale crescent moon, fluffy white swans sailed in clouds across the sea-blue sky.

The king was filled with wonder at such marvellous sights, but Tania wept and wept without cease.

Finally, she went down on her knees before the king and begged:

'Please take my rosy apple and my golden bowl, Your Majesty. Only, pardon my sisters, do not put them to death because of me, I beg of you.'

The king gently lifted her to her feet and said:

'Your heart is of pure gold like your magic bowl. If you will consent to be my wife, you will not only make me happy but my people will have a kind and gentle queen. As for your sisters, they should be punished harshly, but, since you plead for their lives, I will spare them. Instead, they shall be banished to a bleak island at the other end of my kingdom.'

And so, the wicked sisters were banished and Tania became as noble a queen as the realm had seen.

The Crane Woos the Heron

ONE day long ago in the quiet of the world, when there was less noise and more green in the Russian forest, a wise old owl fluttered down, settled on a branch, twitched her tail and stared around. She blinked once, blinked twice, then flew off again. Up and down, round and round, twitching her tail and staring around.

Then she flew away and did not come back – which is as it should be for she is not in our story at all.

Here the telling of the tale begins.

*

There once lived two birds, a crane and a heron, who built their houses at opposite ends of a marsh. One day the crane grew bored with his bachelor life and resolved to take a wife.

'Why not go and woo the heron?' he thought.

So he waded the seven long versts through the marsh to the heron's house on stilts and called:

'Are you home, heron?'

'I am.'

'Will you marry me?'

'No, crane, I will not. Your legs are too long, your vest is too short, you fly badly and cannot provide for me. Go away, lanky-long-legs!'

At that uncheery welcome, the crane stalked off on his spindly legs back across the marsh to his home.

Not long after, the heron began to think over the crane's proposal,

'Why be a lonely spinster? Perhaps I should wed the crane after all.'

So she made her way across the marsh to the crane's humble hut and called:

'Crane, will you take me for your bride?'

The Crane Woos the Heron

'No, heron, I won't. I want to stay single; and even if I did not, I would not marry you for all the fish in the marsh. Go away, granny-long-neck!'

The heron sobbed with shame and turned back.

Soon after she had gone, the crane had second thoughts:

'Perhaps I was rather hasty; it really is no fun nesting alone. I'll go and tell her I've changed my mind.'

And he pattered through the marsh to the heron's home and called:

'Heron, I have changed my mind; I'll marry you after all.'

'I have changed my mind too, crane. I don't want you.'

Back trudged the crane. But no sooner had he left than the heron began to think it over:

'What a fool I was to turn him away. I do not wish to live alone for ever. I ought to go and wed the crane.'

Ever since, the crane and the heron have been wooing each other, back and forth across the marsh. Yet, somehow, they still cannot make up their minds.

The Peasant Priest

For full thirty years a parish church had neither priest nor deacon. The church stood empty and the parishioners had no one to baptize their children or bury their dead.

Now, there lived in that village an old man and his wife who were as ignorant and poor as the croaking marsh toads. One day, however, the old man had an idea.

'What if the parish hires us for its services? I'll be the priest, you the deacon,' he told his wife.

So he called a meeting and asked the villagers if they would accept him as the new priest. The parishioners agreed; it was all the same to them who did the job.

When Sunday came, the new priest brushed his beard, put on a long black smock and began the morning service. A great congregation had gathered inside the church: every Christian from thereabouts wanted to see the new preacher.

Of course, the new priest did not want to make a fool of himself at his first service; seeing the great multitude, he put the bible under his arm, came down from the altar and cried:

'Listen, Brethren! Have you heard the scriptures and hymns before?'

'Yes, Father, we've heard them,' chorused the congregation.

'Well, if you've heard them before, you won't want to hear them again,' said the priest. 'Go on home!'

So the church-goers made their way out, each giving his opinion of the new preacher.

'There's a priest for you!' some said. 'Not like those we had in the old days, forever chanting and singing. With this fellow, there's no wasting time – he lets us home for dinner at once!'

The villagers could hardly wait for the next Sunday. This time, the new priest decided to put on more of a show. Thus, having filled his censer full of charcoal and hot oil, he descended from the altar swinging it as he had seen priests do.

'Listen, Brethren,' he said, 'I want you to do all that I do.'

So saying, he began to swing his censer from side to side. And all the congregation began to wave their arms from side to side. As he swung the censer, however, a burning coal fell out and landed in his boot; the priest at once fell onto his back shaking his legs in the air to get the coal out.

And the whole congregation fell on their backs waving their legs in the air.

It was about that time that a squire happened to be passing the church and, wishing to know what time of day it was, sent his coachman to find out. The coachman stopped just before the church door and, seeing an old woman of some ninety-five years lying on her back feebly kicking her legs in the air, asked her how late it was.

Hardly able to get her breath, the old woman gasped:

'It's like this, Sir; the kicking's just over and the rolling's just begun.'

The coachman opened the door wider and was astonished to see the entire congregation rolling around kicking their legs in the air. He quickly closed the door and returned to his master.

'Well, coachman,' asked the squire, 'did you find out what time it is?'

'You'd better look for yourself, Your Honour,' replied the coachman, quite shaken.

At the entrance to the church, the squire came upon the old woman barely able to wave her legs.

'Excuse me, Grandmother,' said the squire, 'can you tell me how late it is?'

'Well, it's like this, Sir,' she gasped, 'the kicking's over and the rolling's begun.'

Puzzled, the squire pushed open the church door and was amazed to see the entire congregation on their backs, waving their legs in the air.

'Well I never!' exclaimed the squire. 'What a wonderful preacher he must be to put such religious fervour into his flock!'

So saying, he put fifty rubles into the collection box and continued on his way.

Marya Morévna

IN a certain kingdom, in a certain realm, there once lived a king who had one son, Prince Ivan, and three daughters: Princess Marfa, Princess Olga and Princess Anna.

The king grew old and just before he died he called his son to him and said:

'After my death, dear Son, rule the kingdom justly and give the princesses, your sisters, to the first suitors that come to court them.'

Soon after the old king had died, Prince Ivan was walking with his sisters in the palace gardens when dark clouds gathered in the sky and it seemed a terrible storm would break.

No sooner had they reached the palace than the thunder crashed, the roof was rent in two and a black raven flew into the chamber. He flung himself against the floor, turned into a darkly handsome young man and said:

'Good-morrow, Prince Ivan. Many's the time I have been a guest at your palace. Now I come as a suitor, for I seek the hand of your sister, Princess Marfa.'

Remembering his father's wish, Prince Ivan agreed.

'If my sister loves you, so be it.'

So Princess Marfa married the raven and after the wedding he took her away to his kingdom.

One year passed and Prince Ivan and his two sisters were again walking in the palace gardens when a black cloud suddenly covered the sun, lightning flashed and a fierce wind blew.

No sooner had they reached the palace than the thunder crashed, the ceiling fell and a bright-eyed falcon flew into the chamber. He threw himself against the floor and turned into a handsome young man.

'Good-morrow, Prince Ivan,' he said in greeting. 'Many's the time I have come here as a guest, now I come as a suitor. I wish to marry your sister, Princess Olga.'

'If my sister loves you, so be it,' replied Prince Ivan.

Princess Olga gave her consent and married the falcon and after the wedding he took her to his kingdom.

Another year passed, and Prince Ivan was walking one day with his youngest sister in the palace gardens when dark clouds gathered, lightning flashed and thunder crashed, and a fierce wind began to blow.

Just as they entered the palace, the ceiling fell and a golden eagle flew into the chamber. He flung himself against the floor and turned into a fair young man, more handsome than tales can tell or words can relate.

'Many's the time I came here as a guest,' he said, 'now I come as a suitor. I wish to wed your youngest sister, Princess Anna.'

'My sister is free to do as she wills,' answered Prince Ivan. 'If she loves you, she may marry you.'

So Princess Anna married the eagle and after the wedding he took her to his eagle's kingdom. Prince Ivan was alone. He soon missed his sisters greatly and decided to pay them a visit.

Leaving the royal duties to his trusty nobles, he set out on his journey. Whether he was long on his way I cannot say, but eventually he entered another kingdom and came upon a whole host of warriors lying routed and slain on the open plain.

'If there be any living among you, speak up, for I would know who vanquished this mighty host,' he called across the battlefield.

The only living man there replied:

'We are from Old Bones's kingdom. We waged war on Queen Marya Morévna to set free our master, Old Bones the Immortal, but she routed our army. I am the only man left alive.'

Prince Ivan marvelled at this:

'What wonders abound! A maiden defeating a whole army! I would like to meet such a warrior maid. Tell me, which way did she ride?'

'Take the right road, noble prince, that is the way she went,' replied the wounded soldier.

Prince Ivan turned his horse to the right and journeyed three days before he came upon an encampment of white tents. He rode up to the largest and most splendid tent and there, coming out to meet him, was Marya Morévna herself.

'Good-day, bold prince,' she said. 'Do you come here of your own will?'

'Bold warriors come and go as they please,' replied Prince Ivan.

'If you are in no great haste, stay for a while as my guest,' said the warrior maid.

This Prince Ivan was happy to do. He stayed for a week and fell deeply in love with the beautiful queen. Marya Morévna loved him too and it was not long before they were married.

They lived together happily for a time till one day Marya Morévna had to go to battle again. Before departing she told Prince Ivan:

'Rule my kingdom well and see to my royal duties. Go where you please in the palace, but whatever you do, you must not look into the room that is bolted fast and sealed with tar. If you disobey me, you will bring misfortune upon us all.'

Bidding him farewell, she rode off at the head of her army.

After she was gone, Prince Ivan's curiosity drew him to the forbidden room. As he unlocked the door he saw a fire burning inside, over the fire was an iron cauldron, and in the cauldron sat an old man, green and wizened. His arms and legs were fettered to the cauldron by iron chains, and, when he saw Prince Ivan, he began to plead:

'Take pity on me, give me water. For three long years, I have been chained here without a drink, my throat is so dry.'

Prince Ivan was sorry for the old man and gave him a pailful of water. The old man gulped it down and begged for more. Prince Ivan fetched him a second, and then a third.

As soon as he had finished the third pailful, the old man shook his chains so fiercely they snapped like rotting thread. Springing from the iron cauldron, he shouted:

'Thank you, Prince Ivan, you have returned to me, Old Bones the Immortal, my former strength. Now you will never see Marya Morévna again, no more than you can see your own ears!'

With that, he rushed from the room and out of the palace, overtook Marya Morévna and carried her off to his kingdom.

Prince Ivan wept long and bitterly, then set off in search of his wife.

Whether he was long on his way I cannot say, but he eventually came to a splendid palace. Beside the palace there grew a stout oak and in the branches sat a raven.

The raven flew out of the tree, struck the ground and became a darkly handsome young man, and cried:

'Ah, my dear Brother, how glad I am to see you!'

Hearing her brother had arrived, Princess Marfa ran out to greet him.

He was taken into the palace and treated as their dearest guest. After three days and nights with them, he said:

'I must be on my way. I am seeking my wife, Marya Morévna.'

'Well, Brother, you were wise to take such a lovely wife, but you were foolish to lose her,' said the raven. 'It won't be easy to free her from Old Bones the Immortal.'

Before the prince left, the raven gave him a black feather.

'Keep this feather so that I might know if you need my help.'

Prince Ivan thanked the raven and his sister and journeyed on.

He rode for one day, then two, and at dawn on the third he came to a palace even more splendid than the first. Beside the palace grew three oaks and in the tallest sat a falcon.

The falcon flew to the ground, turned into a handsome young man and cried:

'Princess Olga, come and see who is here.'

The second sister came running to greet her dear brother. He was taken into the palace and regaled with the choicest of wines and tastiest morsels. After resting for three days and nights, Prince Ivan thanked them and explained that he had to continue the quest for his wife, Marya Morévna.

The falcon told him:

'You have brought this grief upon yourself and it will not be easy to find her. But go on your way with my blessing and take this grey feather so that we may know if you need our help.'

Prince Ivan took the feather and continued on his way. He rode on and on and came to another splendid palace. Beside it there grew nine tall oaks and in the highest perched an eagle.

The eagle flew from the oak, flung himself upon the damp ground and, turning into a fair young man, cried:

'We've been long expecting you, Brother.'

Leading him into the palace, he called his wife, Princess Anna, to greet their dear guest. Anna rushed to embrace her brother and entertained him with the choicest meads and food.

Prince Ivan spent three days and nights with them, and then began to prepare for his journey.

[152]

'I must depart to find my wife, Marya Morévna,' he said.

The eagle gave him one of his golden feathers and wished him luck with his quest.

'Keep this feather with you and I shall know if trouble befalls you.'

Prince Ivan thanked the eagle and his sister, mounted his horse and set out for Old Bones's kingdom.

Whether the realm was far or near I did not hear, but one day he came to a towering palace. By a window in a tower sat Marya Morévna weeping. When she saw Prince Ivan, she sobbed even louder:

'Oh, Ivan, my bold and handsome prince, why have you come here? You will surely be killed. As soon as Old Bones returns, he will slay you. Why did you not do as I told you?'

'Forgive me, Marya Morévna, my sin lies heavy upon my heart. Come away with me while Old Bones is not here, perhaps he will not catch us.'

Marya Morévna made ready and they rode away together.

But, just at that moment, Old Bones was returning home from hunting and, as he galloped over the plain, his steed stumbled under him.

'Why do you stumble, you bag of bones?' he shouted. 'Do you sense misfortune?'

'Prince Ivan has carried off Marya Morévna,' the steed replied.

'Can we overtake them?'

'We could sow a field of wheat, wait until it ripens, reap and thresh it and grind it into flour, bake it in the oven, eat it and then set off – and we should still catch them.'

So Old Bones rested several days, then set out and in no time at all overtook Prince Ivan.

'I'll forgive you once,' he said, 'for you gave me water, and I'll pardon you twice, but, if I catch you a third time, I'll cut you into little pieces.'

So saying, he snatched Marya Morévna and vanished in a cloud of dust leaving Prince Ivan alone by the roadside. After feeding his horse, the prince again set out for Old Bones's kingdom. Though Old Bones's steed had covered the distance in three leaps, it took Prince Ivan three weeks to reach the towering palace.

Once again Old Bones was away hunting.

Prince Ivan at once set Marya Morévna on his horse and together they fled. Presently, as Old Bones was returning, his steed said to him:

'I sense trouble. Prince Ivan has taken Marya Morévna.'

'Can we overtake them?'

'We could sow a field of barley, wait for it to ripen, reap and thresh it, brew beer from it, get drunk and then set off – and we would still catch them.'

So Old Bones the Immortal rested, then galloped in pursuit and soon overtook the fleeing pair.

'I said you would no more see Marya Morévna than you can see your own ears,' said Old Bones, seizing the lovely Marya and carrying her off.

Prince Ivan sat down on a stone and wept. Then, summoning his courage, he returned once again for his wife. He begged Marya Morévna to come away with him.

'Oh, Prince Ivan, Old Bones is bound to catch us and this time he won't spare you!' she said.

'So be it,' replied the prince, 'I would rather die than live without you.'

So they made ready and rode off as fast as the prince's horse could go. Meanwhile, Old Bones was riding home when his steed stumbled.

'Why do you stumble, you bag of bones? Do you sense misfortune?' he asked.

The steed told his master what had happened. So Old Bones galloped in pursuit and, when he had overtaken the fleeing pair, he took his sword and cut down the prince, leaving the pieces scattered over the plain for the crows to pick.

At that moment, the feathers of the raven, the falcon and the eagle became bloodstained and they knew that some misfortune had befallen their brother. And all three flew to the plain where Prince Ivan lay.

The raven flew off for the water of death, the falcon for the water of life, and the eagle meanwhile washed each piece of the body in clear spring water and put it together. When the raven and the falcon returned, they sprinkled the corpse with the water of death – and the body grew whole. Then they sprinkled it with the water of life and Ivan shook himself, opened his eyes and stood up:

'What a long sleep I've had!' he said.

'You would have slept forever if we had not brought you back to life,' said his brothers. 'Now come and be our guest.'

'No, my Brothers, I must go in search of Marya Morévna.'

Once more he returned to the land of Old Bones and found his Marya Morévna. She was overjoyed to see him alive and could scarcely believe her eyes:

'Is it really you, my good and noble prince?'

'Yes, it is I,' he said, and he told her how his brothers had saved him; he asked her to discover where Old Bones had found his swift steed.

Marya Morévna hid him in a palace cellar where Old Bones would not find him. When the master came home, Marya Morévna prepared a fine supper and treated him kindly, then asked about his horse.

'Beyond the Land of One Score and Nine in the realm of One Score and Ten dwells Baba Yagá, my aunt,' said Old Bones. 'Her hut is across the Burning River, and she has a steed on which she can ride round the world in a day. She has other fine horses too. I tended them for three days and let not one escape, so Baba Yagá presented me with a colt.'

'But how did you cross the Burning River?' persisted Marya Morévna.

'With the aid of my magic scarf,' he replied. 'When I shook it three times to the left, a high bridge appeared out of reach of the flames; when I shook it three times to the right it disappeared.'

The next day, when Old Bones went hunting, Marya Morévna told all that she had learned to Prince Ivan, gave him the magic scarf and sent him on his way to earn a horse from Baba Yagá.

Prince Ivan crossed the Burning River with three waves of the magic scarf to the left, and entered the realm of One Score and Ten. He walked for a long time without food or drink until he came upon a strange bird with her brood of chicks.

'I am so hungry, I shall eat one of those chicks,' he thought to himself.

'Please don't harm my chicks,' said the strange bird. 'Who knows, one day you may need me.'

He took pity on the bird and went on his way. Presently he came upon a bee-hive in the forest.

'I am really starving, I shall help myself to some honey,' he thought. But the queen bee pleaded:

'Please don't touch my honey, Prince Ivan. One day I may be of use to you.'

So he turned his back on the honey and journeyed on. Shortly, he chanced upon a lioness and her cub. By this time he was faint with hunger.

'I shall at least eat that lion cub. I am so hungry I can hardly stand.'

'Don't touch my cub,' begged the lioness. 'One day you may need my help.'

'Very well, I won't touch your cub,' he said and went on his way hungry.

It was not long before he arrived at Baba Yagá's hut; around it stood twelve poles and all save one bore human heads.

'Good-day, Grannie!' he said.

'Good-day to you, Prince Ivan. What brings you here? Do you come as you've willed or do you come to be killed?'

'I come to earn one of your fine steeds,' he replied.

'Very well, you have just three days and if you keep them all safe, you shall have one of my finest steeds. But if you lose any, your head will be stuck on the last pole of my fence.'

Prince Ivan agreed, and Baba Yagá gave him food and drink and set him to work. No sooner had he driven the horses into the pasture than they hoisted up their tails and scattered across the meadows, vanishing from sight. He sorrowed and grieved, then lay down beneath a tree and fell asleep.

At sunset that strange bird of the plains swooped down to him and said:

'Wake up, Prince Ivan, the horses are all back in their stables.'

He returned joyfully to the hut and heard Baba Yagá screaming at her horses:

'Why did you come back?'

'What else could we do? The birds of the air came flying at us from all over the heavens and nearly plucked out our eyes.'

'Well, don't run across the meadows tomorrow, go straight into the dense forests,' said Baba Yagá.

Prince Ivan slept the whole night through and, in the morning, Baba Yagá said to him:

'Take care, if you lose a single horse your head will be stuck on the last pole.'

He drove the horses out to graze and again they lifted their tails and, this time, dashed off into the forest. Once more Prince Ivan sank down beneath a tree in despair, wept and wailed and fell asleep. The sun was already sinking behind the forest when the lioness came running.

'Wake up, Prince Ivan,' she cried. 'All the horses are back in their stables.'

He stood up and went back with light heart to the hut; on the way he heard Baba Yagá shrieking at her horses:

'Why did you come back?'

'What else could we do? The wild beasts from all over the forest came running at us and nearly tore us to shreds!'

'Tomorrow you must run and hide in the deep sea,' said Baba Yagá.

Prince Ivan slept soundly the night through and in the morning Baba Yagá sent him for a third time to tend her horses.

'And if you lose a single one, you will pay with your head,' she warned.

He led out the horses to graze and straight away they lifted their tails and vanished from sight. Into the deep sea they rushed and stood up to their necks in the water.

He sank down beneath the tree, moaned and groaned and at last fell asleep.

The sun was sinking beyond the horizon when the queen bee flew down and buzzed in his ear:

'Wake up, wake up, Prince Ivan, all the horses are back in their stables. This time, when you return to Baba Yagá, go to the stables and hide behind the crib. There you will find a mangy colt wallowing in the mire. Take him, and creep out of the stable at midnight.'

Ivan returned to the stables and hid behind the crib. All the while, Baba Yagá was ranting and raving at her horses:

'Why did you come back?'

'But what else could we do? Swarms of bees came flying at us from

all corners of the earth and stung us till we were full of stings and bumps.'

Baba Yagá went to bed and fell asleep, and at midnight, Prince Ivan saddled her mangy colt and rode to the Burning River. On the bank of the river he waved the magic scarf three times to the left and a tall bridge appeared out of reach of the flames.

He rode across and then waved the scarf twice only to the right – and a low narrow bridge took the place of the tall strong one.

In the morning Baba Yagá awoke and, seeing that her mangy colt had gone, she jumped upon a horse and rode off like the wind.

Arriving at the Burning River, she found the bridge, leaped from her horse and started to walk across. As she reached the centre of the narrow bridge it collapsed and Baba Yagá fell to her death into the river of fire.

Meanwhile Prince Ivan pastured his colt in the lush, green meadows and the colt grew into a strong and fiery steed. He then rode in a trice to the towering palace of Old Bones to rescue his wife, Marya Morévna.

When Marya Morévna saw him, she ran out of the palace to greet him:

'Oh, dear prince, I am so afraid. If Old Bones overtakes us he will surely kill you again.'

'He will not catch us this time, for I have a fiery steed that flies like the wind,' said Prince Ivan.

He sat her behind him on the horse's back and they rode away.

Later that day Old Bones the Immortal was returning home when his horse stumbled beneath him.

'Why do you stumble, bag of bones?' he shouted. 'Do you sense misfortune?'

'Prince Ivan has carried off Marya Morévna,' the horse replied.

'Can we overtake them?'

'That I cannot say for now he has a steed as swift and fiery as myself.'

'We shall see,' said Old Bones. 'Fly faster than the wind, you worthless nag!'

He spurred on the steed with his whip, drove it over forests and mountains, rivers and lakes and soon began to overtake Prince Ivan. When he caught up with the fleeing pair, he made to strike Prince Ivan with his sharp sword, but his horse stumbled and threw him to the ground. As he fell, he smashed his head against a stone. Prince Ivan finished Old Bones off with his sword, burnt his body and scattered the ashes to the four winds.

Then he mounted Old Bones's horse, while Marya Morévna mounted his own, and together they rode on with nothing to halt them. On their way, they rested and dined at the palaces of the raven, the falcon and the eagle. Then Prince Ivan returned to his own kingdom with Marya Morévna and held a feast to which the whole world was invited.

The Frightened Wolves

In a little Russian village there once lived a little old man who owned a goat and a ram. He grew lazy and forgetful in his old age and, one summer, he mowed no hay for the animals' winter food. When the frosts came and there was nothing in the barn, the goat and ram began to bleat about the yard. This annoyed the old man so much that he took a whip and drove them both away.

Finding themselves without a meal or a home, the two animals wondered what to do.

'Let's make for the forest, Baran Baranich,' suggested the goat. 'We'll find a haystack and live there.'

'A good idea, Kozma Bleatich,' agreed the ram. 'Life can be no worse than with that old miser.'

Before they started out on their new life, however, the goat crept back for his master's shotgun and the ram fetched a sack.

On their way to the forest they came across an old wolf's head.

'Baran Baranich,' said the goat, 'pick up that head and put it into your sack. It might come in useful. When we reach the forest we can boil ourselves some wolf-head soup.'

The ram took up the head and dropped it into the sack. On they walked together until they came to the dense forest.

'I'm so cold and hungry,' said the ram stopping to rest. 'Look, there's a fire over there. Let's warm ourselves by it.'

As they came through the trees into a clearing they found, to their horror, that they had stumbled upon a pack of wolves warming themselves round a fire. The ram nearly jumped out of his woolly skin, but the goat sauntered boldly to the front of the wolves' circle and said:

'Good-day to you, lads!'

'Greetings to you, Kozma Bleatich!' chorused the wolves, who were most delighted to see their supper drop in on them.

The goat, however, had other plans.

'Hey there, brother ram,' he shouted. 'Hand me one of the wolves' heads from the sack, we'll boil it up now for supper on this fire. See you pick a good meaty one!'

The ram took the wolf's head from the sack and passed it to the goat.

'Not that one!' said the goat. 'Search around in the sack and dig me out a really juicy one with bulging eyes.'

Again the ram rummaged about in his sack, rummaged and rummaged and brought out the same head.

'Oh you ninny!' shouted the goat stamping his foot in irritation. 'Not that one! Have a really good look . . . shake them up a bit . . . right at the bottom. . .'

The Frightened Wolves

The ram once more delved into the sack, delved and delved and came up with the selfsame head.

'Yes, yes, that's the one!' exclaimed the goat. 'That will do nicely.'

The wolves glanced at one another in alarm. Their thoughts were not hard to guess:

'Look how many of our brothers they have slain. . . A whole sackful of heads!'

'I say, fellows,' asked the goat politely, 'do you have a pot we could boil our supper in?'

At that, all the wolves sprang up, eager to seize on an excuse to escape – some promised to run for firewood, some for water, others for a pot. But they were all of one mind: to put as great a distance as possible between themselves and those two wolf-eaters!

As they dashed through the forest, they ran into a bear.

'Not so fast, my grey friends,' he said. 'What's the hurry?'

'Oh, Michaelo Ivanovich! You have no idea! A goat and a ram descended upon us, carrying a whole sackful of wolves' heads and intending to boil wolf-head soup before our very eyes. We were so afraid they would set upon us, we ran away.'

The deep laughter of Michaelo Ivanovich echoed through the pines:

'What blockheads you are! A couple of helpless animals fell into your laps and tricked you out of your supper. Just line up behind me, we'll return and deal with them!'

Meanwhile in the clearing the goat and ram were startled to hear a distant crackling of leaves and a snapping of twigs. It was too late to escape. The goat clambered up a tall tree and crouched in its branches. The ram, however, was not so agile; no matter how hard he tried he could not climb up. He just managed to get his forelegs over the lowest branch and dangled there.

When the bear and the wolves reached the clearing, they found no trace of the goat and the ram.

'Well, Brothers,' panted the bear, 'you go in search while I keep watch here. They cannot be far away.'

While the wolves searched the forest, the bear settled beneath the very tree in which the goat and ram were hiding. Just above the bear's head, the ram whispered desperately to the goat:

'Oh dear, Kozma Bleatich, my legs ache. I fear I cannot hold on much longer.'

'Hold on,' muttered the goat. 'If you fall it will surely be the end of us!'

The ram clung for dear life to the branch, but his strength gave out and he crashed down right on top of the bear. When the goat saw the plight they were in, he immediately let off a blast from the shotgun and gave a fierce shout:

'Seize that watchman! Don't let him escape!'

The bear got the shock of his life. Hearing the shout and the shot, he quickly pulled himself out from under the ram and made off as fast as his legs would carry him.

As soon as he had fled, the goat sprang down from the tree alongside the trembling ram. Neither wished to remain a moment longer in the forest; so they returned home to their old master. And there they lived to the end of their days.

The Fool and the Magic Fish

THERE once lived three brothers; two were wise and the third was a fool. The Fool would sit on the stove all day long, picking his nose and caring for nothing.

One day the two elder brothers rode to market promising to bring their young brother a pair of red boots if he did everything their wives asked. Soon after they had gone, the wives said:

'Go and fetch some water from the river, Fool!'

But the Fool, lying on top of the warm stove, replied:

'Not I. It is too cold in the snow outside.'

'Go, Fool, or your brothers will bring you no boots from market.'

'Oh, all right,' he consented grudgingly.

Down he climbed from the stove, pulled on his boots and warm coat and, taking two pails and an axe, went down to the river. There, he cut a hole in the thick ice with his axe, scooped up two pailfuls of water and, to his surprise, found a fish swimming in one of his pails.

'What luck, I'll have fish soup for dinner today!' he exclaimed.

But he was astonished to hear the fish suddenly cry in a human voice:

'Let me go, Fool; I shall repay your kindness one day.'

The Fool only laughed.

'What good could you do me? I'll take you home and get the women to make some soup. I love fish soup.'

But the fish begged him again:

'If you let me go, Fool, you may wish for anything you like.'

'If I do let you go,' said the Fool, 'you must first prove what you say. I want my pails to go home by themselves without spilling a drop of water.'

'Very well,' said the fish. 'Whenever you wish something, you have only to say: "By will of the fish, do as I wish!" '

Straightaway, the Fool said:

> '*By will of the fish, do as I wish!*
> *Off home you go, pails, all by yourselves!*'

At this command, the pails turned and trotted off up the hill on little wooden legs.

The Fool threw the fish back into the river and ran through the snow after his pails.

They marched down the village street, while the villagers stood still and marvelled. The Fool followed behind chuckling. The pails went straight into the hut and jumped up on a bench, while he climbed back onto the stove.

Presently the wives said:

'Don't just lie there, Fool. Go and chop some wood.'

He did not want to leave the warm stove, so he said under his breath:

> '*By will of the fish, do as I wish!*
> *Axe, hop down from the shelf and chop wood by yourself!*'

No sooner had he uttered the words than the axe skipped down from the shelf into the yard and began to chop the wood; the logs filed into the hut one by one and jumped into the stove all by themselves.

By and by, the wives said:

'We have no more logs, Fool. Go to the forest and bring back some logs.'

There was nothing for it but to climb down from the stove and pull on his boots again. This time he took a length of rope and the axe, went into the yard and, climbing into the sledge, cried:

'Open up the gates, women!'

'What are you doing in the sledge, Fool? You haven't harnessed the horse yet.'

'I can do without the horse,' the Fool replied with a grin.

They opened the gates and he shouted:

> '*By will of the fish, do as I wish!*
> *Sledge, race to the trees, and do just as I please!*'

The sledge shot out through the gates so quickly it almost pushed the two women over.

Now, the forest lay on the other side of the village and the sledge knocked down many villagers on the way. The village folk cried angrily: 'Seize him! Catch him!' But the Fool paid no heed and only urged on the sledge even faster.

When he came to the forest, he stopped the sledge and said:

> '*By will of the fish, do as I wish!*
> *Show me more tricks and chop up some sticks!*'

At once the axe began to chop the dry wood, and the sticks dropped into the sledge one by one, binding themselves together in neat bundles. Before returning home, the Fool ordered the axe to cut him a good stout club and, with that, he climbed on top of his load and commanded:

> '*By will of the fish, do as I wish!*
> *Our good work is done, so off you go home!*'

The sledge drove off very fast. He again passed through the village centre where he had knocked down so many people, but this time they were ready for him. They seized him, pulled him from the sledge and began to curse and beat him.

Finding himself overpowered, the Fool called:

> *'By will of the fish, do as I wish!*
> *Come, club, in return for these blows, hit them hard on the nose!'*

The club sprang up and laid into them, left and right. Battered and bruised, the poor villagers took to their heels while the Fool went home and settled back on the stove.

The days went by, whether fast or slow I do not know, but the king eventually came to hear of the Fool's doings and sent a servant to bring him to the palace.

The servant arrived at the Fool's village, entered his hut and ordered: 'Come with me to the palace!'

The Fool called down lazily from the stove:

'And what if I don't want to?'

The king's servant flew into a rage at that and struck the Fool. At once the Fool said under his breath:

> *'By will of the fish, do as I wish!*
> *Come, club, let him know what he's earned for that blow!'*

Up jumped the stout wooden club and beat the king's servant so hard it was all he could do to drag himself back to the palace.

The king was much surprised to learn what had happened and sent for the wisest of his counsellors.

'Find the Fool and bring him to my palace,' he ordered.

So the wise counsellor filled a great basket with honey cakes, sunflower seeds and bilberries and journeyed to the selfsame village and entered the selfsame hut and asked the Fool's brothers what their young brother liked best of all.

'He will do anything if you treat him kindly,' the brothers answered, 'and promise him clothes of brightest red.'

The wise counsellor then presented the Fool with the tasty food he had brought in his huge basket and said:

'Why do you lie all day on the stove, Fool? Why not come with me to the palace?'

'I'm quite happy where I am,' replied the Fool.

'Ah, but the king will treat you to sweetmeats and wines if you come.'

'I don't want to go to the palace, so leave me alone.'

'But the king will dress you in bright red robes, a pair of red boots and a red blouse.'

The Fool thought it over and said:

'Very well, then, I shall come. But on one condition: you go on ahead and I shall follow.'

The wise counsellor rode off while the Fool remained on the stove. Finally he raised himself and said:

> '*By will of the fish, do as I wish!*
> *Stove, full speed to the tsar, just as you are!*'

No sooner were the words out of his mouth than the stove moved off by itself through the door, out into the yard and down the village street heading for the palace – with the Fool sitting on top of it.

When the stove drew near, the king looked out of his window and could hardly believe his eyes.

'What in the name of Saint Nicholas is that coming?' he asked.

The wise counsellor explained:

'That is the Fool riding on his stove to your palace.'

The king stepped out of his palace and addressed the Fool:

'I have heard many complaints about you. It is said you knocked down many of my subjects and gave them a thrashing.'

'It was their own fault; they should not have been in the way of my sledge,' answered the Fool boldly.

Now, the king's lovely daughter, Princess Ludmilla, was standing at the palace window at that moment, and, when the Fool looked up and saw her, he fell deeply in love. Under his breath he whispered:

> '*By will of the fish, do as I wish!*
> *Let so lovely a jewel fall in love with the Fool!*'

Then he quickly added, 'Home, stove!'

The stove turned and glided back over the snow towards his village. It entered the hut, went back to its old place and the Fool lay on the stove ledge as before.

Meanwhile a great commotion arose in the palace. Princess Ludmilla had fallen sick, weeping and crying over her loved one. She begged her father to let her marry the Fool. The king was furious that his daughter should want to wed a foolish peasant. He again summoned his wise counsellor and ordered:

'Go and fetch the Fool at once!'

The wise man again collected all kinds of cakes and sweet wines and set off for the village. When he arrived he began to treat the Fool to the tempting food.

After the Fool had had his fill of the good food and wine, he fell into a sound slumber. The counsellor put him into his carriage and took him back to the palace.

The king at once ordered a large barrel bound with iron hoops to be made. The two unfortunate lovers, the Fool and Princess Ludmilla, were put into it and the barrel was tossed into the sea.

When the Fool awoke, the princess told him tearfully:

'Oh, Fool, my love! They have put us in a barrel and cast us into the sea.'

Recognizing the voice of the lovely princess, he said:

'By will of the fish, do as I wish!
Come, wild winds, blow the barrel to land, let it rest on dry sand!'

A storm suddenly blew up, the waves raced over the sea and soon the barrel reached dry land. When the Fool and Princess Ludmilla had stepped out of the barrel, the princess asked:

'But where will we live? We shall surely die of cold and hunger.' And the Fool said:

'By will of the fish, do as I wish!
Let a palace of gold from the skies unfold!'

The Fool and the Magic Fish

A gold-domed palace appeared from the sky and settled upon the sands, surrounded by a leafy garden with blossoming flowers and twittering birds.

The princess and the Fool passed through the golden gates, wandered through the marble halls and rested on satin couches.

Then the princess gazed fondly at her beloved and sighed deeply:

'Oh Fool, if only you were not so plain, your nose not so long and your hair not so red.'

It did not take the Fool long to decide.

> *'By will of the fish, do as I wish!*
> *A tall fair handsome man, no less, I'll be to please my dear princess.'*

And he became as handsome as the sky at dawn, the fairest man that ever was born.

Not long after, the king was out hunting and was astonished to find a palace on the yellow sands where none had stood before.

'What impudent knave has dared to build a palace on my land?' he inquired, despatching his messengers to discover who lived in the splendid palace.

The king's messengers ran to the palace, stood beneath a window and called to the master, asking him to reveal himself to the king.

When the Fool heard them, he shouted back:

'Tell the king to come here and he shall learn who I am.'

The king did as commanded. The Fool met him at the palace gates, led the king into the palace, seated him at a table and regaled him royally. The king dined and drank and marvelled.

'But what great king or duke are you?' he asked at last.

'Do you not remember the Fool who visited you on a stove?' the Fool said. 'Do you not recall how you had him put in a barrel with your daughter, Princess Ludmilla, and tossed into the sea? Well, I am that same Fool. If I choose, I can send you and your whole kingdom to the bottom of the ocean!'

The king raised his hands in horror and begged the Fool to forgive him:

'You may take my daughter with my blessing, and take half my kingdom too, if you will spare me,' he begged.

The Fool agreed, forgave the king and wed the fair Princess Ludmilla. He then invited the people of the realm to as grand a feast as Russia has ever seen. No peasant, however poor, was denied a place at the royal wedding.

The Swan Geese

THERE once lived a peasant and his wife who had a daughter and son.

'Daughter,' said the mother one day, 'I want you to look after your little brother while we are out. If you are a good girl and do not run off to play, your father will bring you a new shawl.'

As soon as her parents were gone, however, the girl forgot those words. She left her brother in the garden and ran off to play with her friends.

While she was away, a flight of Swan Geese swooped down, caught up the little boy and carried him off on their wings.

When the girl returned, she searched high and low, ran through the house and garden, but alas – her brother was nowhere to be seen.

She called and shouted, wept and sobbed, knowing well her mother and father would be angry when they returned. But there was no reply from her brother.

As she ran into the meadow, she saw the Swan Geese in the sky disappearing behind the dense forest. Now she knew who had carried off her brother; folk said the Swan Geese were wicked birds who stole little children for their mistress, Baba Yagá.

Away she ran across the meadow after the birds. Presently she came to a stove.

'Stove, stove, tell me where the Swan Geese have flown.'

'Eat one of my rye rusks and I shall tell you,' said the stove.

'I shall not! At home we eat only wheat rusks!' said the girl.

So the stove would not tell her. She ran on a little farther until she came to a wild apple-tree.

'Apple-tree, apple-tree, tell me where the Swan Geese have flown.'

'Eat one of my wild apples and I shall tell you,' said the tree.

'I shall not! At home we eat only juicy apples from our own orchard!'

So the tree would not tell her. She hurried on till she came to a milk river running between banks of jelly.

'River of milk with banks of jelly, tell me where the Swan Geese have flown.'

'Eat some of my milk jelly and I shall tell you.'

'I shall not! At home we eat only cream jelly,' she replied scornfully. So the milk river did not tell her.

The girl ran across the plain and into the forest; day was moving into evening and it seemed she would have to go home and tell her parents what had happened. Suddenly, however, the forest began to grow lighter and she came to a glade; there in the centre stood a hut on hen's feet, clean and neat, spinning round without a sound.

The hut had one window, and through it she could see Baba Yagá spinning yarn. Her little brother was sitting on a bench playing with silver apples.

The girl went in. 'Good-evening, Grannie,' she said boldly. 'I have walked all day across the plain and in the forest, I have made my way through marsh and swamp. My frock is wet and I am so tired, may I stay and warm myself?'

'Of course, my dear,' said the witch with a crooked grin. 'Sit down and spin some yarn.'

Baba Yagá gave her the spindle and went out to heat the bath-house. As the girl sat spinning, a mouse scampered out from under the stove and squeaked:

'Little girl, little girl, give me some porridge and I'll tell you a secret.'

The girl gave the mouse some porridge and he told her:

'Baba Yagá has gone to heat the bath-house. She will wash and steam you, roast you in the oven and eat you up, then dance on your bones.'

The girl trembled and paled, moaned and groaned, but the mouse continued:

'Make haste with your little brother and run away, while I spin the yarn for you.'

She thanked the mouse, picked up her brother and ran off.

Now and again the witch would listen at the door and call:

The Swan Geese

'Are you spinning, Russian maid?'

And the mouse would answer, 'Yes, I am, Grannie.'

When Baba Yagá had heated the bath-house, she returned for the girl but found the hut empty. In a rage she cried:

'Fly off, my Swan Geese, and bring them back! The girl has carried off her young brother.'

The girl ran and ran and as she came to the milk river running between banks of jelly, she saw the Swan Geese flying after her.

'Milk river, Mother milk river, please hide us!' cried the girl.

'Will you eat some of my plain milk jelly?' asked the river.

She willingly ate some and thanked the river. So it hid her and her brother beneath its banks of jelly. And the Swan Geese flew right past without seeing them.

When they had gone, the girl hurried on again carrying her brother. By this time, the Swan Geese had turned back and came flying towards her. At any moment they would surely spot the fleeing pair.

She ran on until she reached the apple-tree.

'Apple-tree, Mother apple-tree, please hide us!' cried the girl.

'Will you eat my wild apples?' said the tree.

She ate one readily and thanked the tree, which hid her and her little brother under its thick leafy branches. And the Swan Geese flew right by without seeing them.

When the birds had gone, she picked up her brother and hastened on again. Just as she was nearly home, the Swan Geese spotted them. They honked and flapped their wings and in another minute would surely have snatched her little brother from her.

Just then she reached the stove.

'Stove, stove, Mistress stove, please hide us!'

'Will you eat one of my rye rusks?' asked the stove.

She quickly put a rye rusk into her mouth and crawled into the stove with her brother.

The Swan Geese circled round and round screeching and honking; but after a time they gave up and flew back to Baba Yagá.

The girl thanked the stove and ran swiftly home with her brother. Never again did she disobey her parents.

Midwife Fox

LEVON the wolf once shared his humble cottage with Mistress Gossip the fox. In the barn he kept a barrel of honey. Now, the wily fox had a very sweet tooth and was eager to get at the honey.

As they sat one day in the cottage, the fox rapped the floor with her tail.

'Hey, Mistress Gossip,' said the wolf, 'somebody's knocking.'

'That will be a patient calling me out,' replied the fox.

'You'd better hurry,' said the wolf, 'you mustn't keep the babies waiting.'

No sooner had Mistress Gossip left the cottage than she made straight for the honey, ate the top layer from the barrel and returned to the wolf.

'How was it?' asked the wolf.

'Tip-top!' answered the fox with a smile.

The next day the fox again rapped the floor with her tail.

'Hey, Mistress Gossip, somebody's at the door,' called the wolf.

'That will be for the midwife again,' said the crafty fox on her way out.

Once more she headed for the barn and feasted herself until the level of honey had fallen to the middle of the barrel. When she returned, the wolf asked:

'How was it?'

'Middling, middling,' replied the fox artfully.

A third time the fox deceived the wolf and this time finished off the honey.

'Did all go well?' the wolf asked.

'Nothing to it,' laughed the fox.

Some time later the fox pretended to be ill and begged Levon to bring her some honey. Naturally, when the wolf went, he found not a thimbleful in the barrel.

'Hey, Mistress Gossip,' he cried. 'All the honey's gone!'

'How gone? Who's had it?' shouted the fox. 'You must have had a fine feast while I've been lying here sick!'

The wolf swore he had not had as much as a lick of honey.

'Well, we'll soon see!' said the fox. 'Let's lie in the sunshine; the sun will melt the honey and it will show on our muzzles. Then we shall find the culprit.'

So they went outside and settled down in the sun. The fox kept awake but the wolf, made drowsy by the sun, was soon snoring loudly. When honey appeared on the fox's lips she quickly smeared it onto the wolf's muzzle and gave him a hard dig.

'Levon!' she shouted. 'There's honey all over your face! Now we know who took the honey!'

Poor Levon the wolf had no choice but to confess to his wickedness.

Exchange

As a peasant was cleaning out a dung-heap, he found an ear of corn. Taking it to his wife, he told her to heat the stove, drop the corn into the fire, rake out the ash, make soup with the cinders and pour it into a bowl.

'And I'll go to the tsar,' he said, 'and take him the bowl of soup. He's bound to reward me for it.'

So off he went to the tsar with the bowl of soup; and the tsar rewarded him with a golden hen. On the way home he met a man guarding a herd of horses, and told him the story.

'I went to the tsar, took him a bowl of soup and he gave me this golden hen,' the peasant said.

'Will you exchange your golden hen for a horse?' asked the man.

And he did, mounted the horse and rode on.

On the way he met a man guarding a herd of cows, and told him the story.

'I went to the tsar with a bowl of soup, received a golden hen and exchanged it for a horse.'

'Will you exchange your horse for a cow?' asked the cowherd.

And he did, led off the cow by the horns and met a man guarding a flock of sheep. He told him the story.

'I went to the tsar with a bowl of soup, received a golden hen, exchanged it for a horse, then swapped the horse for a cow.'

'Will you exchange your cow for a sheep?' asked the shepherd.

They made the exchange and the peasant continued on his way until he came to a man guarding a field of pigs. Again he stopped and told his story.

'I went to the tsar with a bowl of soup, received a golden hen, exchanged it for a horse, exchanged the horse for a cow and the cow for a sheep.'

Exchange

'Will you exchange your sheep for a pig?' asked the man.

So he did, drove the pig before him and came to a woman guarding a gaggle of geese. Once more, he recounted his tale.

'I went to the tsar with a bowl of soup, received a golden hen, exchanged it for a horse, exchanged the horse for a cow, the cow for a sheep and the sheep for a pig.'

'Will you exchange your pig for a goose?' asked the woman.

That he did, took hold of the goose and came to a boy looking after some ducks. He stopped and told his story.

'I went to the tsar with a bowl of soup and he gave me a golden hen which I exchanged for a horse, I exchanged the horse for a cow, the cow for a sheep, the sheep for a pig and the pig for a goose.'

'Let's exchange your goose for one of my ducks,' suggested the boy.

And they did. The peasant now walked along carrying the duck until he came to some boys playing with sticks. Once more he told his story.

'I went to the tsar with a bowl of soup, received a golden hen, swapped my hen for a horse, the horse for a cow, the cow for a sheep, the sheep for a pig, the pig for a goose and the goose for this duck.'

'Will you swap with us, your duck for a stick?' asked the boys.

And he did, walking home swinging the stick. When he arrived at his hut, he left the stick leaning against the gate and went indoors to tell his wife of his good fortune.

'I took the bowl of soup to the tsar.'

'And what did he give you?'

'A golden hen.'

'Where is the hen?'

'I exchanged it for a horse.'

'And where is the horse?'

'I exchanged it for a cow.'

'Where is the cow?'

'I exchanged it for a sheep.'

'So where is the sheep?'

'I exchanged it for a pig.'

'And where is the pig?'

Exchange

'I swapped it for a goose.'
'Where is the goose?'
'I gave it up for a duck.'
'And the duck?'
'I exchanged it for a stick.'
'And where is the stick?'
'I left it outside against the gate.'
At that, his wife went out, took the stick and began to beat him with it as hard as she could, shouting:
'Next time, don't exchange anything, you old devil!'

Chestnut Grey

An old man had three sons: the two elder sons were handsome, hard-working and thrifty husbandmen, but the youngest, Ivan the Fool, was none of those things. He spent most of his time sitting on the stove blowing his nose.

As death approached, the old man called his three sons to him and said:

'When I die, you must take it in turns to sleep by my grave for three nights.'

The old man died and was buried, and that night it was the turn of the eldest brother to go to his grave. But he was too frightened, and he said to Ivan the Fool:

'You go to our father's grave tonight.'

Ivan agreed and went to his father's grave. He lay down by the grave and waited to see what would happen. On the stroke of midnight, the earth opened and the old man rose out of his grave and said:

'Who is there? Is it you, my first-born? Tell me how things fare in Rus: do the dogs bark, do the wolves howl, do my children weep?'

And Ivan replied:

'It is I, the Fool, Father. All is quiet in Rus.'

Then the father sank down in his grave and Ivan returned home.

When he got back, his brothers asked:

'Did you pass the night well?'

'Very well, Brothers,' Ivan replied.

'And does our father sleep soundly in his grave?' they asked.

'Yes,' said Ivan. 'He sleeps the sleep of the dead.'

Another day passed, and it was the second brother's turn to go to the grave. But he, too, was frightened, and he said:

'You go in my place, Ivan.'

So Ivan again went to his father's grave and sat there waiting. On the stroke of midnight, the earth opened and the old man rose out of his grave and said:

'Who is there? Is it you, my second-born? Tell me how things fare in Rus: do the dogs bark, do the wolves howl, do my children weep?'

And Ivan replied:

'It is I, the Fool, Father. All is quiet in Rus.'

Then the father lay down in his grave and Ivan went away. When he reached home, his brothers asked again:

'How did you spend the night, Fool?'

'Very well, brothers,' Ivan replied. 'Father sleeps soundly.'

On the third night, it was Ivan's turn; he went readily without seeking his brothers' leave.

He lay down on top of the grave and, on the stroke of midnight, the earth opened and the old man rose out of his grave.

'Who is there?' he said. 'Is it you, Ivan my third-born? Tell me how things fare in Rus: do the dogs bark, do the wolves howl, do my children weep?'

And Ivan replied:

'Yes, it is I, Ivan the Fool, Father. All is quiet in Rus.'

Then his father stood up, handed him a horse's bridle and said:

'Only you obeyed my command, Ivan. You were not afraid to lay by my grave for three nights. When the time comes, you must go into the open plain, whistle hard and shout: "Chestnut Grey, Hear and Obey!" When the horse appears, climb into one ear and out of the other, and you will turn into as handsome a lad as ever was born. Then mount the horse and go where you will.'

With these words, the old man bade his son a last farewell and lay down in his grave. Ivan took the bridle his father gave him and returned home.

When he reached home, his brothers asked:

'How did you spend the night?'

'Very well,' Ivan replied. 'Our father sleeps the sleep of the dead.'

The three brothers lived together and soon forgot about their father; the two eldest grew rich while Ivan the Fool had nothing.

Chestnut Grey

Now, about that time, the king made it known throughout the land that all unmarried young men should come to the court. The king's daughter, the lovely princess, had had a tower of twelve rows of oak logs built. There she meant to sit at the top of the tower and await the man who could leap on his steed as high as her window and plant a kiss upon her lips.

News of this came to the ears of Ivan's brothers, who decided to try their luck.

They fed their steeds on oats and led them from the stable, put on their cleanest shirts and combed their hair. Ivan watched and wondered from his ledge on the stove behind the chimney.

'Take me with you, Brothers,' he said. 'I want to try, too.'

'You stay on the stove, Fool!' they shouted at him. 'People will only laugh at you if you go with us.'

The brothers mounted their steeds, gave a whoop and a whistle and galloped off in a cloud of dust. Ivan, meanwhile, took his father's bridle, went out into the open plain, whistled and shouted as his father had told him:

'Chestnut Grey, Hear and Obey!'

And lo and behold! A charger came racing towards him; the earth shook under his hoofs, his nostrils spurted flame and smoke poured from his ears. Chestnut Grey galloped up to Ivan, came to a halt and said:

'What is your wish, Ivan?'

Ivan stroked the horse's neck, put on his bridle and climbed into one ear and out of the other. When he emerged, he had turned into a knight as handsome as the sky at dawn, the fairest youth that ever was born. He climbed onto Chestnut Grey's back and set off for the royal palace. On galloped Chestnut Grey with a snort and a neigh,

Passing mountain and dale with a swish of his tail,
Skirting houses and trees as quick as the breeze.

When Ivan arrived at court, the palace grounds were filled with a great crowd. There stood the tower of twelve rows of oak logs, and in the high window of her chamber sat the lovely princess.

Chestnut Grey

The king stepped out onto the balcony of his palace and proclaimed:

'He among you who can leap as high as the tower and plant a kiss upon my daughter's lips, shall take her as his bride.'

One after another the wooers of the lovely princess rode up and leaped ... but, alas, the window was well out of reach. Ivan's two brothers tried with the rest, but had no success.

When Ivan's turn came, he gave a whoop and a shout and sent Chestnut Grey as high as the tenth row of logs. He tried a second time and leapt as high as the eleventh row. One more chance remained. He whirled Chestnut Grey round and, with fire spurting from the horse's nostrils and smoke pouring from his ears, he took a great leap and placed a kiss on the honey-sweet lips of the lovely princess. As he did so, she struck him with her ruby ring and left a red seal upon his brow.

The crowd roared:

'Hold him! Stop him!'

But Ivan and his steed were gone in a cloud of dust.

Off they galloped to the open plain where Ivan stopped his horse, climbed through Chestnut Grey's ears and changed back to his former self. Then he set the horse free and went home, stopping only to bind his forehead with a rag to conceal the princess's mark.

After a time his brothers arrived and told him of the strange knight they had seen.

'Many were the wooers of the princess, and handsome too,' they said. 'But one there outshone them all. He leaped upon his fiery steed to the princess's window and kissed her lips. We saw him come, yet no one saw him go.'

Ivan called down from his ledge behind the chimney:

'Perhaps it was me you saw there?'

His brothers flew into a rage.

'Stay upon your stove, Fool!' they shouted. 'The only place you'll go is to the devil.'

Ivan smiled to himself and went back to sleep.

The next day the king held a feast to which he summoned all his subjects, nobles and peasants, rich and poor, young and old.

Ivan's brothers made ready to attend the feast.

'Take me with you, Brothers,' Ivan begged.

'What?' they exclaimed. 'People will only laugh at you. Stay on your stove and blow your nose.'

The brothers then mounted their steeds and rode away, while Ivan followed on foot. He came to the royal palace and seated himself in a far corner of the banquet hall. The princess offered each guest a drink from a goblet of mead, looking at their brows in search of her seal.

She had looked at all the guests except Ivan, and, when she approached him in his corner, she frowned – for his face was dirty, his clothes tattered and his hair stood on end.

'Who are you?' she asked. 'And why is your brow bound with a rag?'

'I fell over and hurt myself,' Ivan replied.

The princess unwound the rag and a bright glow at once lit up the palace.

'That is my seal!' she exclaimed. 'Here is my promised one!'

The king approached Ivan, looked long and hard and snorted:

'Oh no, my beautiful Daughter! This cannot be your future husband! He is so dirty and ugly.'

Then, Ivan himself spoke up:

'Give me leave to wash my face, Your Majesty.'

The king was glad to dismiss him and Ivan went into the courtyard and whistled and shouted as his father had taught him:

'Chestnut Grey, Hear and Obey!'

And lo and behold! Chestnut Grey came galloping towards him; the earth shook under his hoofs, his nostrils spurted flame and smoke poured from his ears. Ivan climbed into one ear and out through the other and at once turned into as handsome a knight as ever was born.

When he returned to the palace, the guests gave a great gasp of wonder. He was no longer Ivan the Fool, but Ivan the king's future son-in-law – for he soon wed the fair princess.

His brothers then knew what it meant to sleep by their father's grave.

Little Masha and Misha the Bear

AN old peasant and his wife had a pretty granddaughter, Masha. One fine day, Masha's friends called on her to go to play in the meadows.

'Grannie, Grandad!' cried Masha excitedly. 'May I go out with my friends? I shall bring you a big basketful of best white mushrooms, I promise.'

'Run along then,' they told her. 'But mind you don't go into the forest.'

So off skipped the girls towards the meadow at the edge of the forest. Masha took her basket and began to search under all the bushes for mushrooms. She knew the best and biggest ones would be amongst the trees in the forest and, almost without noticing it, she found herself out of sight of her friends. She moved from bush to bush, from tree to tree, picking a good basketful of mushrooms and going deeper and deeper into the forest. Suddenly she was afraid she might be lost.

'Oww–oo–oo! Oww–oo–oo!' she called.

But there was no reply.

Someone did hear her, however. From the trees came a rustling and cracking, and out stepped a big brown bear. When he saw Masha he threw up his arms in delight.

'Aha!' he cried. 'You'll make me a fine servant, my pretty one.'

Taking Masha by the arm, he dragged her to his wooden cottage in the depths of the dark forest. Once inside, the bear growled:

'Now, you will stay here, stoke the fire, cook the porridge and keep the house clean and tidy.'

Masha wept for her grandparents, but she was quite helpless. A miserable life began in the bear's house: day after day she worked from dawn till dusk, thinking all the while of how she could escape. Finally, she had an idea.

'Misha Ivanovich, let me go home just for one day and take my folks a gift to show them I am still alive.'

'Certainly not!' roared the bear. 'You will not get away from here. I'll take them your present myself.'

That was what Masha had planned. She baked some cherry pies, piled them on a dish and fetched a large basket. Then she called the bear:

'Misha Ivanovich, I shall put the pies in this basket for you to carry. Remember though: don't open the basket and don't touch the pies. When you set out I shall climb a tall tree and watch you.'

'All right, all right, my pretty one,' grumbled the bear.

'Now go outside and see if the weather is fine,' ordered Masha.

No sooner had the bear stepped outside the cottage than Masha quickly climbed into the basket and pulled the dish of cherry pies over her head. When the bear returned, he saw the basket was ready, so he hoisted it onto his broad back and set off for the village.

Through the trees he ambled with his load and soon felt tired and footsore. Stopping by a tree stump, he sat down to rest and thought of eating a pie. But just as he was about to open the basket, he heard Masha's voice:

'Don't sit there all day! Don't touch the pies!'

'Well, well, that maid has sharp eyes,' thought the bear. 'She sees everything.'

Up he got and continued on his way.

On and on he went until he came to another tree stump.

'I'll just have a short rest and eat a cherry pie,' he said, puffing and panting.

Yet, once again, Masha's voice called:

'Don't sit down, Misha Ivanovich! And don't eat the pies! Go straight to the village, as I told you.'

So on he went.

Past the pines and firs he pushed, down into the valley, on through groves of silver birch, up grassy knolls until, finally, he emerged into a meadow and stopped by a tree stump.

[191]

'I must rest my poor feet,' he grumbled. 'And I'll have a pie to refresh me; the maid surely cannot see me now.'

But from the basket came a muffled voice,

'I can see you, I can see you! Don't you dare touch the cherry pies. Go on your way, Misha Ivanovich!'

The bear was bewildered, even rather frightened.

'What an artful maid she is!' he growled hurrying across the meadow.

At last he arrived at the village, stopped at Masha's gate and knocked loudly,

'Open up, open up, I've brought a gift from Masha,' he called.

The moment he entered the village, however, dogs came running from all the yards. Their barking startled him so much he left the basket at the gate and made off towards the forest without a backward glance.

When Masha's grandparents opened the gate, they were surprised to find the basket and no one in sight.

Grandad lifted the lid, stared hard and could hardly believe his eyes. For there under the cherry pies sat his granddaughter, Masha, alive and well.

Grannie and grandad both danced with joy, embraced Masha and said how clever she was to have escaped from the bear. The news of Masha's return soon spread through the village and all her friends came running to see for themselves. Masha was so happy.

But she never, never, went into the forest again.

The Fox and the Pitcher

To stop a fox from stealing his chickens, a peasant hung a pitcher from his gate. When the wind blew, a weird wail came from the mouth of the pitcher:

'Whee-ee-ee, whee-ee-ee!'

The next time the fox crept into the yard, she was puzzled by the wailing and rather frightened. Seeing the pitcher, she pulled it down by its strap and slung it round her neck.

'You don't scare me, you silly pitcher,' she said, 'the river will soon put a stop to your howling.'

With that, she raced off with the pitcher to the river and dangled it in the water. The water gurgled in the pitcher's throat:

'Boork, boork, boork, boork. . .'

And it dragged the fox into the water. As she floundered in the river, the fox pleaded:

'Pitcher, pitcher, don't drown me. I really didn't mean it; I just wanted to scare you.'

But the silly pitcher did not heed her cries; it pulled the fox down, down, down, to the bottom – and drowned her.

Judge True

A T opposite ends of a small Russian village lived two brothers: one rich, the other poor. For all the love they had for each other, they might have been sworn enemies. One day in winter, when the last of his logs had gone to heat the stove, the poor brother had to venture into the forest to fetch some wood. Since he had no horse to carry the logs home, he had to go and ask his brother for the loan of his horse.

He received a chilly welcome.

'You may have the horse this once, but mind you keep the load light. And don't come snivelling round my door again. You'll take my horse from me today and my home tomorrow. . .'

The poor brother heard him out in silence, led the horse home and only then remembered he had forgotten the harness.

'It's no use going back to that old miser for it now,' he said to himself. 'My brother may change his mind and take his horse back. I'll tie my sledge to the horse's tail.'

Having done so, he drove off to the forest. But, as luck would have it, the sledge became stuck between two trees. As the poor man gave the horse a flick with his whip, the animal tugged hard and – rrriippp! – his tail came off.

When the rich brother was shown his tail-less horse, he let out a cry of rage and began cursing and beating his brother. Not content with that, he informed the judge who, in good time, called both brothers to court.

They set off for the court-house in the near-by town, the poor brother trailing miserably behind, lost in thought.

'When your pocket's dry, the judge is shy,' he groaned. 'He is bound to find me guilty.'

At that very moment, they were crossing a bridge and the poor brother, not looking where he was going, slipped over the side. It so happened that just then a merchant was driving his sleigh over the ice-bound river below, taking his ailing father to a doctor – and the poor brother dropped like a stone, right on top of the old man, killing him at once.

The merchant seized the poor brother and dragged him off to court.

Now the three of them proceeded to the town, the poor brother stumbling along between the merchant and the rich brother.

The poor man was even more downcast.

'That's the end of me,' he thought. 'What chance do I stand with nothing to bribe the judge?'

Noticing a rock in the road, he picked it up and thrust it under his tattered coat.

'I might as well be hanged for a sheep as for a lamb,' he told himself. 'If the judge's verdict goes against me, I'll kill him as well.'

When the three of them came before the judge, the two cases were heard together and the judge listened intently to the merchant and the rich brother. Now and again, he would glance at the accused and noticed him holding what looked like a weighty bag under his coat; he heard the poor man whispering to him:

'Judge true, judge true! I've something here under my coat for you.'

He repeated this every time the judge glanced his way. And the judge began thinking to himself:

'Could that peasant be showing me a nugget of gold?'

The more he looked, the more tempting it became.

'Even if it is only silver, it could be worth a lot of money,' he thought.

His greed got the better of him. As he passed sentence, he ruled that the tail-less horse should remain with the poor brother – until its tail grew again.

To the merchant he said:

'As punishment for killing your father, this man must stand on the ice beneath the bridge and you must leap on him from the selfsame bridge and try to kill him, just as he killed your father.'

There the trial ended.

Outside the court, the rich man turned to his brother and said:

'So be it, I'll take the horse and we'll forget about the matter.'

'Oh, no, brother,' the poor man replied. 'It shall be as the judge ruled. I must keep the horse until its tail grows again.'

The rich man began pleading with his brother:

'I'll give you thirty rubles for my horse back.'

'Well, all right,' conceded the poor man after long thought.

The money was counted out there and then and the matter was settled.

Then the merchant, too, pleaded:

'Let's forget about the whole business. I forgive you. Whatever we do, it won't bring my father back.'

'Certainly not,' answered the poor peasant. 'We must carry out the judge's orders. Let us go to the bridge and you will jump down on me. It is a long way to jump and you may miss me and be killed yourself, but do your best.'

'No, please, let us be friends,' begged the merchant. 'Here, take a hundred rubles and we'll forget about it.'

The poor man took the money and was about to leave for home when the judge called him back.

'Now give me what you promised from under your coat,' he said.

The poor man took the rock from under his ragged coat and showed it to the judge.

'I kept my promise. Take it. I said: Judge true, judge true; I've something here under my coat for you. Had you not judged true, you would have received this rock on your head!'

The judge sighed, relieved at least that he had escaped with his life.

As for the poor peasant, he set off for home with a pocketful of money, singing at the top of his voice.

The Seven Simeons

ONCE upon a time there lived seven brothers, seven bold workingmen – all named Simeon.

One day, as they were in the fields greeting the sun at dawn, ploughing the soil and sowing wheat, the king and his grandest noblemen came riding by. The king looked and, seeing the seven brothers, was much surprised.

'How can it be?' he said. 'Seven lads ploughing the field, all looking alike and of the same height too. Find out who they are.'

The king's servants ran and brought back the seven Simeons.

'Tell me who you are and what you do,' the king demanded. And the seven brothers replied:

'We are seven brothers, seven bold workingmen, and we are all called Simeon. We plough the land that was our father's and his father's before him. And each of us has a craft of his own.'

'What, then, are your crafts?' asked the king.

Said the eldest brother:

'I am Simeon the Carpenter, and I can make a wooden column reaching to the sky.'

Said the second brother:

'I am Simeon the Climber, and I can climb to the top of that column and look round the world.'

Said the third brother:

'I am Simeon the Sailor, and I can build a ship in the wink of an eye, and sail her over the seas and under water, too.'

'I am Simeon the Archer,' said the fourth brother, 'and I can hit a fly in the air with an arrow.'

'I am Simeon the Star-Gazer,' said the fifth brother, 'and I can count the stars without missing a single one.'

'I am Simeon the Ploughman,' said the sixth brother, 'and I can plough a field, sow the grain and reap the harvest all in one day.'

'And what can you do?' asked the king of the youngest of the seven Simeons.

'I can sing and dance, and play a flute,' the lad replied.

At that, the king's counsellor said scornfully:

'Workingmen we need, O King, good father, but what do we want of a fellow who can do nothing but dance and play! Send him away, for such men are not worth the bread they eat or the water they drink.'

'You are right,' agreed the king.

At that, the youngest Simeon bowed to the king and said:

'Permit me to play for you and show what I can do.'

'Very well,' said the king, 'play for me just once, then leave my kingdom!'

The youngest Simeon took out his pipe of birch and started playing. At once, everyone began to dance and skip and hop. The king danced, his nobles danced and the guards danced too. The horses frisked and capered, the cows in the sheds stamped in time to the music and, in the village, the hens and cocks hopped about gaily. But the king's counsellor danced harder than anyone. In fact, so hard did he dance that the sweat rolled down his face, and the tears too, and his beard trembled and shook.

'Stop your playing! I can dance no longer, I am exhausted!' cried the king.

The youngest Simeon took the pipe from his lips and said:

'Rest now, good folk, all but you, counsellor. You shall dance some more for your scornful tongue.'

At once, everyone stood still, all but the counsellor who went on dancing and could not stop. He danced and danced till at last his legs buckled beneath him and he sank to the ground utterly exhausted.

The youngest of the Simeons put away his pipe of birch and said:

'So, that, King, is my trade!'

The king laughed at this, but the counsellor was ill pleased and plotted his revenge.

'Well now, Simeon the Eldest,' said the king, 'show us what *you* can do!'

And the oldest of the Simeons took an axe and made a wooden column reaching to the sky.

Then the second Simeon climbed to the top and began to look round the world.

'Tell us what you see!' the king called to him.

And the second Simeon called back,

'I see ships sailing upon the Seven Seas. I see wheat ripening in the fields.'

'What else do you see?'

'On the Seventh Sea, I spy an island. It is the Isle of Buyan gleaming in the sun. And there, at the window of a golden palace, sits the Fair Tamara weaving a silken rug.'

'What is she like? Is she really as beautiful as they say?' asked the King.

'That she is. Indeed, her beauty is greater than words can relate or tales unfold. Upon her head she wears a crescent moon and in her hair gleam lustral pearls.'

Now this made the king eager to take the Fair Tamara for his wife; he was about to send his matchmakers when the sly counsellor said:

'Why not send the seven Simeons for the Fair Tamara, O King, good father! They are skilful and strong; but, if they fail, you can chop off their heads.'

'Yes, that's a good idea!' agreed the king.

So he ordered the seven Simeons to bring him the Fair Tamara.

'If you should fail,' he warned, 'I swear by my sword and my kingdom that your heads will roll from your shoulders.'

There was nothing for it: Simeon the Sailor took an axe, and rap-a-tap-tap! he built a ship in the wink of an eye, fitted her out and rigged her too. They loaded the ship with goods of every sort and kind, and the king sent the costliest gifts he could command. He ordered his counsellor to go with the brothers to see they did all they were told; the counsellor was unhappy, but there was nothing for it.

They boarded the ship, and at her sides the billows lapped, in the wind the white sails flapped, and then they set sail across the Seven Seas to the Isle of Buyan that gleamed bright in the sun.

Whether they sailed for months or days nobody knows, but at last the island lay before them.

They stepped onto the shore, went straight to the Fair Tamara and, laying their costly gifts at her feet, told her of their mission.

She accepted the gifts, and, as she was unpacking them, the sly counsellor whispered in her ear:

'Do not marry the king. He is old and feeble; in his kingdom wolves howl and bears prowl, black storms rage and white blizzards blow.'

The Fair Tamara grew angry and ordered the matchmakers from her palace.

What were the seven brothers to do?

'Listen, my Brothers,' said the youngest Simeon. 'Board the ship and prepare to sail. Load it up with good fresh bread and leave it to me to fetch the Fair Tamara.'

Before the hour was up, Simeon the Ploughman had ploughed up the sandy shore, sowed some rye, gathered in the harvest and baked enough bread to last a long voyage. They hoisted the sails and waited for the youngest Simeon.

Meanwhile Simeon went to the palace and stood beneath the window in which sat the Fair Tamara weaving a silken rug.

'It is so beautiful here', he said, 'in the middle of the Seventh Sea, on the Isle of Buyan that gleams in the sunshine, but it is a hundred times more beautiful in Rus, my own dear land. Our rivers are blue and our

birches are white; our fields are vast and our meadows are green and bright with flowers. In Rus, sunset meets sunrise as the moon keeps watch over the stars. Our dew is as sweet as honey, and our streams gleam like silver. In the morning, the shepherd goes into the green meadow and puts his birch-pipe to his lips and, whether you will it or not, you follow wheresoever he leads.'

As soon as Simeon began playing on his pipe, the Fair Tamara stepped out of the golden palace. He crossed the palace's gardens and meadows with Tamara close behind. He walked on along the sandy shore and onto the ship with Tamara at his heels.

At once the brothers turned the ship round and set sail across the Seven Seas.

Simeon put down his pipe, and Tamara immediately woke up and looked about her. The Isle of Buyan gleaming bright in the sun was left far behind.

She threw herself upon the ship's pine floor and, turning into a bright star, streaked up into the sky and was lost in the heavens. But Simeon the Star-Gazer counted all the bright stars in the sky until he came upon the new star. Then Simeon the Archer loosed a golden arrow at the star, and it fell back to the ship and turned into the Fair Tamara.

The youngest Simeon told her:

'Do not try to run away, for there is nowhere you can hide from us. If you so dislike our company, we shall return you to your Isle of Buyan and let the king chop off our heads.'

The Fair Tamara felt sorry for the brothers.

'No,' she said, 'he shall not chop off your heads because of me. You may take me to the king.'

They continued their voyage across the Seven Seas. All the while the youngest Simeon never left the lovely princess and she gazed fondly upon him too.

But the sly counsellor watched and laid his plans.

When they were nearing home and the shore was in sight, the counsellor summoned the brothers out on deck and offered them each a goblet of sweet wine.

'Let us drink to our homeland, friends!' he said.

The brothers drank the wine, and stretching themselves out on the deck, fell into a deep sleep, for the counsellor had put a sleeping potion in the wine; nothing could rouse the brothers, not thunder nor storm, not their mother's tears so tender and warm.

Only the Fair Tamara and the youngest Simeon, who had not touched the wine, stayed awake.

On reaching the shore, still the six brothers slept and Simeon made ready to take the Fair Tamara to the king. Both were sad, for it broke their hearts to part. But there was nothing for it: a promise must be kept.

Meanwhile the sly counsellor hurried to the king and told him:

'O King, good father, the youngest Simeon intends to kill you and take the Fair Tamara for himself. Have him put to death.'

Simeon presently appeared before the king with the Fair Tamara and was at once thrown into the deepest dungeon.

'Hear me, my Brothers, hear me, six Simeons!' he cried. 'Come to my aid.'

But the brothers slept on and did not wake.

At daybreak, Simeon was led out and taken to where the executioners were waiting.

The Fair Tamara wept, the tears rolling like pearls down her silver cheeks, but the sly counsellor laughed.

Simeon spoke up before his death:

'O King, grant a last request before I die, for so our ancient custom bids you. Permit me to play my pipe one last time.'

'Do not do so, O King, good father, do not let him play!' cried the counsellor.

But the king replied:

'I cannot go against the custom of my fathers. Play, Simeon, but make haste, for my executioners have waited long enough; their sharp swords are becoming blunt.'

Simeon put his birch-pipe to his lips and began to play.

Across hills and dales the music carried until it reached the ship where the six brothers slept and woke them up.

'Our youngest brother is in trouble!' they cried, leaping to their feet.

And off they rushed as fast as they could to the court.

The executioners had just raised their sharp swords and were about to chop off Simeon's head, when up raced the six brothers; Simeon the Carpenter, Simeon the Climber, Simeon the Ploughman, Simeon the Sailor, Simeon the Star-Gazer and Simeon the Archer.

They moved in a body upon the old king and ordered him to free their young brother. Fearing for his life, the king released the youngest Simeon.

'Take the princess, too,' he said hastily. 'I do not like her anyway.'

Soon after, the youngest Simeon and the Fair Tamara were married, and such a feast was held as the world had never seen. The guests drank and ate their fill, and sang merry songs with great goodwill.

Then the youngest Simeon took his pipe and began playing a merry tune.

The king danced, the princess danced, the grand nobles and their ladies danced too. The horses once more frisked and pranced, the cows in the sheds stamped in time to the music and, in the village, the hens and cocks hopped about gaily.

But the counsellor danced harder than anyone. He danced and danced till his legs gave way under him and he fell down dead.

Once the wedding feast was over, it was time to get back to work.

And work they did!

Simeon the Carpenter built houses, Simeon the Ploughman sowed wheat, Simeon the Sailor sailed the seas, Simeon the Star-Gazer kept a record of the stars, Simeon the Climber kept watch round the world and Simeon the Archer guarded Rus from her enemies. There is enough work for all in this great land of ours.

As for the youngest Simeon, he sang songs and played on his pipe, and his music warmed the people's hearts and lightened their labour.

The Foolish Wolf

WHEN a faithful dog had grown old, his master took him into the forest, intending to do away with him. But, as he pulled the rope tight round the old dog's neck, he noticed a tear trickling down his nose. So he took pity on the dog, tied the rope to an ash tree and returned home.

The poor dog was left alone in the forest and set to cursing his fate. He made such a commotion that he attracted a huge grey wolf.

'Hello, mangy cur, I've waited a long time for you,' snapped the wolf. 'I well remember the cold winter when you drove me away from your village. Now you are in my forest and I shall have my revenge!'

'What will you do with me, grey wolf?' asked the dog.

'First I shall eat your fur,' replied the wolf, 'then your flesh, your hide and, lastly, your bones.'

'Oh, you stupid wolf!' exclaimed the dog. 'You are so greedy you don't think of the splendid feast you could have. Why do you eat old and lean dog's meat when you could have a tender meal? Why break your teeth on my old bones? My flesh is like rotten wood. Listen, I'll tell you what to do: go and fetch me some young mare's meat, fatten me up a bit – and then treat yourself to a fine meal.'

'A good idea,' thought the wolf to himself. And off he loped to bring the dog some mare's meat.

'Here's your dinner,' he said on his return. 'And see you grow nice and fat!'

Placing the young mare's flesh before the dog, he left him to his dinner.

As the old dog chewed the tender meat he felt the strength flowing back through his tired body. The next day the grey fool returned and asked the dog:

'Well, Brother, are you fat enough yet?'

'I am getting fatter, but, if you could bring me some lamb's meat, my flesh would be much sweeter!'

Again the wolf sped off and this time he brought back a young lamb he had stolen from the shepherd's flock.

The dog ate the lamb's meat, grew fatter and felt even stronger.

When the wolf asked him if he was fat enough, he replied:

'I am still rather scraggy. Now, if you could bring me boar's meat, I would be as plump and tender as a sucking pig.'

The wolf caught a wild boar, took it to the dog and said:

'This is my last service for you! Tomorrow I shall come and dance on on your bones.'

'All right,' thought the dog to himself. 'Just you come; I shall be ready for you.'

The next day the wolf came for the fattened dog. As soon as he saw him coming, the dog shouted names at the wolf, making him very cross.

'I'll make you pay for your insults,' snarled the wolf.

With that he sprang at the dog, intending to tear him to pieces. The dog, however, had regained his former strength and quickly got the better of the foolish wolf, who soon scampered off into the forest; there he lay for several days, licking the wounds the dog had given him.

When he had recovered, the hungry wolf went in search of new prey. By and by, he spied a goat on a hill. As he crept up to the goat, he called:

'Kozma, Kozma, I have come to eat you.'

'Oh, you foolish wolf!' said the goat scornfully. 'Why break your old teeth on me? Listen, go to the bottom of the hill with your jaws open; I shall run down and jump right into your mouth and you can swallow me whole.'

The wolf stood at the bottom of the hill and opened his great jaws as wide as he could. Meanwhile the old goat charged down the slope, as true as an arrow, and butted the wolf so hard that he rolled back head over heels.

When the wolf opened his eyes, his head felt as if it had been split in two. So dazed was he that he could not remember whether he had swallowed the goat or not.

'If I had truly eaten the goat, my belly would be full,' he thought. 'So it seems the old twister tricked me. I shall not be cheated a third time!'

So saying, the wolf made for the village, prowled around for a while and then, at last, spotted a sow with her piglets. He was about to seize one when the old sow began to scold him:

'How stupid you are, wolf!'

Now the wolf was very vain and, instead of snatching up a piglet, he shouted:

'How dare you call me names! For that I shall eat you together with all your piglets.'

'I called you a fool because you are a fool,' answered the old sow boldly. 'How dare you eat my children before they are baptized! If you will be their godfather, we may straight away go and christen them. Afterwards you may eat them.'

The wolf was vexed, but, being pious as well as vain, he had to agree. When they arrived at a water-mill outside the village, the sow said to the wolf:

'Now, dear Godfather, go and stand on the dry side of the gate; I shall dip the piglets in the holy water and pass them over the gate to you one by one.'

That pleased the wolf and he thought happily:

'At last I shall eat some tasty meat!'

He stood waiting on the other side of the gate, while the shrewd old sow quickly raised the gate and let out the water. The water rushed out, knocking the poor wolf off his feet and sweeping him round and round the water-mill. Meanwhile the sow and her piglets hastened home, back to the safety of their sty.

It took the wolf a long time to struggle out of the water. Dripping wet and with a hungry ache in his belly, he once more crept back into the village. This time his luck was in, it seemed, for there in the road was a piece of meat; a peasant had probably dropped it that morning.

The wolf stole up to the meat and began to devour it greedily. Unluckily for him, however, the meat had been put there by a hunter who had long awaited his grey guest and had a handful of hard pellets ready for him. These he loaded in his shotgun and let off a blast at the wolf's head.

And that, dear Brothers and Sisters, is how the foolish wolf met his end.

The Pregnant Priest

A VILLAGE priest one day sent his servant to the doctor for medicine to cure stomach-ache. When the servant explained the nature of his master's illness, the doctor would do nothing until he had examined a sample of the priest's water. On the man's return with the doctor's instructions, the priest filled a bottle and sent it off with the servant. Along the way, however, the servant stumbled and upset the bottle over the track. Seeing a cow urinating in a field near by, he quickly took his empty bottle and filled it from the cow.

When he examined the sample, the doctor was puzzled – but there was no doubt about it: the priest was soon to give birth to a calf!

The priest received the news and was so ashamed he decided to go away until the calf was born. After journeying for several days, he came to another village, knocked on a door and demanded a night's lodging. Since he was a priest, he was granted entry and given the honoured bed above the stove.

Tired from his journey, the priest soon fell asleep.

Now, the peasant whose hut it was had a cow that was in calf. During the night, while the priest slept soundly, the cow produced its offspring. The night was cold, it being winter, and, so that the poor calf would not freeze, the peasant brought it into his hut and placed it on the stove next to the sleeping priest.

In the morning, when the priest awoke, he found the calf beside him.

'Well I never!' he exclaimed. 'I must have had it in the night. Now that it's over, no one will know and I can take it home with me.'

So he thrust the calf under his coat and left the hut.

When the peasant discovered the priest had stolen his calf, he took the matter to the local judge. That worthy man assembled the parties and, after solemn deliberation, ordered the cow and the priest to stand to-gether.

'Whosoever the calf approaches must be its true parent,' he proclaimed. 'And that shall claim its child.'

Everyone stood still and silent: the calf walked slowly and surely straight to its mother.

And the priest remained without his calf.

Ivan Young in Years, Old in Wisdom

An old hunter was walking in the forest one day when he suddenly saw a strange and wonderful bird. By the time he had taken aim, the bird had gone.

'It's a sorry hunter I am,' sighed the old man peering into the bush where the bird had been. To his surprise, however, he found a nest with thirty-three eggs.

'Better than nothing,' he thought, slipping all thirty-three eggs inside his coat.

On the way home, his coat came loose and, one by one, the eggs began to fall out.

As one egg fell, a lad hopped out; down fell another and out hopped another lad. Thirty-two eggs fell – and thirty-two young men hopped out of them.

Just then the old man pulled his coat tight, and one egg – the thirty-third – stayed where it was. When he looked back, he could scarcely believe his eyes: thirty-two strong men followed in his steps, all the same height and as alike as thirty-two drops of water. And they all spoke with one voice:

'Now that you've found us, you can take us home. You are now our father and we are your sons.'

'What a lucky day for me and my wife!' thought the old man. 'Not a child in all these years, and now – thirty-two sons at a stroke!'

When they arrived at his cottage, the old man took off his coat – and down fell the thirty-third egg. And the thirty-third lad hopped out.

'Why, who are you?' asked the old man in surprise.

'I'm Ivan, your youngest son.'

The old man recalled that he had, indeed, found thirty-three eggs.

'All right, then, Ivan, sit down to supper.'

No sooner had the thirty-three lads sat down to eat than they quickly ate up all the food in the larder. Yet they left the table neither hungry nor full.

After sleeping soundly the night through, Ivan spoke up for his brothers:

'You've found yourself sons, Father, now find us some work to do. Go to the blacksmith and have him make us thirty-three scythes.'

While the old man was away, Ivan and his brothers made thirty-three scythe handles and thirty-three rakes. When the old man returned, Ivan handed out the tools and said:

'Come, Brothers, let us find work and earn enough money to take care of our mother and father.'

The brothers bade farewell and set off.

Whether they were long on their way I cannot say, but at last they were approaching a great city. The king's steward met them at the city walls and promised them work.

'It is nothing very hard,' he said. 'You will have to mow the grass in the royal meadows, then dry the hay, gather it in and stack it. Will three weeks be enough for you?'

Ivan stepped forward and said:

'If the weather keeps fine, three days will be enough.'

The steward was greatly pleased.

'Then you shall have all you require.'

'Roast us thirty-three oxen,' said Ivan, 'bring thirty-three pitchers of wine and give us each a loaf of bread. That is all we require.'

When the steward had gone, the brothers sharpened their scythes and swung them so hard they whistled through the air. By evening, all the grass was mown. Meanwhile the royal kitchen had sent thirty-three roast oxen, thirty-three pitchers of wine and thirty-three loaves of bread. The brothers each ate half a loaf and half an ox, and drank half a pitcher of wine. Then they all lay down to sleep.

The next day, as soon as the sun was warm, the brothers dried the hay, gathered it into sheaves and by evening had it all stacked. Again they each ate half an ox with half a loaf and drank half a pitcher of wine. Then Ivan sent one of his brothers to the king's steward.

'Tell him to come and see our work,' he said.

The brother came back with the steward, and, soon after, the king himself followed. His Majesty counted all the haystacks and walked all round his meadows – not a blade of grass was left standing.

'You've made the hay well and in good time, young men,' he said. 'For this, I shall reward you each with a hundred rubles and a barrel of wine. However, there is one more task I have for you: you must guard the hay. Somebody has been stealing it every year, and we can find no trace of the thief.'

'Let my brothers go home, Your Majesty,' replied Ivan, 'I shall guard the hay alone.'

The king agreed; so Ivan's thirty-two brothers received their reward and set off for home.

Meanwhile Ivan stood guard in the royal meadows. At night he stayed awake and guarded the hay, while by day he ate and drank and took his rest in the palace kitchen.

Autumn came, the nights grew long and dark, and one evening, Ivan climbed to the top of a haystack and lay there wide awake. At the stroke of midnight it suddenly grew as light as day – as if the sun had risen. Ivan looked and saw the Horse with the Golden Mane spring out of the sea and dash straight towards his haystack. The earth trembled under her hoofs, her golden mane streamed in the wind, her nostrils spurted flame and smoke poured from her ears.

When she came to the haystack, she stopped and began eating the hay. Seizing his chance, Ivan leaped upon her back; at once, she reared up and raced across the royal meadows, with Ivan holding fast to her flowing mane. As they went, he whipped her hard and drove her even faster across the plain.

The Horse with the Golden Mane galloped far until, at last, she sank up to her belly in a marsh. There she stopped and spoke these words:

'You were smart enough to catch me, Ivan, and to tame me as well. Do not beat or hurt me any more, and I shall be your loyal servant.'

Ivan led her to the royal palace and locked her in the stable, then lay down beside her in the hay and went to sleep. In the morning he went to the king:

'I have discovered who stole the hay from your meadows, Your Majesty, and I've caught the thief. Come, I shall show you.'

When the king saw the Horse with the Golden Mane, he was delighted.

'Well, Ivan,' he said, 'you may be young in years, but you are old in wisdom. I shall make you my Chief Groom for your faithful service.'

And from that day on he was called Ivan Young in Years, Old in Wisdom.

In the royal stables the horses grew more glossy and sleek, not by the month, but by the week. Their coats became as smooth as silk, their manes and tails were always well combed – a pleasing sight, indeed.

The king could find no praise high enough for Ivan.

'Well done, Ivan Young in Years, Old in Wisdom! I've never had so fine a groom. However, there is one last task I must ask of you. I want you to fetch me the Playing Harp, the Dancing Goose and the Singing Cat.'

Ivan left the king with heavy heart and told the Horse with the Golden Mane of his unhappiness.

'Do not worry, Master,' she said. 'Jump on my back and let us go to Baba Yagá and ask her where to seek these wonders.'

So Ivan Young in Years, Old in Wisdom mounted Golden Mane and sped from the city.

Whether he went far or near, I did not hear; whether he was long on his way, I cannot say, but at last he crossed the plain and entered a dense forest. It was dark and gloomy there with no sunbeams dancing through the trees. The Horse with the Golden Mane grew lean and weary and Ivan felt tired and worn. But, at long last, they reached a glade in the centre of the forest in which stood a little hut on hen's feet with a spindle for a heel. It turned round and round from west to east, and Ivan Young in Years, Old in Wisdom rode up and said:

'Little hut, little hut, turn your back to the trees and your face to me, please!

'Not for years will I stay, but to sleep for one day.'

The hut turned to face him, and Ivan tied his horse to a pole, opened the door and entered.

In the hut sat Baba Yagá, the witch with the switch, a bony hag with a nose like a crag, her pestle and mortar in one corner.

When she caught sight of her guest, she croaked:

'Foo, foo, Russian blood, never met by me before, now I smell it at my door! Who comes there?'

'Is that the way to treat a tired wayfarer, Grannie?' asked Ivan. 'At home in Rus they first give a guest food and drink, let him rest and take a bath. Then they put their questions.'

So the witch made her guest welcome: she set the table with food and drink, then ran out to heat the stove in the bath-house. Ivan steamed and bathed himself, and Baba Yagá made up his bed and let him rest. Then she asked about his mission.

'The king sent me to fetch the Playing Harp, the Dancing Goose and the Singing Cat,' Ivan replied. 'I have come to seek advice.'

'I know where they are, my lad, but it is hard to get them. Many a bold man has sought them, but none has ever returned.'

'Well, Grannie,' said Ivan. 'It is my fate to seek them, so tell me where to go.'

'Ah, my fine lad, I pity you, but I see there is no arguing if you've made up your mind. Leave your Horse with the Golden Mane here, she will be safe with me, and take this ball of yarn; tomorrow, when you leave, drop the ball and follow wheresoever it rolls. It will lead you to my second sister. She will help you all she can and tell you all she knows; then she will send you to my third sister.'

On the following day Baba Yagá woke her guest before dawn, gave him food and drink and led him into the yard. Ivan Young in Years, Old in Wisdom thanked her, took his leave and set out on his journey. A tale is short to relate, but long to complete: the ball of yarn rolled on and on with Ivan following behind.

Several days passed, and the ball of yarn rolled up to a little hut on sparrow's feet with a spindle for a heel. There it stopped, and Ivan called out:

'Little hut, little hut, turn your back to the trees and your face to me, please!'

When the hut turned to face him, Ivan opened the door, and a gruff voice said:

'Foo, foo, Russian blood, never met by me before, now I smell it at my door! Who comes there?'

Ivan showed the second witch the ball of yarn, and she cried out:

'So you're not a stranger at all, but a guest sent by my sister.' And she set to laying the table with food and drink for Ivan, to make him welcome.

'Eat and drink your fill,' she said, 'and lie down to rest. Then we'll talk about your errand.'

So Ivan Young in Years, Old in Wisdom ate and drank his fill and then lay down to rest, while the second Baba Yagá began asking him questions.

On learning of his quest, she said:

'The way is not far, but you will surely not escape alive. The Playing Harp, the Dancing Goose and the Singing Cat all belong to our nephew, the Mountain Dragon. Many bold men have tried, but none has succeeded, for they all fell prey to the Dragon. He is the son of our eldest sister, and we must ask her help, or you will not come back alive. I shall send my messenger, the Wise Raven, to tell her of you. Now go to bed, for morning is wiser than evening.'

Ivan had a sound night's sleep, and early in the morning he rose, washed and ate what the witch set before him. Then she gave him a ball of red wool and sent him on his way.

On and on he walked from sunrise to sunset, from sunset to dawn.

At the end of the third day the ball of wool stopped at a large hut built on twelve rocks on top of twelve pillars and surrounded by a high wall.

A dog barked, and the eldest sister came out to greet him.

'My sister's Wise Raven has told me of you,' she said. 'Come in and have food and drink, you must be hungry and footsore.'

After making him welcome, the third witch told him:

'Now you must hide. My son the Mountain Dragon will be here soon. He is always very fierce and hungry when he returns; I fear he will kill and eat you.'

Opening a trap-door, she added:

'Go down into the cellar and sit there till I call you.'

Scarcely had she closed the trap-door than there came a terrible noise and commotion. The door burst open, and in flew the Mountain Dragon, making the walls shake with his fury.

'I smell Russian blood!' he roared.

'Oh, no, my Son, how can that be!' replied his mother. 'It is years since even a grey wolf came prowling here or a falcon flying. It is you yourself who have been flying about the wide world and brought the smell with you.'

And she hurriedly set the table. She took a roast ox from the oven and fetched a pitcher of wine from the larder. The terrible Dragon drained the pitcher at a single draught and gobbled up the roast ox, then became more cheerful.

'Ah, Mother, if only I had some company, someone to play a game of cards with.'

'I can find you a companion to play cards with, but I fear you will harm him.'

'Call him in, Mother, and have no fear. I shall not harm him.'

So Baba Yagá went and lifted the trap-door.

'Come up, Ivan Young in Years, Old in Wisdom, honour your host with a game of cards.'

They sat down at the table, and the Dragon said:

'Let us play, but mind: the winner eats the loser.'

They played all night, and by morning (with the help of Baba Yagá), Ivan had won the game.

The Dragon pleaded with him:

'Stay a while longer, Ivan, that I might have a second chance to win. We can play again when I get home tonight.'

With that, he flew away, and Ivan had a sound sleep and a good meal to follow.

At sundown, the Dragon came back, ate another roast ox, drank two pitchers of wine and said:

'Let us sit down and play, and I shall try to win my life back.'

[219]

They began to play, but the Dragon had not slept all night and had flown about the world all day, so he soon became drowsy. And Ivan won again with Baba Yagá's help.

'Now I must be off,' said the Dragon, 'but we must play one last game at sundown.'

Ivan had a good rest and a sound sleep, but the Dragon had been flying round the world and had not slept for two nights; so he was very tired. He ate a roast ox, drank three pitchers of wine and called to his guest:

'Sit down and give me one last chance to win my life.'

But he was so weary and drowsy that Ivan soon won for the third time.

The Dragon was now very frightened and fell on his knees, pleading:

'Do not kill me, Ivan Young in Years, Old in Wisdom! I shall do any service you name.'

'Well, Mountain Dragon,' said Ivan, 'I've beaten you thrice. I shall spare your life only if you give me your three wonders: the Playing Harp, the Dancing Goose and the Singing Cat.'

The Dragon laughed with joy.

'You may have them, and welcome!' he cried. 'I can get myself even better ones. And I shall fly you home upon my back.'

Ivan gathered up his prizes, bade farewell to Baba Yagá, and soared off on the Dragon's back into the blue sky. Before an hour had passed they landed beside the hut of the youngest of the three witches. Ivan wasted no time in saddling his Horse with the Golden Mane and, taking leave of the witch and her nephew, he started on his journey home.

He arrived at the palace just as the king was entertaining some royal guests: three kings with their princes, their ministers and nobles.

Entering the royal hall, Ivan presented the king with the Playing Harp, the Dancing Goose and the Singing Cat. The king was exceedingly pleased.

'Very well, Ivan Young in Years, Old in Wisdom, you have done me three fine services. For that, I shall reward you with thirty-three sacks of gold to make you and your brothers rich for the rest of your days.'

There followed such a grand feast that it is still talked about in Russia to this day. The Playing Harp struck up a tune, the Singing Cat began to sing and the Dancing Goose set to dancing. Their music was so lively that all the guests leaped up and joined in.

And none danced more gaily than Ivan Young in Years, Old in Wisdom.

The Animals in Winter

An old peasant had in his yard an ox, a ram, a goose, a cock and a pig. As guests were coming to dinner on the Sabbath, he told his wife:

'Old woman, we need meat for the Sabbath; I am going to kill the cock in the morning.'

Overhearing this bad news, the cock scurried off to the forest that very night. When the peasant went to wring his neck before sunrise, the cock was nowhere to be seen.

That same evening, the peasant told his wife:

'I could not find the cock; I shall have to kill the pig instead.'

Overhearing this, the pig, too, fled to the forest.

The old man searched high and low for the pig, but without success.

'How strange,' he thought. 'First the cock and now the pig. I shall have to slaughter the ram.'

When the ram heard the news he went to the goose and suggested they should run away together – or they would surely be killed. So, as soon as it was dark, the ram and the goose made off to the forest.

Though the peasant searched every corner of the yard he could find no trace of the ram and the goose.

'That leaves only the ox,' he sighed. 'A pity to kill him, but we must have meat for the holy day.'

On hearing that, the ox plodded off to join his comrades in the forest. And, throughout the summer, life was free and food was plentiful. The runaway creatures had not a care in the world. But summer passed all too quickly and winter was not far off. As the autumn leaves withered and thin layers of ice blocked the water-hole, the ox approached the other animals: 'Listen to me, brothers. Winter will soon be upon us. We must build ourselves a hut.'

The ram, however, answered:

'I have a warm woollen coat; I shall winter in that.'

Then the pig spoke up:

'No hard frosts bother me; I'll burrow a hole in the ground with my snout and do without a hut.'

The goose also refused to join the ox:

'I shall use one wing as a pillow, bury my head in it, and use the other as an eiderdown. The icy winds will not worry me.'

The cock, too, shook his head:

'I shall shelter from the winter in a fir tree.'

The ox saw that he could expect no help from his fellow creatures; he would have to do all the building himself.

'As you wish,' he sighed, 'then I shall build a hut for myself.'

And he built himself a strong wooden hut, stoked up the stone stove and settled down on top of it, warm and snug.

Almost overnight autumn yielded to winter, the first snows came and the wind sent icy blasts through the trees. The ram rushed about, but, despite his woollen fleece, he shivered and shook and could not keep warm. At last he went to the ox:

'Maa-kaa-kaa, maa-kaa-kaa! Let me into your hut.'

'No, Baran Baranich,' replied the ox. 'I asked you to help build the hut, but you said you had a warm coat and did not need a hut.'

'If you do not let me in, I shall break down your door with my horns,' cried the ram.

That worried the ox.

'Perhaps I had better let him in,' he mumbled, 'or I shall have no door. All right, come in.'

The ram entered and settled on a bench by the stove.

Not long afterwards the pig arrived.

'Hurroo, hurroo, hurroo! Let me in to warm myself.'

'Certainly not,' said the ox. 'I asked you to help, but you said the frosts did not worry you – you would burrow a hole.'

'If you don't let me in,' warned the pig, 'I shall knock down your door-posts with my snout.'

That set the ox thinking, and he finally made up his mind to let in the pig.

In hobbled the pig and wandered down the stairs to the cellar.

After the pig came the goose.

'Gagak, gagak, gagak! Ox, let me in to get warm.'

'No, Goos Goosich, you cannot come in. You have two warm wings: one for a pillow, the other for an eiderdown. You will not be cold.'

'If you do not open the door,' warned the goose, 'I shall peck all the moss from your window.'

The ox had to give in. And the goose waddled in and perched on a post by the door.

A little later the cock arrived.

'Coo-coo-ree-coo, coo-coo-ree-coo! Ox, let me into your warm hut.'

'I shall not, Petya,' replied the ox. 'Go and winter in a fir tree.'

'If you will not let me in, I shall fly onto your roof and peck holes in it to let the draughts in.'

Of course the ox had to open the door, and in strutted the cock; he flew up to a beam above the door and settled down to sleep.

So the five creatures lived together for the winter in the warm hut. But their peace was shortlived, for a wolf and a bear came to hear of the new residents.

'Let's go to the hut, eat them all and live there ourselves,' Michaelo Ivanovich suggested to Levon the wolf.

On that they agreed, but once outside the hut they argued as to who would enter first.

'You go first,' said Levon. 'You are the stronger.'

'No, you go,' replied the bear. 'I am too clumsy. You are nimbler than me.'

At last the wolf gave in and burst open the door of the hut. No sooner had he passed through the doorway, however, than the ox pinned him to the wall with his long horns, the ram butted him from the side and the pig grunted from the cellar:

'Hurroo, hurroo, hurroo! I'm sharpening the axe, I'm sharpening the knife, I shall skin the wolf alive.'

From his other side, the goose pecked the wolf, and the cock hopped about on his beam above the door, screeching:

'That's the way, give it to him! I'll slit his throat, I'll hang him from the beam.'

Outside the hut the bear could hear the great hullabaloo and took to his heels. Meanwhile, the wolf twisted and turned, his grey fur flying,

his body battered and scratched. At last he tore himself free and dashed after the bear.

When he had caught up with him, the panic-stricken wolf told his story:

'Oh, Michaelo Ivanovich, it was terrible, terrible! Those ruffians almost beat me to death. First a huge peasant in a black smock charged at me, knocking me against the wall, and then set upon me with two great clubs; then another rogue, this one a smaller grey-clad fellow, butted me from one side, while another, in a white caftan, scratched me from the other side. And the smallest of the band, in a red apron, pranced about on a beam above my head screaming, "That's the way, give it to him! I'll slit his throat, I'll hang him from the beam." Then, from the cellar, another brigand bellowed, "I'm sharpening the axe, I'm sharpening the knife, I shall skin the wolf alive!" I was lucky to escape with my life!'

From that day on, the wolf and the bear kept well clear of the hut, fearing the five monstrous creatures who dwelt within. And the ox, the ram, the goose, the cock and the pig lived together with no one to disturb their peace.

Twilight, Midnight and Dawn

THERE once lived a king with three beautiful daughters. So deeply did the king love them that he never let them out of his sight. He even had underground chambers built and kept them there like birds in a cage, so that no rude winds could bite their skin, no radiant sun could scorch them with its rays.

But one day the princesses read in a book about the bright and wonderful world. And, when the king came to visit them, they at once began to beg him tearfully:

'Dear Father, take us to see the bright world that we might walk in the green gardens.'

No matter how hard the king argued, it was no good; the more he refused, the louder they wept and wailed. There was nothing for it but to grant their request.

The three beautiful princesses went out into the palace gardens, saw the radiant sun, the trees and the flowers, and marvelled at the bright and wonderful world.

But, as they played in the garden, a whirlwind suddenly snatched them up and whisked them off far, far away to lands unknown. Their nurses were in despair and ran to inform the king. At once he despatched his loyal servants in all directions: whosoever should find the three princesses was promised a great reward. Though the servants journeyed far and wide, they had to return with no more news than they had taken with them.

The king then summoned his Grand Council and asked his wise nobles whether any among them would seek his daughters. The noble who found them would have his choice of princess in marriage and receive a vast reward. He asked once – the nobles stood quiet, twice – no one stirred, three times – not a murmur.

The king wept, sad and alone.

'No friends have I,' he said, 'none to help me find my daughters.' And he made it known throughout his kingdom that he promised a just reward to any man who would seek the three princesses.

Now, at that time, in a far-off village, a poor widow was living with her three sons – strong and valiant lads. They were all born in one night: the eldest at sundown, the second at midnight and the youngest in the early morning light. So their mother had named them Twilight, Midnight and Dawn.

When the royal appeal reached them, they immediately took their mother's blessing and set off for the capital city. Arriving at the palace, they bowed low before the king and said:

'Greetings, Your Majesty! We have come to serve you faithfully. Allow us to go in search of your three princesses.'

The king was cheered to find such willing helpers; he asked their names and promised them riches.

'We are three brothers – Twilight, Midnight and Dawn,' they said. 'We ask for nothing save that you care for our mother, that she might not starve while we are away.'

The king gladly sent for the mother, gave her a royal chamber and ordered her to be fed and provided for from his own table, to be shod and dressed from his own stores.

The young men set off on their journey. A month passed, then a second and a third. At last they came to a wide plain; beyond the plain lay a dense forest and in the very middle stood a cottage. They knocked at the window and door without reply, so in they went and found the home empty.

'Well, brothers,' said the eldest, 'let us stay and rest awhile.'

They undressed, prayed to God and went to sleep.

In the morning the two youngest brothers went hunting, while the third stayed home to cook the dinner. Finding no food in the cottage, the eldest brother came upon a pen of sheep behind the cottage, chose the fattest, killed it, cleaned and roasted it for dinner. All was ready but, since his brothers had not yet returned, he lay down on the stove to rest.

All of a sudden, there came a knocking and a hammering – the door burst open and in came a little old man with a pointed beard. His fierce gaze swept the room and he bellowed at Twilight:

'How dare you make yourself at home in my cottage! How dare you kill my sheep!'

And he began to beat Twilight with such force he left him barely alive; then he ate the roast sheep and disappeared into the forest. Twilight bandaged his head and lay on the stove groaning.

When his brothers returned, he told them he had made the fire too hot and his head ached from the heat. He had lain all day on the stove unable to boil or roast their dinner.

The next day Twilight and Dawn went hunting, while Midnight stayed at home to cook their meal.

He stoked the fire, chose the fattest sheep, killed it and put it in the oven. Then he lay down on the stove to rest. All of a sudden, he heard a great commotion and the fierce old man with the pointed beard came in; the old man set upon him and left him battered and bruised, ate the roast sheep and disappeared into the forest.

Midnight bandaged his head, lay down under the stove and groaned. When his brothers came back he told them he had fainted from the heat, fallen off the stove and could not cook their dinner.

On the third day, the eldest brothers went hunting, while Dawn stayed home; he chose the best sheep, killed, cleaned and roasted it. After he had set the table, he lay down on the stove to rest. Suddenly he heard a great noise and into the yard came the little old man with the pointed beard, carrying a whole haystack upon his back and a huge trough of water in his hands. He set down the trough, spread the hay about the yard and began to count his sheep. Discovering one was missing again, he flew into a rage, rushed into the cottage and flung himself at Dawn, beating him about the head. Dawn jumped up, seized the old man by his long beard, dragged him into the yard and hammered his beard to a stout post. After that, he returned to the cottage to await his brothers. When they arrived, they were surprised to find him unharmed. Dawn laughed and said:

'Come, brothers, I've caught your heat and tied it to the post.'

Twilight, Midnight and Dawn

In the yard all they found on the post was half a white beard. The old man had run off, but left a trail of blood as he went.

Following the tracks, the brothers reached a deep hole in the ground. Dawn went into the forest, chopped down some vines, twined them into a thick rope and began to climb down the hole, while his brothers held the rope fast. At last he reached the bottom, undid the rope and found himself in another world. After walking for some time, he came to a copper palace. Inside he met the youngest princess – more lovely than a scarlet flower, her skin whiter than the purest snow.

He told her how her father had sent him and his brothers to find her. On hearing the good news she sat him down at her table, fed him well and gave him a glass of water:

'Drink that water', she said, 'and your strength will multiply a hundred-fold.'

Dawn swallowed the drink in one gulp and felt a mighty strength surge through his body.

At that moment a strong wind blew and the princess jumped up in alarm:

'My dragon is coming!' she cried, taking Dawn quickly by the arm and hiding him in another chamber. A three-headed dragon flew down, struck the damp earth and turned into a fierce warrior.

'Ah-ha, I smell Russian blood here,' he cried. 'Who are you hiding from me?'

'How could a Russian get here?' she replied. 'You have flown through Russia and still have the smell in your nostrils.'

The dragon was calmed by her words and called for food and drink. The princess brought him fresh dishes and wines into which she poured a sleeping potion. After dining, the dragon fell into a deep slumber. When she was sure he would not wake, the princess called Dawn who took his sword and cut off the dragon's three heads; then he made a fire, burned the body to ashes and scattered them to the four winds.

'Farewell, Princess,' Dawn said. 'I must go in search of your sisters and when I find them I'll return for you.'

Dawn journeyed on until he came to a silver palace where the second

[231]

princess lived. Here he killed a six-headed dragon and travelled farther. Presently he arrived at a golden palace in which the eldest princess dwelt. There he slayed a twelve-headed dragon and freed the princess. Before setting out for home, she went into the courtyard, waved her red handkerchief and the golden kingdom rolled into an egg. She took the egg, placed it in her handkerchief and went with Dawn to join her sisters. They did likewise: rolled their kingdoms into eggs, placed them in their handkerchiefs and set off to find the upper world.

Twilight and Midnight hauled their brother and the three princesses into the bright world and returned with them to Russia. On the way, the three princesses rolled their eggs into the wide plain and there at once appeared three kingdoms – of Copper, Silver and Gold.

The king was overjoyed to see his daughters again. At once he married Twilight, Midnight and Dawn to his daughters and made each the ruler of the kingdoms of Copper, Silver and Gold.

How a Peasant Cured his Wife of Telling Tales

A PEASANT had a wife who could never hold her tongue: whatever she heard from her husband, the whole village would know at once. If they had a row and the peasant gave her a beating or a whipping – off she would run in a temper round the houses, even to the manor house, to tell tales. And she would make things out to be twice as bad as they really were.

One day the peasant was gathering wood in the forest, when his foot slipped in some loose ground. Puzzled, he took his spade, started digging and soon uncovered a pot of gold.

'Thanks be to God!' he exclaimed. 'But how can I take it home? My wife can't keep a secret; she'll wag her tongue here, there and everywhere.'

He thought and thought and at last hit on a plan. Burying the pot and marking the spot, he turned for home. On the way, he inspected his fishing nets and found he had caught a trout. Taking it out, he continued on his way. Farther on, he inspected his rabbit traps and found he had caught a rabbit. He took out the rabbit and put the trout in its place; then he dropped the rabbit into his fishing nets.

Once home, he called to his wife:

'Tatiana, stoke the stove and fry me a great pile of pancakes.'

'What for?' grumbled his wife. 'Night is coming and you want me to heat up the stove! Who fries pancakes at night? Whatever next!'

'Don't argue,' ordered the peasant, 'do as you're told!'

After a while, he said to his wife:

'Well, Tatiana, you wouldn't credit the fortune the Good Lord has granted me . . . Only I don't dare tell you about it – or you'll go jabbering to everyone.'

'Cross my heart, I won't tell a soul,' said his wife, eager to hear the news. 'Here, I'll kiss the icon and swear by Almighty God I won't tell.'

'Well, all right,' conceded her husband. 'It's like this: I found a pot of gold in the forest today. Now, don't breathe a word or there'll be trouble.'

'I won't tell,' said his wife in a huff. 'It's you who're more likely to boast about it when you're drunk.'

While he was speaking, the peasant kept slipping pancakes into a sack behind his wife's back. When it was full, he prepared to leave.

They set off together in the dead of night, the peasant walking some way ahead of his wife, hanging pancakes on branches as he went.

As his wife caught up with him, she spotted the pancakes.

'Well I never!' she gasped. 'Pancakes growing on trees!'

'So what?' snorted her husband. 'Didn't you see that pancake cloud pass overhead? It must have rained pancakes just now.'

'I didn't notice,' answered his wife. 'My eyes were on the ground, watching out for roots.'

'Come on,' called the peasant. 'I've set a rabbit trap over there in the bushes; let's see if I've caught anything.'

Opening the trap, he brought out the trout.

'Heavens above!' gasped his wife. 'How did a fish get into the trap?'

'Don't you know anything?' said the peasant. 'This is the sort of fish that can crawl along the ground.'

'I didn't know that,' admitted his wife. 'If I hadn't seen it with my own eyes, I wouldn't have believed it.'

As they came to the river, his wife said:

'Your nets are cast somewhere here; let's see if you've caught anything.'

When they pulled in the nets and found the rabbit, his wife threw up her hands in amazement:

'Oy, oy, oy! God help us! What a day it's been: pancakes on trees, fish in traps and now a rabbit in a fishing net!'

'What's all the fuss about!' said her husband sternly. 'As if you've never seen a water-rabbit before in your life.'

'But I haven't,' stammered his wife.

How a Peasant Cured his Wife of Telling Tales

Presently they reached the spot where the gold was hidden. The peasant dug up the pot, filled his sack with the gold and set off for home. The path ran close to the manor house and, as they approached, they could hear lambs bleating: 'maa-aa, maa-aa.'

'Oh, I'm frightened. What's that noise?' whispered the old woman.

'Run for your life,' shouted her husband. 'That's the squire strangling demons. Let's hope they don't spot us or we're done for!'

At last they reached their door, quite out of breath. The peasant hid the gold and warned his wife not to say a word about it.

From that time on, the peasant and his wife lived in comfort. But the old woman took leave of her senses – even more than before: every day, she invited guests to such grand parties that the peasant was driven out of his house. No longer would she even listen to her husband. The peasant put up with it for a time, but one day he lost his temper, seized her by her long hair and dragged her across the floor, making her black and blue.

As soon as she broke free, she rushed from the house screaming:

'You'll pay for that, you bully. You want all the gold for yourself, but you won't have it. I'm going this very moment to tell the squire.'

With that she ran off to the manor house and told her tale to the squire: how her husband had discovered a pot of gold, was drunk every day, how she had tried to stop him but he had seized her hair and almost killed her. She had come to beg the mercy of his lordship, to ask him to take away her husband's gold and make him work instead of getting drunk.

The squire and several strong men marched down to the village to deal with the peasant. They burst into the peasant's hut and hauled him out of bed.

'You miserable skinflint!' began the squire. 'So you found a pot of gold on my land and didn't report it to me. You get drunk on my money, beat your wife and do no work. Hand the gold over at once!'

'I don't know what you are talking about,' answered the peasant calmly. 'I haven't any gold.'

'Don't lie to me,' the squire shouted. 'I know all about it; your wife told me.'

At that, the squire had the peasant's wife brought in.

'Did your husband find a pot of gold?' he asked.

'He did,' replied the woman.

'Did you accompany him at night to fetch it?'

'I did.'

'Then tell us everything in your own words as it was.'

And she began to tell the story.

'First we went through the forest and saw pancakes growing on trees. . .'

'Pancakes?' asked the squire in astonishment. 'How did they get into the forest?'

'It rained pancakes from a pancake cloud,' she explained. 'Then we found a trout in a rabbit trap. After that, we went down to the river, pulled in the fishing nets and found a rabbit caught in them. It wasn't far from the river that my husband dug up the gold. We put the gold in a sack and returned home; on the way, we passed your house and heard Your Highness strangling demons. . .'

That was too much for the squire: he stamped his foot and shouted:

'Be gone, you stupid, long-tongued prattler, and don't ever wag your tongue to me again or I'll cut it off!'

'There you are,' the peasant said with a smile, 'you can't believe anything my wife says.'

Red-faced and angry, the squire stomped out of the house.

Some folk say the old woman did not live long after that; she evidently died of shame. They say the peasant took a young wife, bought a business and began to trade in the town, growing rich and prosperous.

Olga and the Brown Cow

THERE are people in the world who are good, some not so good and some who would betray their own folk. Little Olga fell among just such evil people. She was orphaned early and these folk took her in, brought her up, never let her out into God's world and made her toil every day. She had to sew, spin and weave, do all the housework, tend the animals, yet take the blame for everything.

Her mistress had three daughters of her own: the eldest had one eye, the second had two eyes and the youngest three eyes. Their mother dressed them in pretty dresses, while she clad Olga in rags and sent her to tend the brown cow every day at dawn.

So, every morning, Olga would take the brown cow to the meadow, put her arms round the cow's neck and pour out her sorrows to her.

'Oh, Mother Brown Cow,' she would say. 'They beat me and scold me, they give me no bread, yet they forbid me to cry. I must have five pounds of flax spun, woven, bleached and rolled by tomorrow.'

The brown cow would reply:

'Girl, climb into my ear and out through the other, and your work will be done.'

And so it was. Olga would climb into the brown cow's ear and out through the other, and she would find the cloth, all woven, bleached and rolled.

She then took the rolls of cloth to her stepmother who looked at them, grumbled, packed them away in a chest and gave her even more work to do.

As before, Olga would go to the brown cow, put her arms round her neck, climb through her ears and pick up the ready cloth.

The old woman began to wonder where the girl received her help, so one day she sent her eldest daughter, One-Eye, to watch all she did.

'My dearest child, so sweet and fair,' she said, 'see who is helping the orphan, who spins the flax and weaves the cloth.'

One-Eye went with the orphan through the forest and into the meadow. But, as she was not used to walking so far, she was soon quite tired.

'Lie down in the meadow and rest, sister,' said Olga.

One-Eye was only too glad to stretch herself out in the sunshine. As she rested, Little Olga murmured:

'Sleep, one-eye, sleep.'

One-Eye shut her one eye and fell asleep. While she slept, the brown cow spun, bleached and rolled the cloth.

The mistress learned nothing, so the next day she sent for her second daughter, Two-Eyes, and said to her:

'My dearest child, so sweet and fair, go and keep your two eyes on the orphan and see who helps her with her work.'

Two-Eyes went with Olga, but as soon as they arrived at the meadow she forgot her mother's command and lay down on the grass in the sun. Little Olga murmured:

'Sleep, one eye. Sleep, two eyes.'

Two-Eyes shut her two eyes and fell asleep. While she slept, Olga climbed into the brown cow's ear and found her cloth ready.

The old woman was very cross and on the third day she sent Three-Eyes to spy on the girl.

When they came to the green meadow, Three-Eyes played and skipped in the sun until she was so tired she stretched out on the grass to rest. And Olga sang softly:

'Sleep, one eye, sleep, two eyes.'

But she quite forgot about the third eye.

While the two eyes slept, the third watched all that the girl did. It saw her climb into the cow's ear and out of the other and gather the ready cloth.

Three-Eyes told her mother all she had seen with her third eye. The old woman was now satisfied, and the next day went to her husband and said:

'Kill the brown cow, old man.'

Her husband was astonished and tried to reason with her:

'Have you lost your wits, old woman?' he said. 'The cow is still in her prime and will provide us with milk for several years yet.'

But there was no reasoning with the old woman. She had her way and her husband began to sharpen his knife.

Olga ran to the meadow and threw her arms round the brown cow's neck.

'Mother Brown Cow,' she cried, 'they are going to kill you.'

The cow calmly replied:

'Do not grieve, Girl, just do as I tell you. When I am dead, take some of my bones, tie them in a cloth, bury them in the garden and water them every day. Do not eat my meat and never forget me.'

The old man killed the cow, and Olga did as the brown cow had said. Though she was hungry, she refused the meat; and she buried the bones in the garden and watered them every day.

Within a few days a slender sapling grew on the spot where the bones were buried, and soon blossomed into a sturdy apple-tree with red juicy apples, swaying silver boughs and rustling golden leaves. All who passed by the garden would stop and marvel at the wonderful apple-tree.

Some time passed, and one day, when One-Eye, Two-Eyes and Three-Eyes were walking in the garden, a handsome young prince chanced to ride by. Seeing the apples, he called to the girls:

'Fair maidens, I shall marry the one among you who brings me an apple from that wonderful tree.'

The three sisters rushed towards the apple-tree. The apples hung low within easy reach, yet when they tried to pick them the branches drew away from their grasping hands and swung high above their heads. When the sisters tried to knock them down, leaves showered on to their heads; when they tried to pluck the apples, the boughs tangled their plaits. Strive and stretch as they would, they only scratched their hands and could not pick the apples.

When Olga came up, the boughs bent low and apples dropped into her hands. She presented the fruit to the prince. He was so enchanted by her beauty that he took her away and married her that same day. From that time on she knew no sorrow and lived with the prince in happiness for the rest of her days.

The Wise Frog and the Foolish Frog

THERE were once two frogs who lived in the same damp ditch. One was bold and strong, the other lazy and weak. All the same, they lived as good neighbours should and often went on walks together.

One night they were out for their usual stroll down the woodland path and they came to a barn they had not seen before. From the open door came a smell of mouldering moss – which frogs like better than anything else.

Into the barn they hopped and began to play upon the mossy floor. They hopped up and down, round and round, jumping as high as they could, until – splash! They both landed in a bowl of cream.

And they started to drown. Now, even frogs do not like to die. The two friends squelched and splashed about all they could. But the clay bowl had high, slippery walls, and the frogs could not climb out.

The lazy frog swam for a while, then thought to himself:

'Why waste my efforts? I cannot escape. Better to get it over with quickly and drown at once.'

With those gloomy thoughts, he stopped paddling . . . and slid slowly to the bottom of the bowl.

The bold frog, however, would not give up so easily:

'No, brothers, if I keep on swimming, who knows, someone may come and save me.'

Nobody did come. However much he struggled, he could not swim far: the pot was small, its walls were slippery and there was no way out of the cream.

Even so, he refused to give in.

'I shall keep swimming as long as I've strength left in my legs,' he told himself.

And with his fast-fading strength, the brave frog fought for his tiny frog's life. The cream was soon blocking his eyes and throat, pulling him down. Yet, somehow, his tiny legs kept working, as he repeated over and over:

'No, I won't give in! I won't give in!'

Suddenly – he could scarcely believe it. Something hard was forming under his feet, something as firm as the ground. Puzzled, he looked down and saw that hardly any cream was left in the bowl – he was standing on a firm piece of butter!

'What's this?' he wondered. 'Where has the butter come from?'

Then he realized: he had churned the cream into butter with the paddling of his tiny frog's legs.

'Good Gracious!' he said out loud. 'What a good thing I did not drown at once!'

With a sigh of relief, he jumped out of the bowl and hopped home, back to his damp ditch.

The other frog, however, remained in the bowl. He was never to leap and dive in the ditches and ponds again, never to hop, never to croak.

Truth to tell, you have only yourself to blame, foolish frog. You need not have died before your time.

The Archer who Went
I Know not Where
to Fetch I Know not What

THERE once lived a king who had everything he could wish for, except a wife. That made him irritable and cruel.

Now the king had in his service a young and skilful archer named Andrei. It is this archer that our tale concerns. One day Andrei the Archer was out hunting. Though he had stalked the birds and beasts all day, his luck was out and he had not a single hare or pheasant in his bag. As darkness fell, he walked sadly back to his lowly hut, his empty bag slung across his shoulder.

Suddenly he spotted a dove preening its feathers in a nearby tree.

'It is a shame to kill such a fine bird,' he thought, 'but I must shoot, for the king will be angry without meat to stock the royal larder.'

So he let fly an arrow and knocked the dove from the tree onto the damp earth. Andrei picked it up and was about to thrust it into his bag when, to his astonishment, the bird spoke in a human voice.

'Do not kill me, Archer Andrei,' it pleaded. 'Take me home and let me rest upon your window-ledge that I may heal my wound. If I fall asleep, creep up and strike me with your little finger. Great fortune shall then be yours.' Andrei the Archer could scarcely believe his ears.

'What is this?' he thought. 'The dove looks like any other dove, yet speaks in a human voice.'

He took the dove home, washed the wound on its wing and put it on the window-ledge. Presently the dove tucked its head under its wing and began to doze, and Andrei, not forgetting what it had told him, struck it with his little finger. The dove fell from the window-ledge, struck the floor and turned into a maiden fairer than tales can tell or words can relate.

'I am Princess Maria, the Dove Maiden,' she said. 'Now you have caught me, you must try to keep me. Marry me now and I shall always be faithful and true.'

Andrei the Archer married Princess Maria and he and his young wife lived happily together. But he did not neglect his duties. Each morning before sunrise he would go to the forest, hunt for food for the king's table and take his catch to the royal kitchen. And so it continued for a time, till one day Princess Maria said:

'You and I are very poor, Andrusha. Borrow a hundred rubles and buy me silks; I shall then make us rich.'

Andrei did as she said. He went to his friends, borrowed a ruble here and a ruble there, and then bought silks with the money. He took the silks to his wife, who said:

'Now go to bed and rest.'

No sooner had Andrei climbed upon the warm stove and fallen asleep than Princess Maria, the Dove Maiden, sat down to weave. All night long her clever fingers worked the silks into a beautiful tapestry. It portrayed the entire kingdom with its towns and villages, its forests and lakes, the birds of the air, the beasts of the field, the creatures of the deep, and the moon and stars shining down upon them all.

In the morning Princess Maria handed her husband the tapestry and bade him take it to market to sell to the first merchant to name a price. Andrei tucked the tapestry under his arm and went to market. By and by, a merchant came up and asked:

'How much do you want for that fine tapestry, my good sir?'

'You are a merchant,' replied Andrei dutifully, 'name your own price.'

The merchant pondered long, but could not name a price for the tapestry. Then another merchant approached, and after him another and yet another. Soon there was a great crowd milling round the beautiful tapestry. They all gazed and marvelled yet none would name a price.

At that moment a counsellor of the king came riding by in his carriage and, hearing the hubbub in the market, stopped the coach and made his way through the crowd.

'Greetings, merchants,' he said. 'What is this?'

'We cannot agree on a price for this tapestry,' they replied.

The king's counsellor looked at the tapestry and was filled with wonder.

'Tell me truly, Archer, where did you chance upon such craft?' he asked.

'My wife made it with her own fair hands,' said Andrei.

'And how much are you asking for it?'

'That I do not know, for my wife said I was to take whatever was offered.'

'Then take ten thousand gold rubles.'

Andrei took the money gladly, handed over the tapestry and returned home, while the counsellor rode to the palace to show his purchase to the king.

The king gazed and marvelled, for there was his entire kingdom unfurled before his eyes.

'I must have it!' he exclaimed. 'I'll give you any price you name.'

The king at once called for a sack of gold coins and gave twenty thousand gold rubles to the counsellor, who took the money and thought:

'I shall seek out the Archer's wife and have her make me another tapestry, even finer than the first.'

He climbed into his carriage and ordered the coachman to drive to the edge of the forest where he would seek the hut in which lived Andrei the Archer. When he found it, he knocked boldly on the door. But as the door opened and the Dove Maiden stood in the doorway, the counsellor's senses dimmed, he quite lost his tongue and forgot what he had come for. Never in his life had he seen so lovely a maiden.

Princess Maria waited patiently for him to speak, and when he did not, she shut the door. As the door closed and the spell was broken, the counsellor collected his wits and drove sadly back to the palace. From that day onwards, he could neither eat nor drink for thinking of the Archer's lovely wife.

The king noticed his woeful countenance and asked him what was ailing him. The counsellor replied:

'Ah, Your Majesty, I have set eyes upon the Archer's wife. There is no maid so fair throughout the land. Her beauty has quite bewitched me.'

That made the king eager to see her for himself. So, the next day, the king walked to the edge of the forest, found Andrei's hut and knocked at the door. When the Dove Maiden opened it, the king's sense dimmed as he stared at the lovely maiden. He stood dumb in wonder, for he had never seen anyone so beautiful!

Princess Maria waited for the king to speak, and when he did not, she closed the door.

The king returned to the palace with heavy heart. 'Truly,' he thought, 'there is a wife fit for a king. She is too lovely to be a mere archer's bride.'

So he summoned his counsellor and said:

'I want you to rid me of Andrei the Archer, for I wish to marry his wife. If you do so, I shall reward you with towns and villages and sacks of gold. If you do not, I shall cut off your head.'

Since the counsellor could think of no way to get rid of the Archer, he went to the royal tavern to mourn his fate.

'What ails you, brother?' inquired a ragged old man tugging at his sleeve.

'Be off, you drunken pest! I've enough worries.'

'Buy me a drink and I'll give you some good advice,' persisted the old man.

In despair, the counsellor bought the fellow wine and told him the story.

'Andrei the Archer is a simple fellow,' said the old man, 'but his wife is clever. Tell the king to summon Andrei and say this: "I want you to go to the nether world and see how my dead father, the late king, is faring." You can rest assured Andrei will never return.'

The counsellor hurried back to the palace.

The king was greatly pleased on hearing the scheme and at once sent for Andrei.

'Well, Andrei,' he said, 'you serve me faithfully, but there is one special service I must now ask of you. Go to the nether world and see how my dead father is faring. If you do not succeed I shall have you executed.'

Andrei returned home, hanging his head in despair.

'Why are you so sad, Andrusha?' asked the lovely Dove Maiden.

Andrei told her of his mission.

'That is nothing to worry about!' she said. 'A mere trifle; the real trial is yet to come. Go to bed and rest.'

On the following morning the Dove Maiden gave Andrei some biscuits and a gold ring.

'Go to the king and ask for the counsellor as your companion, so that he may know you have really been to the nether world. When you set forth, cast the ring before you and it will show the way.'

Andrei took the biscuits and the ring, bade farewell to his wife and went to ask the king's permission to take the counsellor. The king granted the request and, as soon as the two had left the city walls, Andrei threw down the ring. They followed it over plain and field, through marsh and bog, across lake and river. Whenever they grew tired, they would eat a biscuit and then set off again.

Whether they were long on their way I cannot say, but at some time or other they followed the gold ring into a deep wooded valley, where it came to a halt. Andrei and the counsellor stopped to rest and eat their last biscuits.

Towards them through the dark shadows stumbled an old, old man with a long white beard, pulling a heavy cart of firewood, while two devils, one to the right, the other to the left, drove him on with wooden clubs.

'Look yonder,' said Andrei. 'Isn't that the king's late father?'

'It is indeed,' replied the counsellor.

'Hello there, Devils!' shouted Andrei. 'I beg you to free that old sinner for a minute. I should like to have a word with him.'

'We have no time!' grumbled the devils. 'We will not draw the cart ourselves.'

'I have a man here who can take over,' said Andrei, giving the counsellor a shove that sent him staggering towards the devils.

The devils unhitched the old king and harnessed the counsellor to the cart in his place. Then they set about him with their clubs, one to the left, the other to the right, and the unfortunate counsellor staggered along hauling the heavy cart.

Meanwhile Andrei asked the old king how death was treating him.

'Oh, Archer Andrei,' moaned the old king, 'I am having a bad time in

the nether world. Tell my son not to be cruel to his people, or else he too will surely share my fate.'

They had barely finished talking when the devils returned with the empty cart, released the counsellor, battered and bruised, and dragged the old man back between the shafts. Andrei took leave of the old king and the two travellers set out for home.

Whether they journeyed for long or for less I cannot guess, but eventually they came to the city and went straight to the palace. When the king saw the Archer, he was beside himself with fury.

'How dare you come back without doing what I told you!' he cried.

'Ah, but I have, Your Majesty. I have seen your dead father in the nether world. His life after death is very hard. He bids you not to ill-treat your people if you wish to avoid his fate.'

'How will you prove you have seen my father?' asked the king.

'I can prove it by the bruises the devils' clubs left on your counsellor's back,' replied Andrei.

That was proof enough, so the king reluctantly had to let Andrei go. He then turned on his counsellor:

'If you do not rid me of that Archer, I shall personally cut off your head.'

The counsellor was now in despair. He went once more to the royal tavern, sat down at a corner-table and called for a pitcher of wine.

'Still trying to drown your sorrows, brother?' called out the selfsame peasant. 'Buy me a drink and I'll give you more advice.'

The counsellor willingly gave him a measure of wine and told of his troubles.

'Don't worry,' said the old man. 'Tell the king to summon Archer Andrei and say this: "Go beyond the Land of One Score and Nine to the realm of One Score and Ten and fetch me Kot Boltun, the Talking Cat." '

The counsellor hurried back to the king and told him his new plan. When the king summoned Andrei, he said:

'Well, Archer, you have done me one service, now do me another. You must journey through the Land of One Score and Nine to the realm of One Score and Ten and fetch me Kot Boltun, the Talking Cat. If you fail, you'll pay with your head.'

Andrei walked wearily home and told Princess Maria of his new task.

'That's nothing to worry about!' she said. 'A mere trifle; the real trial is yet to come. Go to bed and rest, Andrusha.'

While Andrei slept, Princess Maria went to the blacksmith and ordered three iron caps, a pair of iron tongs and three rods – one of iron, one of copper and one of lead.

Early next morning she woke her husband and said:

'Here are three caps, a pair of tongs and three rods. When you are three versts short of the realm of One Score and Ten, you will feel very sleepy – that will be Kot Boltun casting his spell over you. Don't fall asleep. Stamp your feet, crawl along on hands and knees, roll over the ground, but keep awake, for, if you do not, Kot Boltun will tear you to shreds.'

Andrei listened carefully and set off on his strange errand. It is swifter to tell the tale than do the deed, but at last he was journeying through the Land of One Score and Nine and drawing near the realm of One Score and Ten. Three versts before it, he began to feel drowsy. At once he put the three iron caps upon his head, stamped his feet, then crawled on hands and knees and, when he could crawl no more, he rolled over the ground.

Somehow he managed to keep awake and found himself leaning against a tall pole rising high into the sky; before he could look up, a snarling cat came hurtling down the pole and landed on his head. He clawed and scratched at Andrei's head and tore the first cap to shreds, then the second, and was ripping through the third when Andrei caught him with the tongs, dragged him to the ground and started to beat him with the rods. First he whipped him with the rod of iron, and, when that broke, he flogged him with the rod of copper; when that broke he laid about him with the rod of lead.

Though the lead rod bent, it did not break; he pounded harder. As Andrei flogged him, Kot Boltun told him tales of priests and deacons, lords and ladies, soldiers and devils. Andrei, however, turned a deaf ear and beat him as hard as ever.

At last, Kot Boltun could stand no more, and twisting and turning, he began to plead:

'Stop, stop! Let me go! I'll do anything you say.'

'Then you must promise to return with me to the king.'

'Anywhere you choose,' replied the cat, who by this time was quite exhausted.

So Andrei returned to the king with the Talking Cat.

'I have done as you willed, Sire,' Andrei said. 'I bring you Kot Boltun.'
The king could scarcely believe his eyes.

'If this really be the fearsome Kot Boltun, let him loose and show what
he can do,' said the king.

When Andrei let him loose, Kot Boltun began to show his claws, arch
his back and bare his sharp teeth. Then, spitting and snarling, he sprang
at the king and would surely have ripped open his breast and torn out
his heart had not Andrei raised the rod of lead and forced the cat into a
strong cage. Andrei then returned to his beloved Dove Maiden. For a
while the two lived in peace and happiness, but the king was as determined as ever to kill him and take his wife. He again sent for his counsellor.

'You have one last chance to rid me of Andrei the Archer; if you do not
succeed this time, your head will surely roll,' he warned.

The counsellor went straight to the tavern, sought out the ragged
peasant and asked his advice. The old man tossed off his glass of wine,
wiped his whiskers and said:

'Go back and tell the king to send the Archer *I know not where to fetch
I know not what*. That will certainly be the end of him.'

The counsellor hastened back to the king and told him of the plan.
Andrei was again summoned and this time was told:

'You have done me two services, now do me a third. You must go
I know not where and fetch I know not what. If you do that, I shall reward
you handsomely, if not, you will lose your head.'

Andrei went home and wept.

'Why do you grieve so, dear Andrusha?' asked Princess Maria.

'The king has commanded me to go *I know not where and fetch I know
not what*,' he replied mournfully.

'Now, that is a hard task indeed. Never mind, we shall think of something. Go to bed and rest.'

Princess Maria waited till midnight and then went out onto the porch,
waved her hand and an amazing thing happened – all the birds of the air
and all the beasts of the field came to her.

'Hail, birds of the air and beasts of the field,' she called. 'You birds fly in the blue heavens, you beasts prowl in forest and plain – can you tell me how to go *I know not where and fetch I know not what?*'

But the birds and beasts all shook their heads:

'No, Dove Maiden, we cannot tell you what we do not know.'

So she waved her hand again, and there remained not a trace of fur or feather. Then she waved it a third time and straightway two giants appeared.

'My faithful servants,' she said, 'carry me to the centre of the ocean.'

The giants stooped down and gently lifted the Dove Maiden and carried her to the centre of the ocean. There they stood like two tall columns, holding her aloft in the palms of their hands above the sea. With a wave of her hand, she summoned all the creatures of the deep.

'Hail, creatures of the deep, you swim everywhere and know all the islands – can you tell me how to go *I know not where and fetch I know not what?*'

But the fish all shook their scaly heads:

'No, Dove Maiden, we have never heard of such a place or such a thing.'

The Dove Maiden sighed and ordered her faithful giants to take her home. Stepping out of the ocean, the giants bore her to the lowly hut and set her down gently on the porch.

When the giants had gone, she woke her husband and sent him off on his journey with a ball of yarn and an embroidered towel.

'Cast the ball of yarn before you and follow it wheresoever it rolls,' she said. 'And wherever you are, take care and dry yourself only on this embroidered towel.'

Andrei bade farewell to his lovely wife, bowed to all sides and followed the ball of yarn. Many a strange land did Andrei pass on his journey, but the ball rolled on and on and, as the yarn unwound, the ball grew smaller and smaller. Soon it was no bigger than an egg and was hard to see along the path. His eyes now ached but, just as the ball had all but dwindled to nothing, it came to a halt in a forest glade before a hut on hen's feet. The hut had neither doors nor windows and slowly turned round and round.

'Little hut, little hut, turn your back to the trees and your face to me, please,' said Andrei.

The hut slowly came to a halt, a door appeared and Andrei entered. Baba Yagá was sitting on a bench, spinning yarn. As he came through the door, she stopped spinning and sniffed the air:

'Foo, foo, Russian blood, never met by me before, now I smell it at my door. Who dares to come here? I shall roast you and suck your bones dry!'

'Wait, Baba Yagá. You surely would not eat a dusty wayfarer,' said Andrei. 'For I am lean and grey with dust. Heat the bath-house first, so that I may wash.'

So she heated the bath-house and Andrei washed and steamed himself and took out his wife's towel to dry himself.

On seeing the towel, Baba Yagá exclaimed, 'I recognize that handi-work. Only my daughter could have done such fine embroidery.'

'Then your daughter is my wife. It was she who gave me the towel.'

Baba Yagá then made him truly welcome, and set the table with all kinds of foods and wines. While he was dining, she asked how he had come to marry her daughter and whether they were happy. And Andrei told his mother-in-law about their happy life together and the terrible tasks the king had set him.

'If only you could help me!' he sighed.

'Alas, dear son-in-law, even I have not heard of *I know not what and I know not where*. The only person wiser than me is Babushka Lagushka Skakushka, the Old Frog, and she has been living in the mossy marsh these three hundred years. However, go to bed now and get some rest.'

When Andrei was sound asleep on the warm stove, Baba Yagá took her two birch broomsticks and flew swiftly to the mossy marsh and called in her shrill voice:

'Babushka,
Lagushka,
Skakushka,
Do you still live?'

The green slime stirred and a great croak gurgled through the mud:

'I do!'

'Then tell me, do you know *I know not what?*'

'I do!'

'And do you know *I know not where?*'

'I do!'

'Then will you take my son *I know not where to fetch I know not what?*'

'Gladly, I would, Baba Yagá, but I am too old and it is a long hop,' croaked the old frog. 'Take me home, put me into a jug of fresh milk and let him take me to the Burning River. There I shall tell him.'

Baba Yagá took the Old Frog home on her broomsticks, poured some fresh milk into a jug and put her into it. Early next morning she woke Andrei.

'Take this jug of fresh milk with the wise old frog,' she said. 'Mount my horse and go to the Burning River; there you must leave the horse and take Babushka Lagushka Skakushka out of the jug, and she will tell you what to do.'

Andrei dressed, took the jug, mounted Baba Yagá's horse and rode off. After a long journey he at last came to the Burning River. No beast could jump and no bird could fly across that wide river. Andrei dismounted, shielding his eyes from the fire.

'Take me out of the jug, my lad,' croaked the frog. 'We must cross the river.'

Andrei took the wise old frog out of the jug and set her on the ground.

'Now climb upon my back,' she ordered.

'Oh, but you are so tiny, Babushka, I will surely squash you.'

'Have no fear,' she replied. 'Climb on and hold tight.'

Andrei sat on the frog's back and she began to puff herself up. She swelled and swelled until she was as big as a wheatsheaf.

'Are you holding fast?' she asked.

'That I am, Babushka.'

The Old Frog puffed and puffed until she was as big as a haystack.

'Are you holding fast?'

'Yes, I am, Babushka.'

Again she puffed and puffed until she was taller than the dense forest.

Then in one hop she leapt across the Burning River, set Andrei down on the other side and breathed out slowly until she was her normal size again.

'You are now in the land of *I know not where*,' she said. 'You must follow that path until you come to a tower that is not a tower, a hut that is not a hut and a barn that is not a barn. Go inside and hide behind the stove. There you will find *I know not what*.'

Andrei left the wise old frog and followed the path until he came to a tower that was not a tower, a hut that was not a hut and a barn that was not a barn. He went into the hut that had neither windows in the window frames, nor a door in the doorway, and hid behind the stove.

Presently he heard a noise from the forest and through the doorway stepped a fierce, bearded man – Quick-and-Nimble-the-Size-of-a-Thimble – who screeched:

'Hey, Brother Nobody, bring me food and drink!'

Scarcely had he spoken than a table appeared out of nowhere, and on the table stood

> *A barrel of beer,*
> *Light and clear,*
> *A sucking pig,*
> *Crisp and big,*
> *Warm black bread,*
> *And wine bright red.*

Quick-and-Nimble-the-Size-of-a-Thimble sat down at the table, ate up every bit of the sucking pig, swallowed the whole barrel of beer, munched the warm black bread and washed it down with the bright red wine. When he had finished, he called again:

'Hey, Brother Nobody! Clear the table!'

At once the table vanished as if it had never been, bones, barrel, crumbs and all. With that, the little old man wiped his white whiskers and went back into the forest. As soon as he was gone, Andrei emerged from behind the stove and cried:

'Hey, Brother Nobody, bring me food and drink!'

Barely were the words spoken than a table appeared out of nowhere, groaning beneath all kinds of foods and wines and other good things.

Andrei sat down at the table and said:

'Sit down, Brother Nobody, let us drink and dine together.'

And a voice replied:

'Thank you for your kindness, my friend. Many a year have I served my master, and never has he given me so much as a dry crust. Yet, you bid me sit at your table and dine with you.'

Andrei looked on in wonder: there was no one to be seen, yet the food vanished as if swept up with a broom; the wines and the meads poured themselves into glasses and the glasses clinked and clanked, hopped and leapt across the table.

'Brother Nobody, why don't you show yourself?' Andrei asked.

'That I cannot do,' came the voice. 'For I am *I know not what.*'

'Would you like to serve me, Brother Nobody?'

'Indeed I would. You are surely a good and kind master.'

When they finished their meal, Andrei said:

'Now, clear the table and come with me.'

As Andrei left the hut he looked round and saw nothing.

'Are you there, Brother Nobody?'

'Yes, I shall not leave your side.'

Presently Andrei arrived at the Burning River where the wise old frog was waiting for him.

'Well, my lad,' she said, 'did you find *I know not what?*'

'Yes, I did, Babushka.'

'Then climb upon my back once more.'

Andrei sat on her back and the wise old frog began to puff herself up until she was the size of an ox, and then, in one hop, she sailed across the Burning River.

As he jumped from her back, Andrei thanked her and set off homewards. At each bend in the track he would turn and ask:

'Are you there, Brother Nobody?'

'Indeed I am. I shall not desert you.'

Andrei journeyed on and soon became weary and footsore.

'Oh, my poor feet,' he said. 'How tired I feel!'

'Why did you not tell me before?' said Brother Nobody. 'I can take you home in next to no time.'

At once Andrei was picked up by a fierce gust of wind and whisked

over hills and forests, towns and hamlets, rivers and lakes. As they flew over a wide blue sea, Andrei became tired and breathless.

'Brother Nobody, I should like a rest,' he said.

The wind dropped at once and Andrei sailed gently down to the sea. Where only waves had been splashing, there now appeared a small island with a golden-domed palace surrounded by a sunny garden.

Brother Nobody said:

'Rest, eat and drink and keep watch on the sea. Three merchant ships will soon come by. Hail them, invite their captains to dine with you and treat them royally, for they have three marvels in their possession. Exchange me for those marvels – do not fear, I shall soon return.'

Soon three ships came sailing towards the island and their captains saw the golden-domed palace and sunny garden.

'What wonder is this?' they exclaimed. 'Many's the time we have sailed these seas yet never have we seen anything but the frothy waves. Let us go ashore and fathom this mystery.'

The three ships cast anchor and the three captains rowed towards the island. As they reached land, Andrei the Archer was there to greet them.

The more the merchant captains saw, the more they marvelled. The palace cupolas blazed like fire, nightingales sang in the trees and strange yet docile beasts roamed the island.

'Tell us, good Sir, who built this haven of rest and splendour?' the merchants asked.

'My faithful servant, Brother Nobody, built it in a single night,' Andrei replied. He then led the three guests into the palace.

'Hey, Brother Nobody, bring us food and drink!' he ordered.

Suddenly a table appeared from nowhere, set with the choicest foods and wines that ever graced a Russian table. The merchants gazed and stared in amazement, and there was no end to their wonder and delight.

'Let us strike a bargain, good Sir,' said the merchants. 'Trade us your servant, Brother Nobody, and take anything you wish from us.'

'Very well. What marvels can you offer?'

The first merchant took a wood club from under his coat. 'All you have to say is: "Club, give that man a beating!" and the club will set to work and thrash your enemy black and blue.'

The second merchant produced an axe and, when he stood it on its handle, the axe began to chop: rap, a'tap, tap – out came a ship; rap, a'tap, tap – out came another, complete with white sails, guns and sailors brave. The ships sailed, the guns fired and the sailors obeyed the merchant's orders.

When he turned the axe round, the ships vanished.

The third merchant took a flute from his pocket and began to play it.

[258]

At the sound of the shrill music, an army appeared, on foot and horse, armed with cannon. The soldiers marched, the trumpets blared, the banners waved and the cavalry galloped up for orders.

Then the merchant played on the other end of the flute and everything vanished.

'What you offer is certainly very useful,' said Andrei the Archer, 'but my servant is worth far more than just one or even two of your wonderful treasures. If you wish, I will trade Brother Nobody for the club, the axe and the flute together.'

The merchants thought it over and finally accepted the offer.

'Better to exchange our marvels for Brother Nobody, for with him we shall have all we want to eat and drink, day and night, without having to stir,' they reasoned.

So the merchants handed Andrei the club, the axe and the flute, and shouted in chorus:

'Hey, Brother Nobody, you are coming with us! Will you serve us well?'

'Why not?' came the voice. 'It is the same to me whom I serve.'

So the merchants returned to their ships and began to make merry. They ate and drank, all the while shouting:

'Hurry up there, Brother Nobody. Bring us this, bring us that!'

They gorged and gulped until they were bursting and drunk, and fell soundly asleep.

Meanwhile the Archer sat alone in the golden-domed palace, feeling quite sad and lonely.

'Dear me,' he sighed. 'I wonder where my faithful servant, Brother Nobody, is.'

'Here I am, friend. What is it you wish?'

Andrei was overjoyed.

'It is time to go home to my young wife. Take me home, Brother Nobody.'

As before, a gust of wind picked him up and whisked him away.

On board ship, the merchants were now waking up, feeling hungry and thirsty.

'Hey, there, Brother Nobody!' they shouted. 'Bring us something to eat and drink, and be quick about it!'

They bawled and screamed for a long time until they were quite hoarse. But their cries went unheeded and, when they looked across the water, they understood why: the island had gone. Only the foamy waves raced across the spot where it once had stood.

In the meantime Archer Andrei had flown home to his lowly hut. But, alas, the sight that met his eyes filled him with despair. Nothing remained of his home but charred ruins. There was not a sign of the Dove Maiden.

Andrei hung his head and wept. He had come too late. Yet, as he stood there sobbing, a white dove fluttered onto his shoulder. It kissed him gently on the cheek before striking the ground and turning into his lovely wife, Princess Maria.

The young couple embraced and told each other of all that had happened.

'Since you left I have been flying about the forest glades and groves as a dove,' said his wife. 'Three times the king sent his soldiers for me and when they did not find me they burned down our home.'

'Brother Nobody, can you build a palace by the ocean blue?' asked Andrei.

'Indeed I can,' came a voice. 'It shall be done at once.'

And sure enough, he built them a splendid palace of white stone, surrounded by a rose garden and a silver moat in which black swans swam. And there Andrei and Princess Maria lived happily with their loyal servant, Brother Nobody.

It was not long, however, before the king heard of the palace. He was out hunting one day when he chanced to pass the palace of white stone standing by the ocean blue. On enquiring whose palace it was, he was told:

'It belongs to your Archer, Sire. He lives there with his lovely wife, Princess Maria, having returned from *I know not where* and fetched *I know not what*.'

This sent the king into a rage. He mustered his army and marched down to the shore, where they were to destroy the palace and put Andrei and his wife to death.

When Andrei saw the vast army advancing on his palace, he quickly picked up his axe and stood it on its handle. Rap, a'tap, tap, went the axe and a stout wooden ship sailed upon the sea; rap, a'tap, tap, – and another appeared; rap, a'tap, tap, tap, tap . . . until a hundred ships sailed upon the sea.

Then Andrei began to play upon his flute – and a gallant army appeared, infantry and cavalry, their banners flying and cannon at the ready.

His captains galloped up to take their orders, and Andrei commanded them to start the battle: the trumpets blared, the drums rolled and the troops moved in to attack. The infantry tore through the ranks of the king's army, and the cavalry forced the enemy soldiers into the ocean. There the fleet of a hundred ships fired its cannon until not a single soldier of the king remained alive.

The king and his counsellor turned to flee, but Andrei took up his club and cried:

'Break their bones and strike them dead!'

At that order, the club whirled and spun through the air and caught first the counsellor, then the king, and struck them both a mighty blow on the temple.

When the people heard that the king was dead, they came from all over the kingdom to the palace of white stone and begged Andrei to be the new king and his wife the queen.

Andrei agreed. A grand banquet was prepared to which all the people of the realm were invited. And above the merry laughter and happy rejoicing could be heard cries of:

'Hey, there, Nobody! Over here, Nobody!'

But if you ask me where Nobody really came from, I can only say *I know not where.* And if you ask me who he was I can only say *I know not what.*

Perhaps King Andrei and his lovely wife, the Dove Maiden, can tell you for, as far as I know, they are living still in the white stone palace somewhere in Russia.

A Bull-Calf Goes to School

ON his way back to barracks, a soldier stopped at a village. There he spent the night in an old woman's hut, regaling her with his stock of soldiers' tales. She being a simple woman, born in a bush (as they say), hardly having seen beyond her own cattle-shed, sat there, ears wagging, taking it all in. . .

'Tell me, Soldier,' she said finally, 'where did they teach you such wisdom?'

'It's like this, Grandma,' replied the wily soldier, 'our regiment has a school where they make simpletons into scholars; they can even teach animals so that you wouldn't recognize them from humans.'

'Well I be jiggered!' exclaimed the old woman, her eyes as round as saucers. 'Do you think your school could make something of my bull-calf?'

'Certainly,' replied the soldier. 'Bring him to town and I'll enrol him for you. You'll certainly bless me for it.'

Next day the woman tied a string round the calf's neck and led him to the barracks.

'This, Grandma, is our school,' said the soldier. 'Leave your animal here with enough money to cover his board and lessons. I'll see to his studies.'

The woman paid the fees, left the calf with the soldier and returned home. As soon as she was gone, the soldier took the calf to the cook-house, had him slaughtered, ate the meat, sold the skin and drank the money away.

About a year passed before the woman paid another visit to town to see how her animal was progressing. When she arrived at the barracks, the sentries told her;

'You are too late, Grandma. Your bull-calf passed out some time ago; he is a wealthy merchant now. Do you see that great stone house over there? That belongs to him. You go there and maybe he'll recognize you, or you him!'

So the old woman went to the stone house and asked the doorman:

'Is it here the wise young bull lives?'

'Bull? Mr Bull the Merchant, do you mean, Grannie? Yes, this is his place. Come in if you have business with him.'

As the old woman entered, the master of the house appeared.

'What do you want with me, Missus?' he asked.

The woman stared at Mr Bull the Merchant and could scarcely believe her eyes: her bull-calf really had become a man!

'Holy Moses!' she stammered at last. 'My blessed little beast!'

And she began to tug at his ear and stroke his head, clucking:

'Just see how sleek and fat you've grown. Who would think you're only an animal, a cow's offspring. . . Gee-up, gee-up! Come on, back to your cattle-shed where you belong!'

The old woman tried to lead Bull the Merchant by the nose to take him home. But, to her surprise, he suddenly turned nasty and had her thrown out of his house.

The Kingdoms of Copper, Silver and Gold

FAR across the Russian steppe, there once lived an old man and his wife and their three sons – Yegorushko-the-Flyer, Misha-the-Bowlegged and Ivashko-the-Dreamer. When the sons came of age, their parents sent each in search of a wife.

The first son searched high and low, yet found no girl to be his bride. However, when he was walking home he encountered a three-headed dragon.

'What is your errand, bold fellow?' asked the dragon.

Yegorushko told his story and the dragon bade him follow to a place where he might find a wife. After several days and nights they came to a great stone.

'Move the stone,' said the dragon, 'and you shall find whatsoever you deserve.'

Yegorushko tried with all his might to shift the stone, but it was beyond his strength.

'So be it,' said the dragon. 'You deserve no bride.'

The son returned home and related his adventure to his father and mother. The old folk were puzzled but made up their minds to send forth the second son, Misha-the-Bowlegged. The same strange fate befell him too. That decided the parents: they would not send Ivashko-the-Dreamer. He would certainly come back empty-handed.

But Ivashko begged so hard, his parents eventually let him try his luck. When he encountered the three-headed dragon, he received the same question:

'What is your errand, bold fellow?'

'My brothers sought a bride and could not find one; now it is my turn. Will you help me?'

'If that be your wish,' said the dragon. 'I shall show you the place and you may seek your fortune. But I warn you: you will receive no more than you deserve.'

When they reached the great stone, Ivashko seized it and rolled it aside easily, revealing a hole with a rope hanging down.

'Take hold of the rope,' ordered the dragon, 'and I shall lower you into the hole: you will come to three kingdoms – of copper, silver and gold. In them you will find a maiden, each more lovely than the first. From those maidens you must choose your bride.'

Ivashko climbed down lower and lower until he was in the bowels of the earth. At the bottom a path opened up and he saw a kingdom of copper glinting fiery red in the underworld sun. Journeying through that kingdom, he came to a palace and there, at the copper gates, stood a maiden more beautiful than words could relate or tales could unfold. She greeted him sweetly:

'Welcome, long-awaited guest. Come into the palace and tell me whence you come and whither you travel.'

'Oh, Lovely Maiden,' Ivashko said. 'You ask me questions without offering me food and drink. That is no way to treat a Russian traveller.'

At that, the beautiful maid laid a table with all kinds of sweetmeats and wines. Ivashko ate and drank his fill and then told her of his quest for a bride.

'If it pleases you,' he said, 'I would dearly take you for my bride.'

The maid shook her head sadly: 'Journey farther until you come to the kingdom of silver; there you will find a maiden more beautiful than me.'

Ivashko bowed low, thanked her for her hospitality and took his leave. He journeyed farther into the earth until he came to a kingdom of silver glittering in the sun. As he approached the silver palace, he saw a girl waiting by the gates – more lovely even than the first.

'Greetings, passing stranger,' she said kindly. 'Come into the palace and tell me your story: whose son are you, whence come you and whither do you go?'

'Oh, Fair Maiden,' said Ivashko. 'You ask me questions before offering me food and drink. That is no way to greet a Russian wayfarer.'

So the maid of the silver kingdom at once set a table, brought him all manner of tasty morsels and meads and regaled him most royally. When he had ate and drunk his fill, he told her of his errand. Would she be his bride?

The girl shook her head: 'Journey farther until you come to the kingdom of gold; there you will find a maiden even lovelier than myself.'

Ivashko thanked the girl and continued on his way, down into the depths of the earth. When he reached the kingdom of gold, he met a

maiden at the palace gates who was indeed the loveliest girl he had ever seen. Giving thanks to God, he bowed low before the girl and told her of his mission.

She set a table with all sorts of food and drink, better than he had ever tasted before. Ivashko-the-Dreamer enjoyed his meal and when it was over he asked:

'If it please you, Fair Maiden, will you be my bride?'

To his joy, the maid of the golden kingdom consented and they set off together back to Rus. On the way, they called in at the silver and copper kingdoms to fetch the two lovely maidens. As they reached the bottom of the hole, they found the rope hanging there. But the dragon was gone and in his place Ivashko's brothers stood waiting.

First Ivashko tied the copper maid to the rope, gave it a tug and the brothers hauled her up; then followed the silver maid and the golden maid. Finally he tied himself to the rope and the brothers began to pull him up. When they saw it was Ivashko, a wicked thought came into their heads.

'Why pull the Dreamer up? Why not keep the three maidens for themselves?'

So they cut the rope and Ivashko fell with a bump to the bottom of the hole. Of course he wept tears of anger and grief; there was nothing for it, however, but to journey back along the path into the earth. He had not gone far when he came upon a little old man, no bigger than his finger yet with a beard as long as his leg. He was sitting atop a tree-stump humming merrily. Telling the little old man of his misfortune, he was told to journey on until he came to a hut; in the hut lived a fierce giant who would either eat Ivashko or advise him further.

Ivashko walked on until he came to the hut; he went in and begged the giant not to kill him, but to tell how he might return to Rus.

The giant was quite full, having just eaten nine oxen and nine sheep, so he snorted:

'Go beyond the thirty lakes until you reach a little hut on a hen's foot; there you will find a witch. She has an eagle-bird that will carry you back to Rus.'

Ivashko continued his journey, crossed the thirty lakes and came to the hut on a hen's foot. He entered and told the witch he had been sent by the giant to ask for her mighty eagle-bird to carry him back to Rus.

'Go into my garden where you will see a guard,' said the witch. 'He stands before some doors; take his keys and open seven doors. When you come to the last one, enter quietly – the eagle will shake his wings. If you do not scare him, you may sit astride his back and fly away. But take some meat with you, so that you may feed him whenever he wants to look around.'

Ivashko did exactly as the witch had told him, mounted the eagle and flew away; presently the eagle began to look around, and Ivashko at once broke off a piece of meat and fed him. This continued until the meat was gone – yet they were still far from Rus. When the eagle next looked round and was fed no meat, he tore a piece from Ivashko's leg, swallowed it and at once soared up through the hole into Rus.

As Ivashko dismounted, the eagle spat out the lump of meat and bade him place it back on his leg. No sooner had he done so than the leg grew whole as if the wound had never been.

Ivashko-the-Dreamer returned home, took the golden maid from his brothers and together they lived in health and happiness. And they live on still in a village somewhere in the Russian steppe. Just the other day I met Ivashko.

> *We drank beer together and yet*
> *I barely got my whiskers wet.*

Commentary on Russian Folk Tales

THE STORYTELLERS...

WHEN the Slav tribes trekked eastwards from Central Europe some fifteen hundred years ago, they found themselves in a strange terrain, flat and marshy, interspersed with broad rivers. Some clans headed south from Kiev through a tree-less steppe of feather-grass so high it could conceal a horse and rider, a country which Gogol describes in *Taras Bulba* as 'A land of the tall embrace, of a greenish-yellow ocean sprinkled with millions of spring flowers.'

Other families went due east, clearing a way by axe and fire through a forest of fir and pine, silver birch and larch, well watered by bog and lake, nourishing great numbers of wild animals. Still others paddled their canoes along the Volga and Dvina rivers northwards, past Novgorod and Pskov, through solid pine forests to lakes Ladoga and Onega. All these varied lands settled by the Eastern Slavs became known as Rus, were later called Russia and today make up the heart of the Soviet Union. It is from the people of this Great Russian Plain that the folk tales in this book are taken.

According to the Russian historian Vasily Kluchevsky (1841–1911), we must learn about the Russian forest, river and steppe in order to understand the Russian people. In his *Course of Russian History* he wrote, 'The forest provided the Russian with oak and pine to build his house, it warmed him with aspen and birch, it lit his hut with birchwood splinters, it shod him in bast sandals, it gave him plates and dishes, clothed him in hides and furs and fed him honey. The forest was the best shelter from his foes.'

But life in the forest was tough and dangerous: a way had to be hacked through the thick undergrowth; trees had to be cut down to make a clearing for huts and cattle; wolves and bears stalked man and beast. It was an awe-inspiring world of weird sounds and menacing shadows. The forest taught caution and kindled fantasy.

Kluchevsky again:

The silence of the sleepy, dense forest frightened the Russian; it seemed to harbour something evil in the fearful, soundless twilight of its ancient summits. The momentary expectation of sudden, unexpected, unforeseen danger strained his nerves, excited his imagination. And the ancient Russian populated the forest with all kinds of fantastic creatures; it was the dark kingdom of the one-eyed evil spirit or woodsprite who would amuse himself by leading men astray.

The steppe put quite a different imprint on the Russian soul: its endless expanse gave the feeling of vast horizons and distant dreams. Yet it was even more menacing than the forest, for it offered no hiding place from the marauding nomads and the dreaded Tartars. The forest and steppe, therefore, evoked conflicting feelings, were both friend and foe. Not so the Russian river:

He loved his river [wrote Kluchevsky]; there is no other feature of the land so fondly sung of in folklore. And for good reason. In his meanderings, she showed him the way; in his settlements, she was his constant companion; he placed his home upon her banks. For most of the year she fed him. For the trader she was the perfect summer and winter road. She taught the Russian order and sociability; she made men brothers, made them feel part of society, taught them to respect the customs of others, to trade goods and experience, to invent and to adapt.

The rivers and lakes, too, had their mysteries. In a world inhabited by demons it is easy to understand how primitive Russians thought the spirit of the river murmured when pleased or roared when angry. The continual motion of water very naturally suggested that it was alive; so each river had its spirit – old, ugly, green-bearded – who, when drunk, made the rivers overflow, when pleased, guided the fish into the fishermen's nets, when cross, raised storms, sank ships, seized and strangled sailors, tore traps and lines. In the depths of the waters lived the *rusalka* or water nymph, a lovely naked girl with skin the colour of moonlight, silken hair and emerald eyes. She so charmed passers-by with her laughter and song that some men would drown themselves for the *rusalka*'s sake.

Here, then, are the main offspring of Mother Nature that formed the Russian soul and lent Russian folklore its special flavour and imagery. Much of the subject matter is, of course, common to folk tales throughout the world; but the style is purely Russian, a faithful mirroring of customs, fears, prejudices and dreams, all nurtured by the Russian habitat.

The unique artistry of Russian folk tales must in part be attributed to the storytellers (*skomorokhy*), who cultivated their storytelling art and passed down stories by word of mouth from generation to generation. These minstrels, jesters, blind pedlars, vagabonds of every sort, masters of the telling of a tale, were most welcome in the strung-out settlements. Some were so adept at their craft that they were 'able to relate tales not only the whole night through, but for several days together'. So says Professor Yuri Sokolov in *Russian Folklore*.

At a time when modern life had not yet spread into the remotest corners of the countryside, storytelling was a favourite entertainment in the quietness and monotony of the long winter evenings, in a land where snow covers the earth for half the year. As recently as 1908 the brothers B. and Y. Sokolov could describe the following scene (from *Tales and Songs of the White Lake Region*):

In the winter, in the depths of the forest, far from any habitation, there is often a whole village gathered together – peasants, their wives and children. By day there is the heavy work, but, when it begins to grow dark, there is the well-deserved repose by a blazing hearth. In the forest they construct a camp – that is, a spacious mud hut with a hearth in the middle. The people are packed in and here they warm their chilled limbs and satisfy their hunger and thirst. Then they begin to while away the long winter evening. What a valuable person, then, does the storyteller prove to be! In the midst of the dense forest, with trees crackling from the frost, to the accompaniment of the howling of wolves, beside the blazing fire – what an apt setting, what a wonderful atmosphere for a fairy tale full of every imaginable kind of terror! And here the storyteller comes on to the scene, the jester, the merry fellow, whose witticisms and mockery pour forth as from a horn of plenty. The whole audience listens with bated breath, and unanimously and rapturously acclaims his amusing narrative.

When the Sokolov brothers were recording folk tales, they recalled that fishermen would come and bargain with the storyteller who pleased them most, promising him a portion of their catch if he would accompany them on their fishing expeditions. Naturally the storytellers did not work for nothing and it is a device of their craft that they should frequently finish their story with a humorous rhyme calling for their reward, especially for a drink:

> It was at the feast I heard this tale,
> There it was I drank mead ale.
> Though it flowed down my beard, my mouth stayed dry,
> For never a drop passed my lips, swear I.

It is interesting that in Russia folk tales were for so long not simply tales to amuse the common people but to entertain gentlefolk too. A good storyteller was a much prized possession in many well-to-do homes, including that of the emperor himself. The first Russian tsar, Ivan the Terrible, was said to be a great admirer of folk tales and had at Court three blind men who would take turns at his bedside, telling stories to lull him to sleep. The Russian poet Alexander Pushkin acknowledged his debt to his childhood nurse Ariana Rodionova for his great love of folk tales; Count Leo Tolstoy, as a child, fell asleep to the stories told by an old man who had been purchased by his grandfather for his skill at storytelling. Folk stories recounted by serf nurses to young aristocratic gentlefolk provided themes for innumerable Russian masterpieces – from the music of Tchaikovsky (*Sleeping Beauty, Swan Lake, Nutcracker*), Rimsky-Korsakov (*Sadko, The Snow Maiden, The Golden Cockerel*) and Stravinsky (*The Firebird, Petrushka*) to the writings of Pushkin, Gogol and Aksakov. Indeed, there can scarcely have been a Russian writer or composer of any stature whose work was not inspired at one time or another by memories of folk tales told in childhood.

But storytellers had not always been so welcome. The tsar Alexei Mikhailovich, father of Peter the Great, had *skomorokhy* rounded up and their tongues cut out. In the famous royal edict of 1649 it was proclaimed: 'Many persons stupidly believe in dreams, in the evil-eye and in bird-song, and they propound riddles and tell fairy stories; by idle talk and merry-making and blasphemy, they destroy their souls.'

Ironically enough, it was during the reign of Tsar Alexei Mikhailovich that the first records of oral Russian tales were made. But they were not published in Russia or in their mother tongue; ten tales were recorded by an Englishman, Samuel Collins (1619–70), who worked in Moscow as royal physician during the 1660s. His stories, along with travel notes, were published in London in 1671 under the title *The Present State of Russia*. It was to be nearly two centuries, however, before a collection of Russian folk tales was published in Russia. Why, in the land of its birth, were records of the Russian folk tale so late in appearing? After all, Charles Perrault began publishing his French fairy tales in 1697 (*Contes de ma mère l'oye*) and the brothers Jacob and Wilhelm Grimm their German tales in 1812 (*Kinder und Hausmärchen*). The answer to this Russian riddle also explains why Russia's voice was silent for so long in literature generally – while other nations had their Shakespeare and Chaucer, Dante and Cervantes, Corneille and Racine, it was only in the nineteenth century that Russian literature came to life. An explanation for this late start must be sought in the role of the Church in Russia.

When Christianity came to Russia in the tenth century, it outlawed the pagan

Slav gods, although some of their features reappeared in the legendary feats of the saints. But the old cults continued: either they were adopted by the new Orthodox Church as its own rites, or they became magic. Thus, Perun (god of thunder and lightning) became Ilya the Prophet; Volos (guardian of herds and flocks) became St Vlasia; Kupalnitsa (goddess of rivers and lakes) became St Agrippina; the spring rites now coincided with Easter, the winter Calendae was replaced by Christmas, and the Festival of Yaril (god of the sun and all earthly life) became St John's Day. Nevertheless the memory of local gods persisted and the fear of them degenerated into superstition. At this stage of disorganization of local custom, the magic of folk tales became half-fantastic, half-conventional; transmitted as they were, orally and under the ban of the Church, the tales became diluted with faint memories of real history, lost folk songs and laments, Christian legend and superstitions dating back to earlier periods.

The Church, by its control of printed literature in Russia, was for several centuries able to prevent the literate from reading the 'fables of men'; they were not to be deflected from the 'Divine Scriptures'. In any case, the idea of using written Russian, so intimately associated with the Church, for the coarse peasant language of the oral tales was thoroughly alien to the Russian tradition. Even when Pushkin (1799–1837) attempted to imitate the folk tale, he was condemned for intruding peasant vulgarity into refined aristocratic society. Like other writers to follow, he was compelled to 'prettify' the folk tale before it could be accepted. It was, perhaps, hardly surprising that the priests and the nobility should find themselves lampooned by the folk whose lore they sought to suppress, or even by eminent Russian writers in their stylized folk tales. For example, Pushkin's satire on the clergy, *The Priest and his Workman Balde*, was banned during his short lifetime, then published four years after his death as *The Merchant Ostolop and his Workman Balde*, and was only restored to its original version some forty years later.

Despite the dead hand of Church censorship, the nineteenth century saw the intensive recording and study of folk tales. It is quite natural that this should coincide with the blossoming of Russian literature. In 1838 there appeared the first attempt at a collection of true folk tales – five stories under the title *Russian Folk Tales*, by Bogdan Bronitsyn, taken down, the preface says, 'from the words of an itinerant storyteller, a peasant from the Moscow region, to whom they had been related by an old man, his father'.

But the first significant and unsurpassed collection of Russian folk tales was that made by Alexander Afanasiev (1826–71), whose vast enterprise appeared in eight volumes between 1855 and 1867 and contained as many as 640 tales – by far the largest collection of folk tales by one man anywhere in the world. Unlike the Grimm tales, Afanasiev's stories were taken down second-hand – from the records of other people. Only about a dozen stories were recorded personally by Afanasiev himself. Yet this modest lawyer from the Voronezh region became one of the most influential figures in Russian national culture; generations of Russian authors, composers, artists and sculptors have drawn upon his subject matter and been inspired by it. As the writer and humanist Maxim Gorky said:

In the tales, people fly through the air on a magic carpet, walk in seven-league boots, build castles overnight. The tales opened up for me a new world where some free and fearless power reigned and inspired in me the dream of a better life. The immortal oral poetry of the common people, at a time when poet and peasant were one, has greatly helped me understand the fascinating beauty and wealth of our language.

Afanasiev's interest and pride in the intrinsic beauty of Russian peasant language – at a time when aristocratic Russian society was aping foreign fashions and conversing in French – brought him to admire folklore for its rich musical quality, its poetic artistry, sincerity, purity and childlike simplicity. He would surely have agreed with Pushkin that 'Our language is inherently beautiful and nowhere has it such breadth of expression as in folk tales. How marvellous they are – each one a poem! We must learn to speak and love Russian, not simply to admire it in tales.'

But in Afanasiev's early preoccupation with folk poetry, he was, in his own words, only in the Kingdom of Copper. He had to journey on to the Kingdom of Silver to breathe the pure air of folk morality: where good always conquers evil, where the poor outwit the rich, where the golden apple falls into the hands of the orphan not of her cruel stepmother, where the hero is invariably kind-hearted and fearless yet a man whom others spurn as a simpleton.

It was, nonetheless, in the Kingdom of Gold that he sought the key to folk tales. What was the secret of this treasure-house of adventure and image? How did the tales arise? What was the hidden meaning behind the tales? He sought to understand the world of the primitive storyteller whose feeling in regard to his surroundings was of some mysterious and fantastic power that controlled the sun, the sky, the stars, the storm clouds, the rivers and lakes. This last realm led him to a romantic theory of the language and lore that inspired him. In the story of Marya Morévna, for example, he believed that, to the primitive mind, the three bird-bridegrooms who arrive at Prince Ivan's palace to the accompaniment of thunder, whirlwinds and lightning, are really the Rain, Thunder and Wind. The three princesses they marry are, in fact, the Sun, Moon and Stars; seeing how the light went out of the sky during a storm, the early Russian created an explanation of the abducted maidens in the poetic language of folk tale. Marya Morévna (meaning 'Daughter of the Sea') herself is really the Sun which, at dawn and dusk, 'bathes' in the sea. The ogre, Old Bones the Immortal, fettered by iron chains, is the storm cloud chained by the winter frosts; he gains strength when he drinks his fill of water as spring melts the winter snows and ice-bound rivers, then he tears himself free and carries off Marya Morévna, so clouding over the Sun. Winds bring rain clouds that pour the water of life upon the earth. Prince Ivan is Perun, the pagan Russian god of Thunder and Lightning, who smashes the storm cloud with a mighty blow and saves the Sun, leading her out of the darkness from behind the mountains.

In another story, 'Fair Vassilisa and Baba Yagá', Afanasiev suggests that the witch symbolizes the dark cloud that wants to destroy the sunlight (Vassilisa); but the Sun frees itself from the power of the storm and other dark clouds (the wicked stepmother and her daughters). In the dragon stories it is the storm cloud (dragon) fighting the Sun (the hero) who destroys and disperses it with lightning (his sword). When Fenist the Falcon is woken by the maiden's kiss, it is really Nature woken by spring, the earth kissed by the sun.

To Afanasiev, therefore, folk tales were primitive man's story of Nature: the heroes are the gods of sun, sky, light, thunder and water, while their foes are the gods of darkness, winter, cold, storms, mountains and caves. Because of this mythological approach, Afanasiev attached no value to information concerning the storytellers from whom the tales had been taken; he did not think style of delivery important, since folk tale, like language, was to his mind a product of collective work over the ages. Moreover, he saw nothing wrong in a stylistic revision of a tale, although he did not go so far in this respect as his principal model, the Grimm brothers. In fact his editing is clinical; he does not seek to prettify his stories, to make them interesting for children. In at least a third of the tales he does not even indicate where the tales come from. However, his biographer, Vladimir Porudominsky, in his book *Shall I Tell You a Story?*, states:

Commentary on Russian Folk Tales

If we take a map of Russia and colour in the provinces from which Afanasiev's tales come, we have an area stretching eastwards from the western borders to the Ural Mountains, from the northern regions down through the Volga almost to the Caucasus. Over thirty provinces sent their storytelling envoys to him: they came from Vologda and Astrakhan, Orel and Perm, Grodno and Orenburg, Kazan and Kharkov.

In his search for material, Afanasiev had much assistance from the Russian Geographical Society, founded in 1848. At the end of his day's clerical work in the Moscow archives of the Imperial Foreign Ministry, he was able to work in its library, sifting through the notebooks on folklore; the Society also sponsored expeditions to distant regions of the country in order to record and gather tales from peasant storytellers. As his publishing mission became known, he received collections sent by village teachers, provincial governors, army officers and others who had recorded tales for their own amusement and stored them away. Soon he had accumulated as many as 125 stories, which he edited and published in three volumes between 1855 and 1858. This was only the beginning. By the end of the 1850s, however, the sources seemed to be drying up; the Geographical Society called off its expeditions for lack of funds and officialdom began to have second thoughts about publishing folk tales. In desperation, Afanasiev wrote to an elderly scholar, Vladimir Dahl, living in the old market town of Nizhny Novgorod, whom he knew to be an ardent collector of tales. His proposal was that a new book of tales should be published – collected by Dahl and edited by Afanasiev. Dahl replied to his letter at once:

I accept your suggestion wholeheartedly. Let me explain. I have several hundred tales; of course, they contain much rubbish and repetition. I have not the time to publish them myself as I have much too much work (my Russian dictionary). I do not want any credit at all save to ask you to mention in general that such-and-such book of tales was given to you. That is only because there has been some talk about the tales and people have a right to demand or expect something from me on that matter. Therefore I am giving you my entire collection and you may do what you like with it.

After carefully editing Dahl's valuable collection, Afanasiev was able to publish a further 228 tales in two volumes. Besides the fairy stories, the new work contained many satirical animal tales and anecdotes; not all of them evaded the censor and those that were published stirred up opposition in some quarters. The Moscow Metropolitan Filaret declared: 'The legends published by Afanasiev are thoroughly blasphemous and immoral; they offend pious sentiment and propriety. Religion must be safeguarded from such profanity.'

To this Afanasiev replied indignantly and incautiously: 'There is a million times more morality, truth and human love in my folk legends than in the sanctimonious sermons delivered by Your Holiness.'

But the tide of official encouragement was now turning and many in authority inclined to the view that the folk tales tended to corrupt by their coarseness, their satire (particularly against the clergy and nobility) and their peasant wit. It has to be remembered that Russia in the 1860s was in the throes of radical social change: peasant uprisings, a radical intelligentsia and industrial development had all combined to force the government to free the peasants from serfdom in 1861. Although this freedom from slavery was long overdue, its immediate effect was to produce even greater violence and discontent in virtually all sections of society. For Afanasiev trouble was brewing. In 1860 the censor responsible for vetting his works was dismissed and the police raided the printing works which published the tales; the owner Grachev was arrested and the second edition of the tales, then in preparation, was confiscated and later burned.

Dismayed and embittered at this brutish treatment of his life's work, Afanasiev sought permission to take a holiday abroad. Although his health was failing, it was not for this reason that he went on a European tour, for, during his three months' (July–October 1860) tour of Germany, Belgium, England, France, Switzerland, Italy, Austria and Poland, he arranged for publication abroad of several works that would clearly not please the Russian censor. In London he handed to a publisher notebooks of tales rejected by the Russian censor; and in Geneva, he published a highly amusing, even bawdy, collection of folk wit under the title *Sacred Tales*, which contained a biting satire on the clergy and nobility. It was printed under the fictitious authorship of 'Balaam, by the Typographical Art of the Monastic Fraternity in the Year of Obscurantism.' The preface explains:

Our book is appearing as a fortuitous and simple collection of that aspect of Russian folk humour for which there has hitherto been no room. Under the extreme conditions of Russian censorship, with its distorted understanding of ethics and morals, our book has been quietly printed in that cloister, far removed from the disturbances of the world, into which there still has not penetrated the sacrilegious hand of any kind of censorship.

Not long after Afanasiev's return from abroad, his house was searched by the police and he was summoned to the capital, St Petersburg, to appear before a special investigating committee. Although this body was unable to produce any evidence of his involvement in revolutionary or other subversive activities, its chairman, Prince Golitsyn, recommended to Alexander II:

Considering that the accused civil servant, employed in the archives of the Ministry of Foreign Affairs, may collaborate with people of evil intent to obtain from the Archives documents which should not be opened without government permission, I deem it necessary to draw the attention of the Foreign Minister to this circumstance so that he may take appropriate measures.

To this the emperor appended just one word, in pencil, in the margin: 'Absolutely!' Consequently, Afanasiev found himself disgraced, dismissed from his job and deprived of his Moscow house where he had resided for the previous thirteen years. For the next three years he vainly sought employment and was forced to sell his priceless library in order to live. He commented wrily: 'Books once nourished me with ideas, now – with bread.'

At the end of 1865 Russia's greatest folklorist and eminent historian at last found work as a humble assistant clerk in a Moscow court – a position he would probably have spurned on graduation from the Law Faculty of Moscow University nearly twenty years earlier. Two years later he was promoted to clerk to the Congress of Commune Judges in the Second Parish of the City of Moscow, where he spent his days filing reports, filling in forms and registering visitors. No other work was available to a man who had fallen under the shadow of the tsar himself. His home was now a cramped and damp room and this, along with his hard work, caused his health to suffer: he contracted consumption, which he used to laugh off as a 'mild lung disorder'.

Despite his illness and poverty, Afanasiev was not idle. During the period of penury he spent every free moment on a monumental new work: *The Poetic Interpretations of Nature by the Slavs*, which ran to over 2,500 pages in three thick volumes. Here he expounded his theories of the symbols of folk mythology in folk tales. Aided by the press censorship reforms of 1865, he managed to get his work published (1865–9) and received an award from the Russian Academy of Sciences. Though unable to publish any more genuine folk tales, he did produce two volumes of *Russian Children's Tales* in 1870, but this was to be his last undertaking.

Attitudes towards him seemed to be changing once more as Russian writers, eminent or unknown, acknowledged their debt to the man who had brought to light the prodigious repertoire of tales of the Russian people. In the spring of

1872 the famous writer Ivan Turgenev wrote a letter from Paris to the Russian authorities declaring that Afanasiev's literary works gave him the right to receive financial assistance 'for security from hunger, cold and his other discomforts'.

Turgenev could not have known that Alexander Afanasiev, at the age of forty-five, had died in poverty and virtual obscurity six months previously.

*

Apart from Pushkin's prologue taken from *Ruslan and Ludmilla,* all the stories in this collection are taken from Afanasiev's *Russian Folk Tales.*

... AND THE TALES

Russian folk tales may be divided into three principal genres: fairy, animal and everyday, each with its own distinct style, themes, scenarios, origins and audience. Occasionally actors and themes intermingle – a princess wanders into an everyday tale ('Good and Evil') or two peasants tangle with the magic elements ('Ivan the Rich and Ivan the Poor'). But this is rare.

Fairy Stories

The traditional fairy stories are full of fantasy and stock descriptions: the heroes and heroines are bold young men and innocent maidens (or vice versa) assisted by helpful beasts and magic implements; the villains are dragons, witches, sorcerers and evil kings. And the lucky number is three, thus presenting triads of witches, tasks, sons, princesses, nights and dragons' heads. Many themes and characters belong to Russian peasant myth and are undoubtedly as ancient as the inhabitants of the Great Russian Plain. Pushkin mentions some – the storytelling cat, the woodsprite and mermaid, Baba Yagá and Old Bones the Ogre – in the prologue (*priskazka*) to his long verse tale *Ruslan and Ludmilla,* set in pagan Russia and upon which Glinka based his famous opera. Although not strictly folklore, this prologue provides an appropriate introduction to the heroes and demons of Russian folk tale. We meet Baba Yagá, the witch who dwells in a revolving hut on hen's feet, sometimes with and sometimes without windows or doors; typically, this old hag sits on a bench or stone stove, one leg curled under her, the other dangling, her crooked nose reaching to the ceiling. She rides through the air in an iron mortar propelling herself along with a pestle and sweeping her tracks away with a broom, stirring up terrible storms and leaving a trail of disease and death in her wake. She is, of course, a cannibal, specializing in devouring young children. It is noteworthy that, in several tales, the witch is helpful ('Fenist', 'The Frog Princess', 'The Archer'), thereby reverting to her earlier functions in the Mother Age of folk tales when she represented the priestess in whom all love and religion was embodied. The strong matriarchal influence on Russian folk tales is further apparent, in that the main role is frequently played by the woman – who may be a bold warrior in the case of Marya Morévna, a wise maiden like Fair Vassilisa, an enchanted wife like the Dove Maiden ('The Archer') or the Frog Princess. This matriarchal influence is also apparent in that, in most non-Russian variations of the Frog tale, the frog is a man, a prince; similarly, in 'Sleeping Beauty' and 'Snow White' the princess is awakened by a prince; yet in the Russian 'Fenist' it is the man who is awakened by a maiden's kiss. With social change that made man the centre of the social group, especially as a result of Christian influence, the power and knowledge of women were broken down and the priestess became the wicked witch; her superior wisdom – dabbling in witchcraft – was reason enough to have her burned at the stake or, in Russia, set loose across the plain tied to a horse's tail.

Another purely Russian folk villain is Old Bones the Immortal, who carries off fair maidens. Chained and imprisoned ('Marya Morévna'), he features in a forbidden chamber incident, common to the Bluebeard cycle of European tales. His Russian name *Koshchay* appears to derive from either the Old Russian or the Turkish (*koshchi*) meaning 'prisoner'. (The constant struggle between Russians and nomadic Turkic tribes, including the Polovtsians and Tartars, has bequeathed many names and figures to Russian tales.) The name became confused with the Russian word *kost*, meaning 'bone' and so also came to mean a skeleton or miser. The epithet 'Immortal' means he can only be killed in an exceptional manner, since his death is usually at the end of a needle, which is in an egg, the egg is in a duck, the duck in a hare, the hare in a stone chest and the chest at the top of an oak tree.

This brings us to another feature of Russian primitive belief: that the soul or heart dwelt outside the body in some special place. In some tales ('Olga and the Brown Cow', 'The Rosy Apple and the Golden Bowl') trees and plants are tenanted by the souls of the dead, thus becoming personified and endowed with human qualities. This superstition led to certain trees being regarded as sacred, to the legends of the speaking or bleeding plants and to the planting of trees as life tokens. Even today in Russia the silver birch is generally accepted as personifying women, the maple – men. Memories of holy trees and groves are recorded in the names Holywood and Holyoak. Trees and other objects also feature as life tokens: if the hero dies, the tree falls or, as in 'Marya Morévna', the birds' feathers become bloodstained – because the hero's soul resides in them. In another version of this story Prince Ivan leaves his silver spoon, fork and snuff-box with his brothers-in-law which, by their tarnishing, indicate his death. These primitive beliefs are associated with the present-day notion of breaking a mirror and, in Russia, a person whistling indoors – both said to presage a death. On the other hand, today's lucky charms, crosses, icons and other miraculous objects may be compared with the magic swords, self-laying tablecloth, sack, etc., in the tales. A black cat or flying cranes today play similar roles to the helpful beasts of the tales – the grey wolf ('Firebird'), the pike ('The Fool and the Magic Fish') or the horse ('Chestnut Grey'). The probable significance of all these animals is totemistic – i.e., a belief in the sacred nature of certain beasts and plants from which men claim descent.

Another link with the past, especially marked in religious practices, are offerings made to a supernatural being. In ancient Russia, as elsewhere, man behaved rather like the child of today who treats a doll as something living and holds long conversations with it ('Fair Vassilisa'). The offerings made to it, and to the fairies of other nations, or to God during the Harvest Festival, are survivals of the propitiary sacrifices offered by primitive man to the spirits that beset him at every turn. Even many of the modern names for supernatural beings have their derivation in these primitive ideas; thus, the English 'bogie-man' is related to the Russian name for God, *bog* – an illustration of how the word 'devil' was originally the same as a god, being a corruption of *deva*, the Sanskrit name for God. Hence *div* and *divitsa* (the ancient pagan deities of Russia), the Latin *Zeus*, the French *dieu* and the English word 'deuce' (meaning 'a little devil') can all be traced to the same root.

The point of departure for all 'fortunate youngest son' stories lies in the fact that the youngest born was originally the heir – a position which he gradually lost with changing social conditions. He would therefore be regarded by many as an heir deprived of his rights, so that a sentimental feeling for him would arise. This is evident in 'The Firebird' and 'Frog Princess', in which elder brothers try to deprive the youngest brother of his inheritance or some other prize. 'Puss in Boots' is a well-known Western example. Similarly it was once the last born in Russia who, when his parent died, performed the funeral rites; it was he who watched by the grave. When the other brothers refuse to take their turns at watching by the father's grave, it is the youngest who keeps the vigil ('Chestnut Grey'). In 'The Firebird', the youngest son guards a golden apple-tree.

Other features common to folk tales include 'smelling out' formulas and sleep charms. With the former the Russian version ('Foo, foo, I smell Russian blood') may be compared to the 'Fee, fi, fo, fum, I smell the blood of an Englishman' in 'Jack the Giantkiller'. This seems to arise out of the keen sense of smell which primitive man possessed and which modern man has lost. Sleep charms appear in 'Olga and the Brown Cow' ('Shut one eye, shut two eyes') and in many Western tales; the margin between them and folk lullabies is certainly not wide.

Animal Tales

Animal tales are said by Sokolov in *Russian Folklore* to constitute about ten per cent of the entire Russian stock of folk tales, a much lower proportion than in Western Europe. Further, of the seventy themes in the Russian stories about animals, half are common to West European tales, the rest belonging exclusively to Russian tales. This relatively small place given to animal tales in Russian folklore is due to the special nature of the medieval literature of Russia where, unlike Western Europe, the animal epos never gained great popularity – partly due to the fear that most Russians had of the wild animals (wolves, bears) that inhabited the Russian forests.

To the mind of the primitive Slav, as to all primitive peoples, beasts with human attributes seemed perfectly natural. They shared the world with him, on his own level, and he admired them, feared them, respected them, ascribed to them the power of speech and a nature resembling his own. As the Polish anthropologist Malinowski observed in *Magic, Science and Religion*:

> By their general affinity with man – they move, utter sounds, manifest emotions, have bodies and faces like him – and by their superior powers – the birds fly in the open, the fishes swim underwater, reptiles renew their skins and their life and can disappear in the earth – by all this the animal, the intermediate link between man and nature, often his superior in strength, agility and cunning, usually his indispensable quarry, assumes an exceptional place in the savage's view of the world.

Commentary on Russian Folk Tales

In the folk tale, therefore, each animal is distinguished by a certain characteristic and its own name. The heroine of Russian tales is the crafty fox, known as Liza (from *lisa*, the Russian for 'fox') Patrikeyevna, variously known as the beautiful fox, the fox with an oily tongue, the gossip, the godmother, little sister, a deceiving midwife, a smooth-tongued seller of Communion bread or a mother-confessor. Unlike most Western tales (Reynard the Fox or Brer Fox), the Russian fox is female – perhaps another indication of the proximity of Russian tales to the Matriarchal Age. By contrast to the sly fox is the stupid wolf, Levon, the grey fool, the stupid old wolf, the victim of the fox's tricks ('Little Sister Fox', 'Midwife Fox'). The bear, Michaelo Ivanovich or Misha, is the twig-crusher, the old grey peasant, clumsy and slow-witted, but also kind-hearted. The hare is a coward, the little grey fellow, the cross-eyed one; the cat is often the purring one (i.e., the storyteller), the zither player, known as Catafay Ivanovich; the cock is fearless, Petya (from *petukh*, the Russian for 'cock'); the goat is Kozma from the Russian word *kozyol*, and the ram is Baran Baranich from *baran* (meaning 'ram'), and so on.

Some of the tales here are peculiar to Russian folk tales ('Midwife Fox', 'Liza the Fox and Catafay the Cat', 'The Castle'), while others are more or less universal and may be found in the fables of the Greek slave Aesop and of Lafontaine, and in the tales of Uncle Remus, Grimm and Perrault. Not only are animal traits universal, so, too, are explanations of their shape. Take any animal with a stumpy tail, for example, and folklore will have an answer: the wolf lost his long bushy tail fishing through the ice, says the Russian tale ('Little Sister Fox and Brother Wolf'); a French and a Scottish story account for it in the same way. Brer Rabbit, according to Uncle Remus, lost his tail through the same practical joke played by Brer Fox. In the same way, the Russian tale, 'The Bun', is almost identical to 'The Little Gingerbread Man'. The diffusion of these and other folk tales occurred from tribe to tribe by means of migration, by prisoners and slaves taken in war, by marriage and trade. Nonetheless similar stories may have developed independently, just as similar forms of games, of pottery and flint implements and of social organization did in analogous environments.

Russian animal tales are usually short, related mainly for children and in the form of a dialogue in which the storyteller sings the little songs and imitates the voices and actions of the animals.

Everyday Tales

The third group of tales concerns everyday life, and is recounted in the form of an anecdote featuring peasants and soldiers, priests and merchants, rich and poor brothers. Rarely do the characters have names: the most usual appellation is Lord, Priest, Soldier, Poor Man, Peasant. In this dream world it is the poor peasant or soldier who gets the better of the rich, the bigoted and the selfish. Authority is satirized in comical vein; the story is recounted for what it is worth, sometimes baldly and starkly, without the ceremonial trimmings of the fairy tale or the childlike simplicity of the animal tale. Indeed some everyday tales are definitely not for children, telling as they do of the amorous adventures of a priest, peasant or soldier.

Typical of this genre are the soldiers' tales, normally told by soldiers about soldiers. The hungry, homeless soldier, going on leave or after discharge from the army, told his stories to gain a supper and a night's lodging. Like many other vagabonds of old Russia, he had to be cunning and resourceful to stay alive. Before the reform of military service in 1872, army recruits were taken only from the lower classes and military service lasted for as long as twenty-five years! (This often meant forsaking one's village and family, mother and girl friend, for ever – a heart-breaking affair which gave birth to a special form of folklore: the laments for departing soldiers, which are not included in this selection.) In his tales the Russian soldier expels devils ('Death and the Soldier') and punishes witches and mean old women ('Axe Porridge'). Being accustomed to all kinds of people and the rigours of army life, nothing surprises or frightens him – dead bodies, devils, witches, wizards, unclean spirits, even death itself. It is an interesting observation that devils in Russian tales are usually comical, hard-done-by figures, not the invariably evil and fearful characters they are elsewhere. Afanasiev remarked:

In the greater part of tales featuring unclean spirits, the devil is not so much a fearsome tormentor of Christian souls as a rather pitiful victim of tricks played by wily heroes or heroines: he falls victim to a clever wife, he is beaten by a soldier's rifle butt, he comes under the blacksmith's hammer or he is cheated by a peasant out of his hoard of gold.

Tales of the mean, stupid and lustful priest abound in Russian folk satire, although of course few such tales passed the censor prior to 1917. In pre-revolutionary Russia every village had its little church with its onion-shaped steeple and its married parish priest or 'pope'. The Russian peasant, though exceedingly religious, regarded his priest more as a prayer leader, a necessary personage for births, weddings and funerals, than as a spiritual guide. The flock required only that he have a majestic manner, a fine beard and a deep strong voice. By popular repute, he was often greedy (being quite poor and having to bargain with the peasant for his fees), a boozer and a womanizer (life in the village being hard and dull). According to the author Alexander Herzen, writing in the middle of the last century:

The Russian peasant is superstitious but indifferent in religious matters which are, in general, incomprehensible to him. He ritually performs all the rites, the entire external aspect of the cult. But he despises priests as greedy and indolent, living at his expense. The priest, deacon and their wives invariably are the butt of the mockery and scorn in all indecent folk tales and street songs.

Hence the proliferation of satirical stories about the clergy, of which three are represented here. 'The Goat's Funeral' has several versions, some featuring a mare or a dog instead of the goat. It has Western variants too, which, unlike the Russian, tend to satirize the high clergy rather than the local priest (see, for example, the French medieval story 'Barbasan et Méon' in which an ass is buried). For greater effect, the storyteller would often intone the words of the priest or deacon in the manner of the church liturgy, while singing those of the congregation in the manner of a folk tune. Devices resorted to by priests to extract donations from parishioners supply another common object of satire. There is the tale of the priest who tells his congregation that God will multiply their contributions: 'Bring in a cow and God will send you six cows.' The peasant and his wife obey the priest and then, when the priest's cows wander into their yard, they take them as having been sent by God, and refuse to give them up.

Tales on the 'rich and poor brother' theme highlight the problems of economic inequality between rich and poor peasants, even within a family – although family in this sense is more likely to be the extended family of the old Russian village; thus, a 'brother' may be a distant cousin. Nevertheless, by contrast to tales which pit the peasant against the squire or merchant, the tales of discord between brothers heighten the intense feelings of greed, cruelty and disdain even for family ties. In the folk tales the themes are usually of good and evil with the poor man eventually becoming rich and the rich man poor. Often the attitude and punishment of the rich man are severe – as in 'Good and Evil', in which the rich brother cuts out his brother's eyes, but is, in turn, torn to pieces by demons. Tales of corrupt judges who inadvertently help a poor man evade his fate are numerous; they often revolve around the poor man who conquers Fate and a greedy, merciless rich brother who treats misfortune as a crime.

These everyday tales make up the majority of Russian folk tales, constituting about sixty per cent of all material. Much of it is uniquely Russian, thereby providing a useful source of social investigation, a mirror of Russian peasant values.

*

With the march of time the old storytelling traditions seem to be fading in modern Russia: in town and village Russian children are more likely these days to cluster round the television set than to sit at the feet of *Babushka* (Grannie) – that last great fount of oral magic. Such is progress. All the same, the children of Russia probably have more communion with folk art – tales, songs, dances and crafts – than their brothers and sisters elsewhere. Folk tale books, often exquisitely illustrated, are printed in abundance and form the most popular category of children's literature. In the absence of 'comics', children's magazines regularly feature fairy and animal tales, and the first school primer, *Rodnaya rech,* contains some twenty folk tales. Everyday tales, particularly those lampooning the clergy and aristocracy, have naturally come into their own in Soviet times; yet propriety has prevented publication of the more lascivious peasant and soldier stories. Afanasiev's collection, last published in three volumes in 1957 (in a printing of 150,000 copies), is today one of the most precious acquisitions of any library. And new collections have appeared; Peter Bazhov, for example, recorded the legends of Ural miners in such beautiful tales as 'The Stone Flower' and 'The Mistress of the Copper Mountain'. New heroes have entered folk myth – like the founder of the Soviet state, Lenin, and the first spaceman, Yuri Gagarin.

And so the tales live on. Today, more read than recounted, they remain a colourful part of Russian life and language, the heritage of a people proud of the folklore that originated with those early Slav tribes on the Great Russian Plain.

JAMES RIORDAN

Bradford
1975